TALISMAN

GUY ALLEN

This is a work of fiction. With the exception of the references to the occasional historical person and incident, all characters, incidents, and dialogues are products of the author's imagination.

Copyright © 2013 Guy Allen
All rights reserved.
ISBN: 1482543222
ISBN-13: 978-1482543223

DEDICATION

Talisman is dedicated to my wife, Geri Allen,
my soulmate, and my talisman.

ACKNOWLEDGMENTS

Talisman is the culmination of an idea
generated during my gold prospecting years in
British Columbia. This book would never have
been completed without the patience and
encouragement of my wife, Geri. Other friends
who have been generous with their time in
editing and proofing the manuscript include:
Perry Watkins, Dave Wellington, and Jeanne
Yassick of Camano Island WA; Nancy Westler
of Surprise AZ; and my daughter Jennifer Allen
of Port Moody British Columbia. I would also
like to thank posthumously three of the original
'forty-niners', William Downie, William G.
Johnston, and Edward W. McIlhany for
publishing the histories of their years in the
California goldfields.

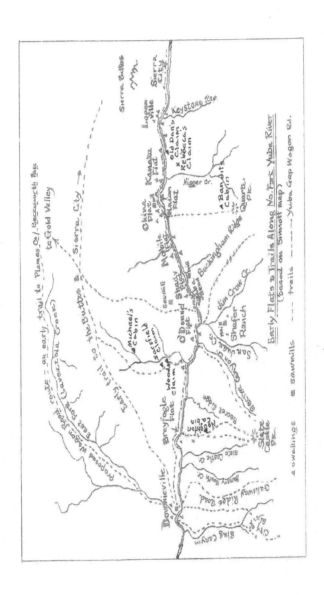

1

.

The wind was cold, and by sundown it had picked up a few snowflakes and was driving them into the face of the old mare as she plodded along the dirt road. The weary horse stumbled as she dragged the rickety wagon over the bumps and ruts. Dusk had fallen quickly. The young woman had been driving all day, pushing ahead when she should have stopped and rested. She was weak and deathly tired, and she felt the bleeding had started again. Finally she could see the flickering lights of the small village ahead, giving her just enough hope to keep going. She pulled up outside the general store, which was the only building of the dozen or so that dotted the main street that glowed with light. When she went inside, her thin, shivering body welcomed the heat radiating from the old wood stove. The few regulars lounging about the stove looked up as she entered and walked slowly to the counter. Their interest increased when they saw the baby that she carried strapped to a sling on her back. Wearily she slumped down on a stool and laid the baby on the counter. As the storekeeper came over to serve her, he could see how very pale and sickly she appeared.

"You don't look very well," the old man observed. "What can I do for you?"

She hesitated, unsure of herself. After a long pause, she replied in a whisper, "I am searching for my husband's family. They live near here. Their name is Woods. Can you tell me the way to their farm?"

The old man thought for a minute and then answered, "I don't know of any family named Woods around these parts."

He turned to the group of men sitting around the stove who had been listening intently.

"Do any of you know people named Woods out here?"

The men were quiet for a few moments then agreed they knew of no one by that name.

"What else can you tell us about them?" The storekeeper asked the young woman.

"My husband's name is John. He is a soldier. He had to leave the baby and me and go back to his Company, but he told me to come out here and stay with his folks. He wrote down where I was to go, but I lost the paper, and now I don't know how to find them."

"There's a family up north of here about ten miles that's got a son in the army. I don't know their name. I only heard it once, but I don't think it was Woods."

This came from one of the men by the

stove. All of them were trying hard to come up with something to help the young woman.

"It don't make much sense for you to try and go any farther tonight, what with you looking sickly and a storm coming in. You can stay here," the storekeeper suggested. "My wife will fix up the extra room in the back for you and the baby. You get a good sleep tonight, and maybe tomorrow we can find out where your people are."

The young woman started to refuse, but she now could feel that the bleeding had definitely started again.

"Thank you," she replied in a whisper. "I should keep looking for his family, but I am so tired I can't ..."

Slowly she slipped off the stool. No one was able to move quickly enough to catch her before she fell to the floor. The men gently picked her up and carried her into the living quarters at the back of the store, where the storekeeper's wife had them lay her down on their spare bed.

By the time an hour had passed, the weather had gotten steadily worse. Snowdrifts were beginning to pile up as the blizzard vented its fury on the village. The other men had headed for their homes long before the full impact of the storm had hit, leaving Ed and Gladys Jensen alone to look after their unexpected guests.

Ed unhitched the mare, fed, and bedded her down in the shed at the back of the store. When he came back in, Gladys was still tending to her patients. The young woman and the baby were both asleep, but the worried look on his wife's face gave Ed cause for concern. She closed the door quietly as they went into the kitchen.

"She's very sick. That baby is no more than a couple of days old, and she looks to have lost a lot of blood with the birth. She was still bleeding when you carried her in. I got it stopped, but I don't know what else to do for her. She hasn't come awake since you laid her down. She needs a doctor badly, but Doc Williams is treating old Mrs. Farling down south, and there is no one else we can get tonight."

Gladys Jensen sat up with the young woman throughout the night. Shortly before dawn, she regained consciousness, sat up quickly, and looked around frantically for her baby. Gladys laid the child gently in her arms, and she smiled weakly at the sleeping infant. She held on tightly to Gladys' hand, and the old woman realized she was burning with fever. As she tried to pull her hand away to go for some cooling cloths, the young woman held on more firmly and looked pleadingly into her eyes.

"Please look after my baby," she mumbled so faintly that Gladys had to bend close to hear. "He's . . .tenant Woods . . . "

Gladys could not make out the last sentence as the young woman's voice trailed away, and she fell back into a deep sleep. By morning light, she was dead.

Morning also brought the end of the storm. The day broke clear and cold, and the little village began to dig its way out of the drifted snow. Ed and Gladys, looking haggard from the lack of sleep, sat around the breakfast table trying to decide what to do next. They searched through the young woman's meager belongings trying to find out who she was and from where she had traveled, but there was nothing helpful. Neighbors came to visit and to hear about the new arrivals. It was decided that she was to be buried the next day in the village cemetery with a wooden marker identifying her only as Mrs. Woods.

The next few weeks were spent making inquiries throughout the neighboring areas, attempting to locate the Woods family or identify the young woman. None of these efforts met with success, and eventually the Jensens and their friends gave up the search. It was as if the young woman had never existed except for the small living legacy she had left behind.

All that Gladys had understood from the young woman's last words was, "He, tenant Woods." Hence, young Tenant Woods, soon to be known as Tenny, became an integral member of the small community. Because no one claimed him, and there was nowhere else to take him, he stayed with the Jensens. They were secretly delighted as they had longed to have children, and he was the first child to grace their home.

Tenny grew quickly to know the ways of his adoptive parents and their small town. He was told the story of his mother and went to visit her grave occasionally, but it had little meaning for him. He considered Ed and Gladys as his parents, and he grew to love them. Tenny, in turn, was the joy and fulfillment of their lives together. As the Jensens grew older and less able to take care of their business, Tenny took over most of the work of looking after the store and the responsibilities of providing for the family.

When Tenny was fourteen, Ed Jensen disappeared. As he had gotten older, he had become increasingly disoriented in his daily life. On many occasions neighbors would bring the old man home after he had gone for a walk or to visit someone and had forgotten his way back. It was sad for Tenny to slowly lose the closeness with the only father he had known. He angered over the unfairness that life had dealt the old man and strove to protect the elderly couple as he saw the quality of their lives deteriorate.

It was another bitterly cold January day with blowing snow, one of many that they had to endure that winter. There was little movement about the village as most of the residents stayed home huddled around their fireplaces and stoves. Tenny kept the store open in case someone ran out of supplies, but as darkness fell he decided to close. Ed had been dozing by the old stove, which he had kept supplied with wood throughout the day. As Tenny went to lock the door, Ed announced that he was going out to the shed to bring in one more load of logs for the night.

By the time Tenny had cleaned the store, twenty minutes had passed and Ed had not returned. Tenny took the lantern and went out to the shed, thinking that Ed might have slipped on the ice with his load of logs and was unable to get up. He followed the old man's rapidly disappearing tracks to the shed door, where they appeared to end. Inside the shed, there was no evidence that any one had recently been there.

The stacks of logs were covered with undisturbed snow that had drifted in through the leaky roof throughout the day. Frantically Tenny searched the shed and the immediate area around it and the store but to no avail. He found no further signs of Ed. He continued his search over a wider area until exhaustion and the cold drove him back into the store. When he told Gladys, they bundled up into their warmest clothing and searched the town, visiting everyone who might have taken the old man in. He was never found.

The loss had a traumatic effect on Tenny and Gladys but in different ways. From a vibrant woman always busy in the store and active in her social circle, Gladys lost all interest in life. The cheerful friend to everyone in the village became a morose recluse almost overnight. She shunned visitors and close friends, asking Tenny to send them away when they came to call. She took less interest in her home and the store as the months passed, retreating to her bedroom to fill most of her days.

Tenny just didn't understand how it all could happen. He had been part of a loving home with a strong respect for the Bible and its teachings. The old couple had lived a life in harmony with their beliefs. They had respected the laws of God and the laws of the land and had taught Tenny to live in the same manner. It didn't make any sense that this should be their reward. Why? What had gone wrong? Tenny continued to ponder the confusion of it all as he attempted to put some order back into their lives.

As spring breathed new life into the earth, darkness continued to prevail in the Jensen home. With the disappearance of the last pockets of snow from the gullies and hollows, Tenny set out each day spending as much time as he could away from the store, searching for some clue as to what had happened to Ed. Each succeeding trip took him farther afield from the village into the small neighboring farms and eventually up into the low rounded hills that surrounded the valley. But none of his searches or questions to those he encountered gave any hint as to what had happened to Ed Jensen.

As spring blossomed into summer, Tenny felt the need to spend more time away from Gladys and the gloom of his home. He opened the store only long enough to keep the people of the town supplied with essentials. He made sure Gladys was comfortable and safe before he hiked into the hills, where he was beginning to feel more at home.

He had given up hope of finding any explanation of Ed's disappearance. Now his trips into the wild areas were those of discovery. On his own, and from the few books in the store and those he was able to borrow, he was learning about the animals and plants of the forests. He was especially interested in the rocks that he found on his travels. Some of the old books told all about these rocks. When he was smaller he would spend hours looking at the pictures and would pester Gladys to read him the stories, until finally she taught him to read the books himself. This family, the store, and the books had been his world until his world fell apart.

His trips into the mountains became longer and more frequent. Occasionally he would be away for two and three days at a time, leaving the store and Gladys to be taken care of by a neighbor. He would trap and fish for most of his food and eat the wild, edible plants that his books had described. At night he would make a simple camp, wrap himself in an old quilt, and fall asleep, lulled by the sounds of the forest. Gradually the pain of his loss ebbed away, and he began to experience again the joy of living.

In 1841 Tenny turned sixteen and made a discovery that was to have a profound influence on the rest of his life. One morning, in a small valley just beyond his campsite, he noticed a thin wisp of smoke curling lazily up through the pines. He had planned to return to the village that morning, but his curiosity got the better of him. He had been told of the mountain people and some of their strange ways, but he had not met up with any of them as yet. He decided to skirt the valley to reach a vantage point above the source of the smoke before going in close. This took most of the morning, but by noon he had reached a rock scarp a couple of hundred feet above a small cabin with its cluster of outbuildings. All the buildings were constructed of well-weathered logs and mostly covered with moss. A large man was steadily splitting firewood logs in the yard with the biggest axe Tenny had ever seen. The man seemed to exert little effort in wielding this mammoth tool without rest. Tenny debated if he should make contact, not having any sense as to whether this man would be friendly or dangerous. Tenny knew he was strong and quick, but he had no weapons to defend himself. Suddenly another man appeared at the doorway of the main cabin. He was older and of a much more fragile build. He walked toward the big man with a limp, waving his arms and shouting words that Tenny could not hear. The other man deferred to him, dropped the axe, and sat down on one of the logs.

The men seemed to relax. Both pulled out pipes, rammed them with tobacco, and smoked in silence. Although still apprehensive, Tenny felt a bit more confident about breaking his cover and approaching them. He slid noiselessly from his perch and angled down the hillside. He walked softly, careful to avoid making any noise. Neither man heard him approach until he entered the clearing. Immediately the big man jumped up, reached behind the log for a rifle, and aimed it at Tenny.

Tenny froze in his tracks.

"Taint no bear, Scud. Dawnt shoot the boy!"

Slowly the big man lowered the rifle and walked toward Tenny.

"I'm Scud. Who you?"

"My name is Tenny Woods. I'm from the village over in the valley. I didn't mean to sneak up on you like that. I thought you probably knew I was nearby. I should have yelled to let you know I was coming."

"We waz spooked," the older man answered. "Theys ben big bear rown here. Scud figgered you him."

"There's lots of bear sign up on the ridge," Tenny replied. "It looks like a mother and two, year-old cubs. As close as I could tell by the freshest tracks, they were headed up the valley."

The old man seemed satisfied with this. He puffed on his pipe and was silent for a moment.

"I'm Caleb, thisears Scud. Why ubee up in theseear mowtens fer?"

"I like to get away from the village and walk in the mountains. I've been looking for different kinds of rocks."

"Theys all kines rocks up ere. Taint none be werth nuttin. No gold, jes coal we burn. Keep wawm."

Their talk continued for most of the morning in the same fashion. Tenny learned they had lived in the valley ever since Scud was born. His mother had left soon after. Caleb was eager to tell his story, but Scud seemed shy and let his father do the talking. His only contribution to the conversation was about the animals in their part of the forest and to point out a pretty bird that was singing above their heads.

Tenny left in the early afternoon in order to reach home before nightfall. Caleb bid him to come back and visit again and to bring them some salt.

It was summer before Tenny made another trip to Caleb's valley. Gladys had become increasingly more of a burden with each passing day, remaining in her bed during the daylight hours and then pacing back and forth in the store most of the night. Tenny felt obliged to stay with her, although she was getting on his nerves and seemed almost oblivious to his presence. July was unseasonably hot and dry, and by the middle of the month Tenny felt he had to escape to the cool air of the mountains for a few days.

He walked all the first day, exhilarated by being back in the wild. He hiked across three valleys and then along the last ridge, taking him by nightfall to the headland of Caleb's valley. He had brought the salt they had asked for and decided to get rid of its burden before exploring the lands to the west. He bedded down just below the crest of the ridge on a small grassy shelf and immediately fell asleep. It was noon by the time he awakened, ate his cold breakfast, and traversed the mile of thick side-hill brush to reach the cabin. Unlike his previous visit, there was no sign of activity when he walked into the yard.

"Hello! Is anyone home?"

A young girl appeared from one of the outbuildings.

"Hello! I'm home. You must be Tenny. I'm Rachel."

As she walked over to him, Tenny could see that she was older than he had first thought, probably only a couple of years younger than him. Her slight build and the shapeless dress that Tenny recognized as having once contained bulk flour were misleading.

"Pa and Scud are off hunting down in the valley. Pa told me you live over in the village and that you came to see them a while back. Scud said you'd be here today."

Tenny was at a loss for words. She was the most beautiful girl he had ever seen, much prettier than the few girls in the village that came to visit with him at the store. Her slim body was darkly tanned. Her rich black hair fell about her shoulders, framing a perfectly

14

sculptured face, which seemed to carry a perpetual smile. She was shorter than Tenny but walked with the grace of a taller woman. She immediately and totally captivated him.

They talked through the remainder of the afternoon. She told him that she lived most of the year with her mother in the Mohawk village to the north but came to spend the summer with Caleb and Scud. Caleb was her father, but her mother had taken her home soon after she was born.

Caleb and Scud returned later in the afternoon with a pair of turkeys they had shot. With Scud's help, Rachel proceeded to prepare one of the birds to roast over the spit.

"I hope you will stay and eat with us," she said.

"I would like that very much, but I left my bedroll in camp up the valley. I'll need at least two hours of daylight to get there," Tenny replied.

"Big moon tonight. No dark," Scud offered.

Tenny looked up at the gray, cloud-covered sky and shook his head.

Rachel saw the doubt on his face and said, "He'll be right. He always is. You'll see."

The turkey was delicious, and Tenny ate until he could eat no more. Drowsily he got to his feet as the shadows began to lengthen.

"I must go. I have just enough time to find the trail and get back to my camp."

"Will you come and see us soon again?" Rachel asked, as she took his hand.

"Do you want me to come back?"

"Yes."

For the first time Tenny did not see the self-

15

assured young woman that he had just gotten to know, but a shy girl unsure of her feelings.

As Tenny started to leave, Scud came up, grabbed him gently by the shoulders, and looked intently into his eyes. Finally he spoke, "Bear in woods tonight. Be careful."

Tenny made his way warily back up the valley, stopping for every sound that wasn't immediately familiar. To avoid the thick foliage on the slope, he had climbed directly up to the ridge and skirted the valley as he made his way around to the headland above his camp. He moved quietly as he had learned to do when stalking the animals that he wished to observe closely. The moon was full and bright as Scud had predicted, and the night was still except for a light breeze that occasionally rustled through the trees along the trail. Suddenly he heard a twig snap behind him. In the stillness of the night it sounded like a gunshot. Tenny froze then moved slowly behind a large oak beside the trail. As close as he could tell, he was downwind from the sound, so hopefully his scent had not been picked up. He waited perfectly still, barely daring to breathe. As he began to relax, he could see a shadow moving slowly through the thick bush along the slope below. The movement stopped, and the shadow grew taller as the bear stood on its hind legs. It moved its head from side to side, testing the wind, which had picked up and was now blowing up from the valley floor away from the bear and toward Tenny. Tenny could detect traces of the rancid smell of the bear in the breeze. Obviously the bear could not pick up Tenny's scent as he fell back on all fours and ambled obliquely up the slope ahead. Tenny dared not move for what seemed like an eternity. Finally he crept back to the trail and continued slowly in the direction of his camp, always on the alert for further signs of the bear's passage. He picked up fresh tracks in the mud a few hundred yards up the trail where the bear had crossed and moved down slope into the opposite valley.

The remainder of Tenny's trip to his campsite was without incident. He half expected to find his belongings torn apart and spread around the clearing, but everything was as he had left it. His food was still secure in a nearby tree, and his bedroll lay undisturbed on the ground. This was reassuring, but Tenny still did not feel safe spending the rest of the night at this site. It was in the bear's territory, and Tenny did not want to take the chance the creature would return. He thought about the other campsite that he had used the night before he discovered Caleb's cabin. It would be much safer. If he traveled along the ridge on the other side of the valley, he figured it would take only a couple of hours. He knew he would feel much more at ease with the extra distance between him and the bear.

When he returned home the next day, he asked around the village about these people he had met that lived in the mountains, but nobody seemed to know much about them.

It was a week before Tenny could get away from the store again to visit Rachel. Since his return, he couldn't stop thinking about her. On Monday morning, after unloading the monthly supplies for the store, and getting everything stacked and sorted, and arrangements made for someone to look in on Gladys, he set off across the ridge to visit her.

"I knew you'd be coming today."

"How could you know? I didn't know myself until this morning when the wagon with the store supplies came in."

"Scud said you'd be here."

"Is he ever wrong?" Tenny asked. He told her about meeting up with the bear the same night that Scud had warned him.

"I knew something was wrong," Rachel replied. "He sat up real late without saying a word."

That day was the first of many that Tenny and Rachel spent together during the summer. They explored the valley looking for the different rocks that Caleb had told them about. Some days Scud would take them to his secret places, dens with baby foxes, hawks' nests up on the ridge, and spots in the stream where there was always a big fish waiting to be caught. But mostly, Tenny and Rachel spent their time together just learning about each other.

By early September the days were getting shorter, and Tenny would make most of his trips home after the sun had gone down. He knew the path so well that he could follow it in the dark. One morning on his way to the valley, Rachel met him on the trail halfway up the ridge. She looked beautiful. She had on the same old flour sack dress, but her hair was tied up in a bright red ribbon, and her smile was more radiant than ever. She was carrying two big baskets.

"We're going somewhere else today," she said, pointing across the ridge over to the next valley behind the cabin.

"There is a big patch of wild berries that are ripe. Pa and Scud gather them every year to make their wine. Scud didn't think we should go over there alone. They can't come with us because Pa hurt his foot. I said we'd better do it, or all those berries would be wasted. It's such a beautiful day. It will be fun."

The hike to the berry patch took over an hour, but it was warm and sunny, and the trail was well marked. The patch was an entire hillside covered with waist-high huckleberry plants. Tenny had eaten the small black-skinned berries but had never seen such a large area of them in his travels.

By noon they had the baskets half-filled and stopped to eat the lunch Rachel had prepared. They took little notice of a large bank of clouds building in the western sky. By mid-afternoon they had filled the baskets and were stretched out on the hillside when it started to rain. Quickly they grabbed the baskets and ran up the hill to the cover of a rock ledge that jutted out over a small cave. A fallen tree blocked the cave entrance, but enough of the ledge was exposed to protect them from the pelting raindrops. Just as he reached the ledge, Tenny heard the roar and saw the movement of a bear at the same moment. It was at the other end of the ledge, fifty feet away and coming toward them.

"Crawl under this log," Rachel called. "Quick!" She squirmed her way through the tangle of roots and squeezed between the trunk and the cave entrance. "I don't think it can get through here."

There was no time for Tenny to argue the point. He could see no other option. The bear was moving too rapidly toward him. With difficulty he worked his way through the roots and branches along the route Rachel had taken. As soon as he was in the cave, the bear began to rage at the entrance, trying unsuccessfully to move the tree. Tenny and Rachel sat back against the cave wall shaking with fear and cold as the bear continued its attacks on the tree. Time passed, and the attacks diminished in intensity and frequency. Finally the bear appeared to abandon its quest, but they continued to hear him moving about outside.

By now Rachel's wet body was shaking violently from the cold air in the cave. Tenny put his arms around her and pulled her close to him, trying to share some of his warmth. As he looked into her eyes, he could see the tears streaming down her face.

"I have never been so scared, Tenny. I thought the bear was going to get us."

She looked up into his face and their lips met in a soft, gentle, warm kiss that neither attempted to break. They kissed again, this time with the passion of wanting each other completely. Tenny could feel himself harden with desire as Rachel pressed her body against him.

"We should take off these wet clothes," she whispered, as she lifted the sack dress over her head. Her nakedness glistened with the wetness that had soaked through. Tenny was riveted to the sight of her perfect body. Her small firm breasts immediately hardened to his touch as she started to take off his sodden garments. He felt the throbbing pressure growing between his legs and started to pull her closer. She came willingly to him. He ran his hands down her body as she started a rhythmic movement. She pulled him down on top of her, wrapped her legs around his waist, and guided him inside her. Tenny felt the pressure increase as he joined in the rocking motion of their bodies. They moved rapidly back and forth until Tenny could control it no longer. He exploded inside her as she dug her fingers into his back and let out a small scream. Suddenly, the pressure was gone, and their bodies relaxed completely. They lay down on the wet clothes and immediately fell asleep.

Tenny was the first to awake. He gazed fondly at her slim body curled up in his arms. He had never experienced such joy. The discovery of the pleasures of her body and the feelings he had were overwhelming. As he stirred, she slowly awoke and rolled herself on top of him.

"Now it's my turn," she said as she slowly ran her fingers over his body, massaging him ever so lightly. As her hands moved lower, he felt himself start to swell again. Slowly she stroked his hardness, first with her fingers and then with her tongue. Tenny was determined to control the building pressure and make these sensations last. When he thought he could stand it no longer, Rachel straddled his body and guided him inside her. Slowly she rocked back and forth, breathing rapidly. Tenny could see in the dim light of the cave that her face was flushed, and her eyes were glazing over. She was moaning softly, then louder as she rocked harder driving him deeper. Suddenly, she let out a scream, and Tenny could hold out no longer. He felt the release from his body as she collapsed on top of him.

They lay in each others arms until Rachel turned to him and asked, "You've never done this before, have you?"

"No. How did you know?"

"I could tell."

"You've done it?"

"Sometimes in my mother's village, some of us will do it when we get together. This wasn't the same. This time it was just you and me, and it was different somehow."

They had forgotten about the bear, but now a noise outside the cave brought the memories of their escape rushing back. They huddled together, not daring to move.

"Hey!"

It was Scud.

"We're in the cave," Rachel shouted. "A bear chased us in here."

"Bear gone," came the answer.

Quickly they pulled on their still damp clothes and squirmed their way back out through the tangle of roots into the last remains of daylight. Surprisingly the full baskets of berries were still where they had abandoned them. The return path seemed much longer as they trudged behind Scud to the point on the trail where they had met this morning. It had been only a few hours ago, but so much had changed that it seemed like a lifetime to Tenny. Rachel took his hand and pressed a soft kiss to his lips as they parted, and Tenny began his long night trek back to the village.

Summer faded into autumn as the days grew shorter. Never before had Tenny been so aware of the beauty in the colors of this season. It seemed to him that all his senses were keener, especially when he was with Rachel, which was now more often. He had decided to open the store only twice a week and spend the rest of his days with her. Every time they were together they made love, finding new ways and places to expand their joy.

"My mother will be coming soon to take me home to our village," Rachel announced one day.

"Can you not stay here, or come live with me at the store? I don't want to be away from you until next year."

"No, Tenny. My mother would not allow it. I must return with her."

Tenny could sense the sad determination in her voice.

A few days later, when he returned to the valley, she was gone.

As winter descended on the land, Tenny made a few more trips to visit Caleb and Scud, but without Rachel his heart wasn't in it. He took them some supplies after the first blizzard of the season and told them he wouldn't be back until spring.

It was a lonely winter for Tenny. Gladys kept to her bed and spoke little, and although the village girls still came to visit him, Tenny showed little interest in them. He waited patiently for Rachel's return.

Spring was late, delaying its arrival with sudden snow squalls and torrential rains. Tenny had no heart for hiking through the woods. He spent most of his time at the store looking after the small amount of daily business and reading the limited supply of books he was able to collect. One that particularly held his interest was a thin volume extolling the beauty and opportunities of the lands to the west along the Pacific Ocean. It told of rich farmlands, practically free for the taking. It described the lush vegetation and the mild, healthy climate. There was so much wild game, it reported, that no one went hungry, even in the winter. The Territory was, according to this book, a true Garden of Eden. Tenny had heard a few of the people in the village talking about folks they knew that had sold everything and made the long journey to this new land. There was also that story in the Springfield paper inviting people to join a group planning to band together and make the trek west. It sounded exciting, and Tenny longed for the adventure, but he knew it wouldn't be right to pick up and go. He had Gladys and the store to look after, and he didn't want to go anywhere without Rachel.

One evening in May just after he'd closed the store, he heard a heavy knock at the front door. To his surprise, it was Scud.

They stood for minutes looking at each other without words. Finally Scud spoke,

"Rachel here."

Tenny looked to Scud's hand, which held a rope, and beyond, to the dark outline of a horse and rider.

"You are surprised to see me," Rachel said as she struggled to dismount from the horse. Tenny couldn't understand why it was so difficult for her and why she needed Scud's help to reach the ground. Then he saw in the dim light how she had increased in size, her body bulging out front.

"I am going to have our baby," she said.

Tenny stood there without speaking as Scud helped Rachel into the store and had her sit by the stove. It was more than he could understand.

"When will the baby come?" Tenny managed to stammer.

"It will come very soon," she replied. "I asked Scud to bring me here so you would know before the baby is born. My mother's family and the people in the village said I had to leave, so as to not shame them by having this baby without its father."

"What are you going to do?"

"I don't know. I can stay with Pa and Scud, but it would not be very good for the baby to be living out there. I was hoping I could stay here with you, and we could be together to look after our child."

In an instant, Tenny's life was totally changed. He wanted to be with Rachel, but to be a father was an overwhelming thought. He couldn't change that. He would be a father. He couldn't just walk away from it like he had been told his own father did. And what about Gladys, would she object? Then he realized how foolish that concern was. Gladys was hardly aware of anything that went on around her. And as for the people of the village, he didn't really care what they thought. They were kind to a point, but they had given up visiting Gladys long ago and showed little interest in his or her welfare. Most of them only came around when they needed supplies.

All these thoughts churned around in his mind as Rachel and Scud sat quietly and watched him.

Finally he said, "I want you to live with me, and we will raise the baby together. We will go to the valley tomorrow and bring all your things here. It is getting late. I will fix a bed here in the store for Scud, and we will get an early start in the morning."

That night they lay entwined in each others arms, whispering quietly about their hopes, their dreams, and their future life together.

It took all of the next day to move Rachel's meager possessions to the store. As they were finally loaded and ready to leave to go home, Scud put both hands on Tenny's shoulder and looked at him intently as he said, "We come to see baby. You tell us."

In her own way, Gladys appeared to understand what was happening. She welcomed Rachel to her home.

Melissa Woods arrived with the full moon of May. Rachel labored all night, and with the help of some of the village women, the delivery was successful. Tenny was able to help ease her considerable pain by being with her and holding her hand. Even Gladys arose from her bed to take part in the birth of her granddaughter. The next day Tenny hiked to the valley to give Caleb and Scud the news.

The summer of 1842 was idyllic. Tenny and his little family were inseparable. The townsfolk remarked on the happiness and joy at the store. More and more often, Gladys' interest in life was awakened, and she joined them, doting on the baby, although in her confusion she always referred to Melissa as Tenny. Tenny began to feel his life was almost complete, but he couldn't shake the feelings of restlessness that made him wish for a more exciting existence. Rachel sensed these feelings and for a long time said nothing. Then late in the autumn, Gladys passed on. She simply went to sleep one night and did not awaken the following morning. All the town's people turned out to hear the preacher say a few words, and Tenny laid her body to rest in a small plot behind the store.

2

The warm, dry wind ruffled the knee-high grass as it blew steadily across the broad plain. Day and night, it just didn't quit and was beginning to get on Tenny's nerves. It had been their constant companion since the small wagon party had set out from Independence a week before. Tenny had kept pushing them, traveling from sunrise to dark. As a result, they had made good time, passing other slower groups as they followed the well-traveled Oregon Trail.

Tenny stretched out in the shade of the wagon as Melissa sat at his feet busily creating little prairie dirt castles. Most of the time he felt good about the trip. All had gone well, contrary to Scud's premonitions of disaster, but there was still that uneasiness and concern about their future lurking in his mind. It was a little voice telling him that he had made a mistake and was endangering the lives of his family. As hard as he tried, he couldn't shake the feeling. Last year when Scud had mumbled his misgivings,

Rachel wanted no part of leaving their life in the village and traveling into an alien wilderness. She pleaded with Tenny to abandon his dream and stay in the village, but his mind was made up, and he had decided to go even if he went alone.

Things had started to change when Caleb died. They had buried him in the valley, and Scud had come to live with them. Scud was no trouble. In fact, he had done more than his share of the work. He learned quickly and soon began taking over most of the store duties from Tenny. His efforts resulted in a steady increase in business. He enjoyed the work and the respect he was earning from the townspeople.

Sometimes Tenny resented the bond between Rachel and her brother. He often felt like an outsider, when they found so much joy in each other's company.

Four years had passed. He and Rachel had argued and made up, and they had loved but not as often. Something precious had been lost as if an unseen hand had driven a small wedge between them. They both felt the loss but never talked of it. So life went on. Finally she had agreed to go, and Scud gave up his new life in order to look after his sister.

Tenny sold the house and store and purchased a wagon, horses, mules, and equipment from farmers near the village. He made sure to keep enough money to buy needed supplies along the route they would take. They made the trip to see Rachel's mother, to obtain more horses, and for Rachel to say goodbye. They stayed in the Mohawk village for three days. It was the first time Rachel's mother had met Tenny, and she was not happy with her daughter's choice for a mate.

In St. Louis, and again in Independence, they had been advised not to take the Santa Fe trail. Although it had been well traveled for quite a few years, recent troubles with Apache and Comanche warriors, and the Mexican military had reduced traffic along this route. Quite a number of groups had been attacked. The men were killed and the women and children taken as slaves. If traders and settlers were fortunate to make it through, the Mexican authorities often imprisoned them.

Independence was bustling with the activity of groups being assembled and making preparations for their journeys across this relatively unexplored area. The City was alive with traders and trappers coming east to sell their wares and the emigrants heading west. Tenny had talked with experienced travelers and learned that his wagon would have to be caulked with tar or pitch to make it waterproof for the creek crossings. He had also been advised to carry plenty of extra rope and to have extra mules to pull the wagon through some of the sandy or muddy stretches. One of the strongest recommendations Tenny received was to join up with one of the many groups of emigrants for safety. However, he felt that sticking with one group would slow him down. He was anxious to get to the mountains as soon as possible. His plan was to hook up with whatever group was nearby at the end of the day and to set out early in the morning before they were on the trail. Prior to leaving Independence, he had traded some of the horses for the extra

Spanish mules, and he and Scud had purchased Springfield muskets, and pistols. He was advised to follow the Santa Fe Trail only for a short distance until it branched off onto the Oregon Trail, which had been surveyed by John Charles Fremont. Tenny had read the reports of Fremont's daring expeditions and had a rough copy of the published map that traced his route. What had most vividly stuck in his mind was Fremont's warning that it was critical for travelers to reach the west coast by autumn or risk being stranded by early winter snows in the mountain passes. Because of this, he was obsessed with getting to California as quickly as possible. They left Independence during the last week in April and were on the move every morning at dawn following the rough trail westward.

The first week had taken them to the ferry crossings on the Kansas River. Throughout this part of the journey they encountered Kansas Indians each day, either on horseback or living in small shacks along the trail. These Indians were friendly, but the travelers had been warned about their thieving ways. Consequently Tenny and Scud were each obliged to spend half the night guarding their animals and possessions. The mules were another problem. Considerable time had been spent in breaking them in to pulling the wagon. They continued to perform all types of antics rather than move ahead in an orderly fashion. This irritated Tenny, but by the time they reached the ferry landing, the animals were generally under control. To cross, their wagon was carefully lowered down the steep bank by rope onto the boat, which was poled across the river.

Beyond the river crossing, they were in the more dangerous Pawnee country. As they traveled, they could see small bands of Indians at a distance. They tried to stay close to other groups of wagons for protection. Average travel was almost twenty miles per day until they hit the many stretches of deep sand or mud that often sunk the wagon to the hubs. Each time the wagon got stuck, the load would have to be lightened and extra mules hitched to pull it out.

Water was scarce, and each evening they tried to locate near other groups of emigrants camped by a stream. Usually the stream banks were steep, and water for the mules had to be carried up in pails, an exhausting task at the end of the day. Even crossing these small streams often required a double team of mules and the use of ropes to deal with the steep sides. Tenny and Scud had caulked the wagon before they left Independence. Fortunately they had packed along an extra cask of tar to patch the leaks that developed with each creek crossing.

It took them three weeks to reach Fort Kearny on the Platte River. By this time the mules were manageable, and Rachel was able to drive them. Tenny and Scud, on horseback, rode close by, searching for game, and checking the condition of the road ahead. The two men were only getting four hours sleep each night except for those occasions when they made camp with other groups. This proved to be no problem for Scud, but Tenny was becoming more anxious, tense, and irritable as the days went by. He began to imagine suspicious disturbances among the animals at night and see figures moving through the bush toward camp. Every time he woke Scud to go and investigate, they found nothing.

They were able to stock up on a few supplies at the Fort Kearny sutler's store. At Scud's insistence they camped near the Fort for a couple of days in order for Tenny to get some much-needed sleep. It seemed to help him calm down.

Beyond Fort Kearny, they followed the Platte valley on a course surrounded by sand hills. Antelope and buffalo were more abundant, and most days they were able to dine on fresh meat. At the junction of the North and South Platte Rivers, they were forced to ford the south branch at a point where the water was almost a mile wide. They were now in an area controlled by the Sioux, who were considered one of the most dangerous tribes.

Their journey continued along the Platte River following a trail with numerous sections of deep sand that slowed their progress. They passed Scott's Bluff with its few cabins and a blacksmith who sold whiskey. The landscape then deteriorated into an extensive area of sterile soil, which would grow only sage, cacti, and very little grass.

By the end of May they had reached Fort Laramie, an American Fur Company trading station that the U. S. Government had purchased to be set up as a military post to protect the increasing number of emigrants traveling westward.

The Fort consisted of a rectangular enclosure of adobe buildings, up to three stories high, around a central yard.

HERD OF BUFFALO—PLATTE RIVER.

Experiences of a forty-niner - William G Johnston, 1892

Services such as blacksmithing and wagon repair were available, and most basic supplies could be purchased. Wagons and tents were spread out in the flats surrounding the Fort, which was situated on a treeless plain on a bend in the Laramie River near its junction with the Platte. Groups of Sioux were also encamped near the Fort, trading buffalo robes and buckskin for tobacco, whiskey, powder, lead, blankets and beads.

Rachel convinced Tenny to stay for a day so they could repack the wagon and wash the trail dirt from their clothing. Besides, it was a chance for her to talk to other women camped near the Fort. As usual Tenny was edgy to keep moving, but he agreed to stop with the hope of restoring some degree of harmony between them.

Late that afternoon, half a dozen Sioux warriors came to their camp. They all started talking at once, gesturing wildly at Rachel. No one could understand them until one of the braves, in very broken English, revealed that their leader wanted to trade their ponies for Rachel. Tenny was incensed and started to move toward them. Scud, noting his companion's rising anger, stood between him and the group, fearing their number and the danger Tenny could provoke. Scud explained slowly that the woman was not for trade, no matter what was offered. The Sioux seemed to grudgingly accept this and wandered off without incident.

"I stay awake tonight," Scud announced. "They maybe come back."

But they didn't, and the small party was on the trail again at the crack of dawn. The track from Fort Laramie led into the Black Hills with a steady rise in elevation and the crossing of a number of granite ridges and small streams. Eventually it took them back to the valley of the North Platte, where the traveling was easier and the grass plentiful. That evening they camped on a level grassy spot beside the Platte. They had missed joining up with another group because Tenny insisted they push ahead. Consequently they had passed trains of emigrants that had stopped for the day and were alone when darkness finally fell.

The summer heat was slowing their progress, often forcing them to seek out shade at midday. By then the grass had dried up, and the river was now their only source of water. Tenny kept pushing, continually refusing to travel in the company of other emigrants for very long. At the upper crossing of the Platte, they were taken across the river for a small fee by a ferry operated by the Mormons. They traveled through a desert covered with wild sage, and salt and soda springs. A day's travel took them to the valley of the Sweetwater River. This wide expanse of rushing water was bordered on either side by tall treeless mountains. They were now in territory controlled by the Crow and Cheyenne tribes.

As each day passed, they became increasingly aware of small bands of Indians moving throughout the surrounding hills. Fewer emigrants had traveled this far so early in the season, and more distance separated the individual groups of wagons. They followed the

Sweetwater valley, which grew progressively narrower as they approached South Pass.

Thunderheads had been building in the west all day. The wind had picked up, and by evening the sky was being lit up by continuous flashes of lightning. They had stopped an hour or so after passing the last wagon as the animals were becoming increasingly more difficult to control. The mules and horses sensed the tension in the air and tried to break loose with each clap of thunder. Keeping the fire going for the evening meal required constant attention. By the time they squatted around the dying embers to eat, the rains had moved in and quickly extinguished any sparks that remained. There was nothing more to do except crawl into the sleeping robes and hope the storm would play itself out by morning.

Tenny was shaken awake in the middle of the night by Scud.

"Two horses gone."

"They must have gotten scared and pulled their halters," Tenny observed sleepily as he pulled on his sodden clothes.

The rain had quit, and the heavy water-soaked clouds had given way to a clear, cool moonlit sky.

"No," Scud replied, as they examined the two pieces of rope. "They been cut."

"Those damn Cheyenne. They've been waiting for a chance to steal. Hopefully we've got enough light to follow their tracks. Grab your gun and we'll go get our horses back."

After waking Rachel and instructing her to gather some dry wood and build up the fire, Tenny and Scud rode out of camp on the two remaining mares. The trail led in a northerly direction toward the line of mountains that bordered the valley.

"Only our horses," Scud remarked as he stared at the two sets of tracks.

Tenny could see he was right.

"They must have walked in just to get the two horses."

Following the trail was easy over the wet ground. Even in the low scrub along the base of the rock wall, the tracks were clear. The Indians, probably thinking they wouldn't be followed, had made no attempt to hide their trail. It swung in a wide arc, first running east along the direction of the mountains then gradually swinging back toward the south.

"They're heading back toward our camp," Tenny observed with concern. "Rachel and Melissa are there alone."

As they rode over a slight rise they could make out the flicker of the campfire in the distance. At the same instant they heard the screams.

The two men drove their horses hard. From the edge of the brush they could only make out two figures near the fire.

One of the warriors was holding Melissa, with his arm across her mouth as she writhed about and tried to yell. They couldn't see Rachel, but they could hear her screaming. As they moved quietly out into the open, her naked body came into view. She was lying on the ground thrashing about and trying to squirm away, but the other Cheyenne warrior was too strong. He pinned her down, spread her legs, and lowered his body to her. He began to thrust into her, gaining momentum when she stopped struggling and lay still. All at once, with a blood-curdling cry, the young Indian collapsed on top of her as Tenny drove a knife into his spine. Rachel scrambled out from underneath the burden and grabbed a blanket while Tenny picked him up and threw him into the blazing fire. The screams of the paralyzed man echoed through the night until he was dead.

Meanwhile Scud had silently crept up behind the other warrior, grasped his head in his hands, and snapped his neck. As Tenny led Rachel back, Scud was comforting the still frightened Melissa. Tenny and Scud buried the two bodies in shallow graves and quickly packed up camp in the fading light of the fire. They traveled the rest of the night and the following day without stopping. The immediate danger was over, but that night would leave its mark on all of them for the rest of their lives.

The traders at Fort Laramie had told them that this stretch would be the most dangerous part of their journey. Tenny had reckoned on forty days of steady travel to reach the Sierra Nevada mountains. After the incident with the Cheyenne warriors, he was more aware of the danger as they drove straight for the Pass. They stayed near the Sweetwater River as much as possible since drinking water was scarce on the dry rocky land. Even the water from the river carried much sand, and it grated the teeth to drink it. The valley had soon become so narrow as to be impassable, and they were forced to go over a high rocky ridge covered with snow. On the far side of the ridge, French Canadian trappers from Fort Bridger had set up a temporary trading post where they offered buckskin clothing made by their native wives.

The trail followed a steady incline on a sandy plain to the seven thousand foot elevation at South Pass. This marked the Continental Divide, where streams on the east side flowed east, and those on the west flowed west.

They forded a number of shallow streams with ease until they reached the Green River. This body of water was four hundred feet wide, up to twenty feet deep, with a strong current. Other groups had tried, without success, to use trees that lined the banks in the construction of rafts to cross. A number of wagons, mules, and supplies had been lost in attempts to drive them across the swiftly flowing water. A few groups were assembled at the bank caulking their wagons. In this manner, they were to serve as boats, and were paddled across to the opposite shore. Tenny and Scud spent the morning getting their wagon as waterproof as possible. They carved paddles from a couple of dry logs they found on the riverbank. Then they packed most of their supplies on the mules, which when roped together, would swim across with the horses. The two men paddled with all their effort and almost reached the opposite shore when a sudden change in direction of the current caused Tenny to fall over the side into the raging current. Frantically he grabbed for the rope holding their water barrel, but the force of the river ripped it out of his hands. The current sucked him under, but he was able to come up for air in time to keep from drowning. He tried to swim to shore, but the current was too strong. At a bend in the river, where the water had undercut the bank, a large tree had fallen over. The current carried Tenny close enough to grab hold of the top branches, stop his downstream progress, and allow him to slowly pull his body into the larger, stronger branches.

With Rachel's help, Scud was able to get the wagon up onto solid ground, where they harnessed the mules to pull it out of the river. Scud chose the fastest horse and rode downstream searching for Tenny while Rachel set up camp in a grove of cottonwoods. He found the body caught up in the tree half a mile from their point of crossing. Tenny was unconscious but alive. Scud climbed out on the trunk and dragged the limp body to safety. Back at the camp, they took off Tenny's wet clothes, wrapped him in a blanket, and set him by the fire.

When he regained consciousness, he continued to shake with the cold. The next morning his body was raging with fever. Rachel and Scud decided he was too sick to travel and that they should lay over an additional day before breaking camp. Other travelers offered medicine from their supplies. A doctor traveling with a large wagon train from Ohio examined Tenny and announced that he was suffering from pneumonia and that he needed rest and warmth until the fever subsided. Their group offered a supply of mustard for plasters to help in the healing process. Throughout the day, Tenny passed in and out of consciousness and began to hallucinate with periods of strange visions passing through his mind.

They set out again the next morning. Two

days travel took them to Fort Bridger, where Rachel was able to purchase two buffalo robes for ten dollars. She wrapped these around Tenny's feverish body. She was also able to buy a portion of a butchered beef to supplement their diet.

All the work of keeping them moving fell on Scud's shoulders, and the strain was beginning to show. They traveled for fewer hours in the day, keeping close to other groups and camping with them at night. Many times over the next few days, he and his sister discussed the idea of turning around and returning home, but they finally realized there was really no home to go back to. The store had been sold, and Scud's home in the mountains belonged to someone else. So in spite of their lack of any enthusiasm for the venture, they kept going.

The few water holes they were able to find were either too salty to drink or fouled with animal droppings. The horses and mules tired easily, and travel slowed in spite of Scud's constant efforts to keep them moving. Bleached buffalo and oxen bones were scattered throughout the area, but game was scarce, and the food supply dwindled rapidly. Scud hunted all day as they moved along but was still barely able to provide enough fresh meat.

When they reached the mountains, their joy was short-lived as they continued to move slowly on the rough, poorly marked trail. The scorching heat of the desert was replaced by cooler days and frigid nights. Now more time was lost removing boulders that had been dislodged by the rains. As they reached higher elevations the rain showers turned to snow, which slowed them even more as the animals struggled to find their footing on the slippery trail.

At the end of June they reached the Mormon settlement at Salt Lake City. They stopped long enough to have a local doctor examine Tenny. The fever had dropped, but he was still too weak to take on any heavy work. He also experienced short periods of memory loss, forgetting for a few moments how to perform even the simplest tasks. They stayed in the City for three days, sampling the variety of foods available. The small local farms were well maintained and productive. They were able to obtain vegetables, milk, cheese, and eggs to supplement their meager diet. Scud took the respite from travel to complete necessary repairs to the wagon and harnesses.

Tenny's condition improved rapidly as they returned to the trail, but communication within the group grew less and less as the days wore wearily on. Tenny and Rachel spoke to each other only when necessary.

.

CLIMBING THE SIERRA NEVADA.

Experiences of a forty-niner - William G. Johnston, 1892

As they moved west, the quality of the surrounding land again grew poorer. Fresh water springs and creeks were replaced by stagnant sources, too brackish for man or beast, and bugs of all varieties were everywhere. The path took them to the headwaters of the Humboldt River, which they descended through a barren landscape of sand and marsh. The river gradually grew smaller as they moved west until it disappeared altogether. Tenny had not regained his full strength, and his patience was being tried by the continual problems. When they reached the Great Desert, conditions got worse. A week of burning sand, intense heat, and thirst affected them all. Tenny began to see shimmering bodies of fresh water where there was only sand. In one instance, he threw himself into a depression of sand to cool off, thinking it was a pool of cool, fresh water. Scud and Rachel had to forcibly pull him out. The fever returned and with it terrible headaches and periods of mental confusion that would keep him awake all night. His condition didn't improve until they reached the foothills near the end of July.

The trail up the Carson River valley through the hills was narrow and strewn with boulders. After the first day, Scud realized they would not be able to cross the main range without Tenny's full effort. His own strength was not sufficient to do the work of both men. He decided, against Tenny's objections, to team up with another small group to make the ascent. Rachel agreed to cook for both crews, allowing the men to concentrate on moving the wagons up the steeper slopes with ropes and double teams of mules. Tenny was of little help at the beginning, but by the end of the week, he was able to do his share of the work.

The Sierra Nevada summit was cold, and the ground was covered with snow. This slowed their progress to a crawl. Their spirits were lifted by occasional glimpses of the fertile valley to the west, and they were encouraged by the prospect of traveling down into a warmer land. They left their companions to a day of rest and, at Tenny's urging, started their descent. The slope was a blessing and a curse. They made rapid progress where the trail was well marked and clear, but these intervals were few and far between. Mostly it was difficult to follow, and their progress was punctuated by periods of desperate scrambling to keep the wagon upright on the icy patches. Twice the mules stumbled on the steep slopes and overturned the wagon, spilling much of the contents into the snow. They had to be unhitched each time, and Tenny and Scud had to struggle to push the wagon back on its wheels and collect the supplies that had rolled down the hillside. Surprisingly the only casualty on this part of the trail was one of the horses that had been recovered from the Indians. It suffered a broken leg and had to be shot. Scud butchered the animal and even this tough stringy meat was a relief from the diet of biscuits and the occasional grouse.

Tenny kept pushing them forward, traveling from dawn to dark, leaving little time to find dry wood and make camp.

"We go slow or lose more animals," Scud announced one bitter, crisp morning.

They were halfway down the western slope, but snow still covered the ground and drifted onto the trail. With regret, Tenny knew he was right and relented. He agreed that, from now on, they would travel only during the warmer parts of the day.

As they reached the lower elevations, and the trail passed from forest to prairie, the mood of the party improved. As Tenny felt they were out of danger of being stranded or delayed by the mountain storms, he eased off on his relentless pursuit to rush ahead.

Now they had to deal with the rain and the mud of the California valleys. Even so, the warmer weather, fresh water, and abundant grass made this stage of the trip the most pleasant.

Other travelers had told them that the trail they were following led into the recently discovered gold fields and the City of Sacramento. The trail was well traveled, and every so often groups of anxious gold seekers passed them. One morning as they rounded a bend, they caught sight of a light carriage overturned in the ditch beside the trail. As they pulled beside it, they could hear frantic calls coming from beneath the wagon. A single horse was still in harness but was lying on its side with a broken leg.

Bracing themselves against a large rock, Scud and Tenny were able to lift the side of the wagon just high enough for Rachel to pull a young woman free. The flowered pattern of her silk dress was barely visible through the mud that was plastered over most of her slim body and embedded in her long black hair. She was shivering violently from the wet and cold. Rachel wrapped her in a blanket and led her to the comfort of their wagon.

"Muchas gracias por su ayuda. Mi nombre es Dona."

"I don't know what you're saying," Rachel replied.

"I think she said her name is Dona," Tenny observed.

"Si. Dona. El rancho de mi padre está cerca de aquí."

"I got 'ranch' and 'padre', which could mean father. I think she wants us to take her to her father's ranch."

Scud shot the horse, and he and Tenny tried to pull the girl's wagon back onto the trail.

"Wagon not run til axle fixed," Scud observed.

"I think we should try and find out where she lives and take her home," Rachel announced.

By repeating the word 'rancho' and pointing in the two directions along the road, Tenny was able to determine that her home was in the same direction they had been traveling.

After they had gone a couple of miles, Dona excitedly pointed to a narrow track leading off to the north.

"Este es el camino a mi casa."

IMMIGRANT TRAIN NEARING THE SACRAMENTO RIVER.   Source: Hunting for Gold - Wm. Downie, 1893

This trail to her ranch wound for half a mile through rich grasslands, where herds of fat cattle grazed.

The passage of their wagon raised clouds of dust along the narrow pathway, which led to a two-story wood building with balconies at the front on both levels. There were no trees surrounding it, but carefully tended patches of shrubs and spring flowers covered the land around the building. As they approached, a small squat man appeared on the lower balcony. His short legs supported an ample stomach, and his head was covered with curly gray hair, which revealed his advancing years.

"Aquí está mi abuelo." Dona announced.

"Good Day," the old gentleman said as he waddled over to the wagon and helped Dona to climb down. He was dressed in a faded dark cloth jacket, a white vest that hung low over his stomach, and a pair of old dark pantaloons. His smiling eyes and wrinkled mouth lit up his face with a look of merriment.

"¿Qué pasó?" He asked his granddaughter.

"El carro se volvió más sobre mí y mi caballo está muerto," she sobbed. "Estas buenas personas me rescataron."

Turning to Tenny, he said, "Thank you for looking after my granddaughter and bringing her home. She is very sad with the loss of her favorite horse. Please come in."

Inside, most of the length of the lower part of the house was occupied by the sala, the chief room. A number of painted chairs and settees were arranged around the naked-plank floor. The visitors seated themselves facing the old man as he paced about the room.

"Tell me about yourselves, while Dona makes the coffee, and our housekeeper prepares the evening meal. We invite you to stay and eat with us."

While the preparations were being made, Tenny proceeded to tell Don Arturo the story of their trip.

As a middle-aged woman set out an earthenware bowl with large lumps of beef, a dish of frijoles, and an abundance of bread and potatoes, the old man said, "You have had an interesting trip with hardships, but you are fortunate. We have heard the stories of many of your countrymen that have not survived. What are your plans? Are you going to the city to find work or heading out to the gold fields?"

"I don't know," Tenny replied, "Getting through the mountains has been our big problem until now. I haven't thought much about what we're going to do out here."

"If you have enough money to keep going through the coming winter, you should be able to get by in the city. There is much work there. Many people have quit their jobs to go to where the gold is being found and make their fortunes, but prices are high with all the new settlers coming in."

"That is one of our problems. The money is almost gone. We will have to find work of some kind."

Don Arturo thought for a few moments about Tenny's reply and then countered, "We may be able to help you. My son-in law, Dona's father, Don Pedro, has a business freighting beef, hides, and other goods up north to the small settlements and camps. He has run two wagons until now, but his drivers have quit. He is on a trip up there with one of the wagons but will be back in a few days, and I think he might have jobs for both of you. In the meantime I would like you to stay here as our guests."

After so many days on the trail, this generous offer was a godsend. Tenny accepted without hesitation.

"Bueno, there is a small adobe building at the back that our drivers used for sleeping. It is not fancy, but you may stay there and are welcome to take your meals with us. There is plenty of pasture for your animals."

By the end of the week Don Pedro returned and welcomed his guests, especially with the prospect of having two drivers for his mules.

The winter went quickly as Tenny and Scud earned their board and wages taking the mule-driven wagons, heavily loaded with supply essentials, to villages and settlers in the mining camps in the more northerly parts of the land. The work was tough and dangerous with the ever-present threat of bandits and snow-clogged trails, but the profits were great, and Don Pedro was generous in sharing his considerable earnings with his drivers.

Rachel's pregnancy was obvious by the end of the year. She had tried to hide it from Tenny, because she knew the child was not his and feared his anger when he learned of it. They had not lain together since the Cheyenne attack and had become more distant as the winter progressed. She had spent her time helping out in the house and attempting to teach English to Dona. She was soon to discover the girl was a very slow learner. One day Don Arturo explained to her that Dona had been injured at birth, which had also resulted in her mother's death.

"We are worried about what will happen to such a beautiful young woman who is so unaware of the dangers in our world."

The household grew excited about the approaching birth. Tenny was the only one that showed little interest in the upcoming event.

Joachim was born in the spring. There was no doubt to any observer that he was not Tenny's child. The skin color and sharp native features were constant reminders to Tenny of that fateful night, and his rage became almost uncontrollable when he thought about it. Rachel became fearful of what he would do to the child the day he picked it up and stared into its tiny face.

"I should throw this creature into the fire, the same as I did with the animal that produced it."

As he carried the baby toward the fireplace, Scud grabbed him and held him firmly, while Rachel took the child from him. Tenny struggled to get free, but Scud's grip was too strong.

"You hurt baby; I hurt you," Scud whispered in his ear.

When he loosened his hold, Tenny turned to him and snarled, "If you ever try that again, I'll kill you."

Don Arturo and Don Pedro had stood by quietly observing and were troubled by the escalating conflict among their guests. The event marked a more rapid and permanent deterioration in the relationship between Tenny and Rachel. They continued to have very little contact and barely spoke to each other. The effects were far-reaching and the once peaceful household took on a more somber tone. Don Pedro was much concerned by these new developments to the point that he finally took Tenny aside.

"As you can see, things are not going well here. I think it is time you and your family find other lodgings. I will not allow your presence to disrupt my household."

Tenny was not surprised at this announcement but was more concerned about their future as freight drivers.

"Do you still wish us to ship your supplies?" he asked.

"I have been thinking about that," Don Pedro replied. "The business has been good, but

I am tiring of it. I am prepared to sell you the outfit and let you pay for it out of your profits, providing you purchase all the beef from me. You will need to move as soon as Rachel is able to travel with the baby."

Tenny jumped at the chance.

The outfit consisted of two wagons, eight mules and their packsaddles, and two sure-footed horses with riding saddles. With Tenny's wagon and their additional mules, they were well supplied. Tenny agreed to Don Pedro's price of $1,500 for the outfit, payable in one year's time out of their profits. They loaded the mules with beef and hides from the ranchero and picked up other supplies in the town of Marysville. Once they were loaded, they made their way north to the Yuba River valley, selling their goods along the way. Business was brisk, and profits generally equaled at least three times their cost. By late summer Tenny was able to hand Don Pedro the $1,500.

Tenny and Scud soon realized that although their venture had been exceedingly profitable, greater returns could be made if they were shipping to their own store in one of the more settled areas. With this in mind, they acquired some land on Lost Miner Creek, which was a short distance upriver from Downieville. Tents were erected for a temporary store and home. By fall Scud had built a solid two-story house, and Tenny was making regular supply trips throughout the valley and to the camps farther upriver. Goods were selling to the locals as fast as they could keep the store supplied. As winter began to set in they hurried to bring in more goods, using all the wagons and the extra mules as pack animals.

That winter was cold and wet. Deep accumulations of snow in the valleys reduced the frequency of their supply trains to once a week. They had found that barrels of whisky provided the best profits, and some trips were devoted strictly to satisfying the unquenchable thirsts of the miners. As relations between Tenny and Rachel continued to deteriorate, Tenny became sullen, and his drinking increased. He avoided Rachel and communicated with Scud only when necessary. Joachim's presence continued to be a thorn in his side, and he began to spend as much time as possible away from their home. He would prolong his supply trips, spending more time with his drinking friends in town.

The week before Christmas was marked by a constant snowfall. Fortunately the wind had finally calmed down, but the large flakes continued to drift in covering the valley roads and trails. Two weeks had passed since Tenny was able to make a trip to Marysville for another load, and it was wearing on his nerves. The whisky helped relieve the tension, and he had managed to exist in various stages of drunkenness for most of the week. The snow stopped the day before Christmas Eve, and the next day a few adventurous souls from upriver were clearing the main river trail and making it passable with their travel. Tenny learned from one group that they were on their way to a camp meeting near Downieville that evening, where a popular preacher that had worked around the Valley for the past year was scheduled to speak. The services had been going on for most of the week, but today was the first day the miners from upriver could get out to attend. Tenny jumped at the chance to get away. He saddled one of the mules and joined the group, making sure he had an adequate supply of liquid refreshment to get him through the evening. A holiday atmosphere prevailed as the men celebrated escaping their snow-bound cabins.

The meeting area occupied a gentle slope east of town, where the snow had been cleared away. It was a beautiful spot in the midst of a grove of live oaks. A number of tents, sewn together from a bunch of old sails, were pitched around a preacher's stand, in front of which were erected a number of rough backless seats. Tenny took a seat in one of the back rows with his friends. As they waited for one of the preachers, the bottles were freely passed around. Evening settled in, and the lanterns hanging from the trees were lit, casting a dim flickering light over the gathering congregation. Finally the first speaker walked to the stand and harangued the crowd about their sins and the evils of drink, gambling, and ignoring the Lord's day. This had little effect on the amount of alcohol being consumed in the back rows.

"Heed what I say, and the Lord will do great work here tonight. The devil is here among us, tempting us to abandon the Lord, but he will not let that happen if you listen to his word."

The words burned into Tenny's mind through the drunken haze and made him feel uneasy. He felt the man was looking directly at him and speaking these words for him alone. Looking at his friends, he saw that they were totally unaware of the message being delivered. He turned away from the next bottle being offered and sat transfixed by the sudden awareness he was experiencing. It was after midnight by the time the third preacher had delivered his message. Most of the miners had left by then so Tenny reluctantly decided to return home. Fortunately the mule could find its way back, and Tenny just went along for the ride. The moon was bright, and he could see the outline of their house just as the mule stumbled and tossed him into the ditch at the side of the trail. He hit the ground hard, and his head came to rest on a rock at the edge of the stream. He was aware of nothing until he felt Scud shaking him awake. It was bitter cold. He grabbed at a rock trying to pull himself to his feet, but all he came up with was a handful of sand and gravel from the bank. That was when he saw the gleam from the pebbles in his hand. He showed them to Scud, and the big man pawed around in the stream bank, coming up with more of the shiny stones. There was little doubt in their minds as to what they had found. These were nuggets of gold. They had heard stories of how the metal had been discovered near Sutter's Mill the previous year, but no one had found gold in this valley until now.

A sober Tenny sat up most of the night thinking about what had happened.

The message at the service was engraved in his mind, and now this discovery was an unquestionable sign to Tenny that God was telling him to change his ways and help spread His word.

Scud had been down by the creek all

morning panning the gravel and returned just
after noon with a small sack of nuggets and gold
dust. The next day they staked and registered
their claim. The more Tenny saw of the yellow
metal, the more convinced he became that God
was calling to him. It had begun to snow again,
but Tenny was determined to make the trip into
town for the last day of the camp meeting.
Because of the change in the weather, the crowd
was smaller than expected. He sat in the first
row in front of the preacher's stand and listened
intently to every word. After Bishop Callahan
had given his fire and brimstone sermon, the
next speaker was a man named Vanderslyke,
who had drifted in to a camp meeting earlier in
the year, and his life had been taken over by the
Lord. He spoke of the years of drinking, the sins
of the flesh, the degradation that had been his
life up to that fateful day, and how he had been
transformed into spreading God's word. Tenny
was totally under his spell. He arose from his
seat, walked forward, kneeled before the stand,
and pleaded for forgiveness for his sins.

After the meeting, the two men talked into
the night. Vanderslyke explained that he had
devoted his life to this mission and described
what Tenny must do to dedicate himself to the
work of the Lord. He gave Tenny an old Bible
and showed him the important passages to study
to bring meaning to his life.

Tenny was barely aware of the snow falling
and building up on the road as the mule
followed the trail back to the house. He spent
the rest of the night and the next day reading his
Bible in the flickering lantern light.

By the third day of studying his Bible, he

had made up his mind. Vanderslyke had made the invitation to join him and the other preachers on their circuit in order to learn first hand how they worked and what he must do. Tenny had no qualms about leaving his family for however long it took. In fact, he was happy to get away from them and pursue his new life. They were not surprised. Rachel and Scud were not unhappy to be rid of him for a while. Only Melissa was sorry to see him leave.

Source: Hunting for Gold,
LOOKING FOR THE COLOR Wm. Downie 1898

He started out the next morning with two
mules, one to ride and the other to carry his
pack. The four preachers were getting ready to
leave Downieville when Tenny arrived. Two of
them had decided to visit the few villages to the
north, while Callahan and Vanderslyke looked
to the numerous southern settlements that were

springing up as fertile ground for their message. The news of the gold discoveries had spread rapidly throughout the territory, and soon the gold seekers were everywhere, setting up small camps wherever they found the precious metal.

These new experiences were exhilarating to Tenny. The group stayed in the low country where snow cover was minimal. They would erect their tents with the help of the locals and stay for at least a couple of days at each camp or as long as their meetings were well attended. Services would be offered on the two successive evenings or more if there were larger crowds. The Bishop was the headliner and would conduct the service for a couple of hours with one of his carefully prepared sermons. After refreshments were served, Vanderslyke would recite his story, which had been carefully crafted with the Bishop's help. At that point Tenny would get up and give his message, the words coming from his heart. The response was encouraging. Tenny could tell that the people believed him and were moved by what he had to say as many came forward to talk with him after the services.

And so as the pattern emerged, they made their way from camp to camp throughout the valleys. Tenny could sense the acceptance of his presence becoming stronger as he became more comfortable with his role in the proceedings. He also became aware that this popularity he was experiencing was beginning to bother the other preachers. One evening after services, Callahan came to see him.

"I think it is time we organized your sermons to fit in more with our teachings."

"How do you feel that I am not in line with you?" Tenny asked.

"You have been telling your story, which is good, but your emphasis on the steps people can take to change their lives sometimes gives them the feeling that they don't need to contribute to our ministries in order to save their souls."

Tenny had harbored vague expectations of something like this. He knew the financial offerings for his segments of the programs had been considerably lower than that received by the others.

"Are you saying that the money raised is more important than giving these people hope for a better life?"

"Certainly not," the Bishop replied, "but we feel you should elaborate more on the sins they are committing."

The conversation confirmed his growing suspicions that the whole program was primarily based on making money.

The next morning he packed his belongings and headed back to the Yuba River country and home.

3

Tenny had a lot of time to think on his long trip back home. His convictions hadn't wavered on wanting to help people follow the Lord's teachings and find the way to a better life. He could also see how the preachers relied on the collections to support their lifestyle and allow them to continue with their work.

It was late February when he returned home. His feelings, although not as strong, hadn't changed toward his family. He did feel some remorse about the way he had treated Scud. On the other hand, he was more convinced that it was Rachel's influence and the sins of the flesh that had destroyed his life before he found his true purpose. His feelings against Rachel and her bastard child were even stronger. He was anxious to spend as little time as possible at home. His driving thought was only of actively pursuing his new mission in life.

Scud had spent the winter hauling supplies,

which Rachel sold to the local miners from their little store. As spring arrived and the warmer weather took over the land, new groups of men arrived in the Yuba valley to seek out the more remote placer deposits and hunt for the veins that were the source of the gold. Business picked up as more and more claims were staked, and small settlements and farms sprouted up along the river and the adjoining creeks. Scud had staked a piece of ground adjoining their claim in the hopes that Tenny's discovery on the riverbank continued upstream. Subsequently others that had learned of Tenny's find marked out a string of additional claims in a continuous line up Lost Miner Creek. However, the area of Tenny's discovery appeared to be unique, and very little gold was found on these nearby claims.

Tenny panned the gravel from their claim with Scud for a few days, but he soon became restless to get on the road again. By now he had read his Bible through at least half a dozen times and had in his mind the kinds of messages he wanted to preach. He reached an agreement with Scud to split all the gold and profits from the store equally so that he could get back on the road. By early March most of the snow had melted from around their cabin, and the early spring wildflowers covered the valley. Tenny decided it was time to leave. With the two mules and a week's worth of supplies, he chose to visit the camps that had provided the most personal support on the previous trip. Starting with a single tent and a few benches provided by the locals, his congregations grew rapidly. News spread from camp to camp of the vibrant and uplifting services offered by this young man, and men who had never attended services before flocked in to hear him. The generous offerings and support from his followers encouraged him to continue and deliver his message to other camps to the south.

Rachel had hoped that Tenny's return would bring back some of the closeness they once had, but such was not to be the case. He was even more distant than before and went out of his way to avoid physical contact with her. Rachel longed to be loved. She didn't completely understand why he no longer cared for her. She knew the presence of Joachim stood between them, but she couldn't abandon the little boy. He was her son. She had the love of her children, and her brother was devoted to her, but she felt life was passing her by. Her beauty began to bring in much more business than the other stores, which had opened up in the area. The miners, hungry for the sight and company of a beautiful woman, traveled that extra distance to enjoy the warmth of Rachel's smile.

The trouble began soon after Tenny set out. The three Reilly brothers worked a group of claims a couple of miles upstream from the store at the junction of two small creeks. They had come over from Ireland and were immediately drawn by the stories of the tremendous riches to be dug out of the ground in the new western frontier. They had been successful, amassing much wealth in dust and nuggets over the winter. Their first venture was to haul in their own supplies, but they soon realized their time was better spent mining rather than freighting.

By the summer of 1851 the country was dotted with a number of small establishments offering accommodation and meals to travelers as well as necessary supplies to the locals.

With a keen eye for feminine beauty, the brothers soon became regular customers at Rachel's store. The scarcity of available females in the area enhanced Rachel's attraction, especially to the brothers. Individually and collectively they came to the store and tried to charm her and make her aware of their presence. They would dress up in their best clothes to make their supply trips and try to gain her attention. Rachel was not unaware of their efforts and was flattered by them, but she had chosen not to respond. However, her natural seductive nature was difficult to mask. Consequently the brothers managed to convince themselves that she was interested, if not in love with each of them, and it was a challenge to each to possess her. This was especially true for Michael, the youngest, who was firmly convinced that he was Rachel's choice. William, the eldest, and Tom were the first to attempt a courtship, much in the Irish tradition. These efforts were met with little encouragement. They made a point of visiting the store on weekdays when business was slower and hung around until the store was empty. At that time they individually told her of their attraction to her and urged her to come and stay with them. She basked in the warmth of this longed-for attention but told them firmly but gently that she was not available. Though crestfallen, the two older brothers accepted her decision and did not strive any further to win her affection. This, however, was not the case with Michael. When his attentions were refused, he became angry and morose and proceeded to brood about this presumed rebuke to his manhood for many days. One Saturday evening he could no longer contain his smoldering anger. On that occasion, after an especially profitable week at their diggings, the brothers were making regular trips to their whiskey barrel. The more Michael drank, the more he thought about Rachel and her rejection of him. Suddenly he exploded from his chair, knocking the table over and spilling their drinks on the floor.

"I'm going down there and get her and bring her back. Who the hell does she think she is, sending us on our way? She's not even a white woman, and she thinks she's too good for the likes of us. Well, we'll see about that."

With those words, he burst out through the door, stumbled over to the small shed, threw the saddle on his horse, and galloped off down the creek trail.

Rachel and Melissa were just closing up the store for the evening as Michael rode up. He lurched through the open door and grabbed Rachel by the arm.

"You're coming with me right now. I'm done with you treating me like I was dirt. You're damn lucky I even want you."

Rachel's dress tore as she pulled away from him. She kicked him in the knee, dropping him to the floor, and she screamed as he got up and caught hold of her by both arms. Melissa ran out the door and within minutes she and Scud were back. By this time Michael had ripped off most of her clothes and had her pinned to the floor. In an instant, Scud picked him up and threw him against the wall. Michael collapsed in a heap on the floor just as his brothers arrived. As Scud reached for the injured man, William leveled his shotgun and said, "Leave him be. We'll take him home and deal with him. He won't bother you no more."

They picked up their unconscious brother, carried him out to their wagon, and went home.

When reports of the incident had circulated throughout the valley, groups of miners pressured the Reilly brothers to make their peace with the Preacher's family. So on a Sunday afternoon two weeks later, a reluctant Michael Reilly showed up at the store and mumbled his apology to Rachel and Scud.

Attendance at Tenny's camp meetings increased dramatically as word spread throughout the area of the spiritual inspiration being experienced. This resulted in a substantial increase in donations for him to continue his work. As it was more than Tenny needed, he felt the call to return most of it to his congregations with the stipulation that the money be used to build more permanent structures in which to conduct future services.

His successes soon caught the attention of the other preachers, especially his former mentor Bishop Callahan, who saw this untrained upstart as a threat to his reputation and income. As he made his way from camp to camp, he began denouncing Tenny as a charlatan and an imposter. These words were taken as the gospel among the Bishop's followers, but to those whose lives had been enriched by Tenny's sermons, it was the Bishop who was the phony. As Tenny's words reached more and more of the miners and the folks in the small settlements, he was encouraged to take his message further afield. This spurred him on to visit other valleys along the Motherlode. The more he was encouraged by this adulation, the stronger became his resolve that he, and only he, was doing the Lord's work. Thus his convictions grew stronger and his performances more effective. The power he felt was intoxicating as he stood on the platform and looked out over the sea of faces. Their admiration made him feel he could do no wrong. Some of the married women approached him with thinly veiled invitations to spend some time with them, but Tenny's focus and dedication was unswayable.

The autumn months found him many miles from home. Cold and the threat of bad weather steadily reduced the attendance at his services to the point that Tenny realized he would have to make his way north before winter set in. He came in sight of the Yuba Valley just as the first major blizzard of the season started to blow. Unable to see the main trail in the blinding snow, he turned off on a side trail that bordered a small creek. His hope was to find a miner's cabin where he could wait out the storm. The trail was mostly overgrown, but the mules were able to make their way up to an old abandoned cabin as the winter winds howled about. The cabin had obviously been occupied for some time in the past, but there were no signs of recent use. Rotting timbers supported a sagging roof, which showed cracks and gaps where the covering had blown away. Debris from the overhanging trees was scattered all over the dirt floor. Even so, Tenny was fortunate to push his way in through the sagging door before the full fury of the storm hit. For ten days the wind drove snow and ice crystals around and through the many holes and cracks into the small one-room structure. There was no bed and only a small rickety table in one corner. A single shelf hung precariously on the back wall. It was lined with an array of basic foods that had been severely ravaged by rodents.

An ancient cast iron single plate stove leaned against the wall inside the door and supported a leaky stovepipe that made its way through a gaping hole in the roof. A substantial pile of dry branches had been piled next to it. Tenny's first reaction of dismay was quickly supplanted by the thought that he would only have to endure it for a day or two until the storm blew itself out. Little did he know that he would be forced to remain there for over a week and that it would drastically change his life. There was little he could do for his two mules except turn them loose and hope they could find enough feed and shelter to survive.

Throughout the first couple of days he busied himself reading his well-worn Bible and sketching out future sermons. By the third day he had exhausted his supply of paper and ideas. Time began to hang heavy, and his meager food supply was running low, forcing him to severely ration it. He soon discovered the dried beans and other foods on the shelf were rotten and not edible.

The nights were the worst to endure. Even

with a small fire, the wind continued to blow through holes in the walls and roof, keeping the inside temperature much the same as that outside. Only by wearing all his clothes, wrapping himself in his bedroll, and lying close to the stove on the bare ground could he get a minimum of sleep. He was forced by the cold to waken every hour or so to add a bit more wood to the fire.

On the fifth day he ran out of food and wood. After spending a cold sleepless night, he was relieved to find the morning had brought a lull in the storm and a brief glimpse of the sun. He was able to force open the door and push away enough snow to venture outside. He sank to his waist with every step through the drifts. The mules were in a shelter of trees behind the cabin that had tufts of grass poking through the white blanket. He considered trying to ride out, but as the clouds came in and the wind picked up, he wisely decided to stay put. He set about gathering as much wood as possible before he was driven back into the safety of the cabin by the gathering force of the storm.

The following days were a continuous nightmare. The lack of food and sleep were taking their toll, and the doubts and fears were steadily creeping into his mind. He began to think that God had abandoned him and was punishing him for some transgressions he had committed. What had he done wrong? He had been steadfast and persistent in spreading His word. Why had he been left to suffer like this?

"Why are you doubting me?" The voice woke Tenny from a fitful sleep. The little cabin was dark with no traces of light seeping in through the cracks. Tenny looked around frantically for the source of the voice, but there was no one there. He stoked up the fire with a few sticks of his meager wood supply so that he could see all corners of the room. It was empty.

He settled back in his bedroll still shaken by this event that he couldn't understand. Gradually he began to drift back into sleep.

"You have abandoned your wife. Are you abandoning me as well?" Tenny was wide-awake now but no longer with fear. He began to understand that the Lord was really talking to him, and he was filled with joy.

"What should I do?" he asked and waited. There was no answer.

"I will do anything. Please tell me." There was only silence as Tenny began to weep. Sleep was even slower in returning this time.

The next morning marked the tenth day since the storm had begun. It had finally blown itself out during the night, and the new day announced its presence by sending shafts of sunlight into the dreary room. Tenny was hardly aware of the change as his mind refused to accept the reality of his situation. Slowly he forced away the memories of the night and climbed out of his bedroll. Where was he? How did he get here? He called out for Rachel, but there was no answer. He searched the room for something familiar before he realized where he was and what had happened. He pulled his bedroll up tight around his body and tried to push his way out of the cabin. The bank of snow that had drifted in front of the door made it almost impossible to open. With all his waning strength, he pushed against it until it gave him enough space for his escape. The crisp morning air took his breath away but seemed to clear his head.

"I've got to find the mules and get out of here," he thought as he slowly ploughed his way through the waist-high snow. He remembered leaving them in a small, protected grove of trees behind the cabin. Although the distance was short, it took Tenny the better part of an hour in his weakened state to slog his way to the mules. The packmule was dead; its bloated body was frozen to the ground. His pack lay beside the animal. He dug around inside it to find his gold dust as well as some hard stale biscuits, which he quickly devoured. His riding mule was also down, but she was alive. She had pawed her way down to some grass on the leeward side of the trees to survive. He helped her to her feet and was thankful that he hadn't taken off her saddle in his haste, as he doubted he would be able to put it back on in his present state. He had limited strength. His condition continued to deteriorate, as he grew dizzy and disorientated. Painfully he pulled himself up into the saddle only to be dumped over the other side as the mule lurched forward. He had to summon all his remaining strength to climb back on and pull himself into riding position. Leaning forward, he wrapped his arms around the mule's neck and guided her back to the front of the cabin. He wanted desperately to retrieve his Bible and notes, but he was afraid he would not be able to get back in the saddle. The urge was almost physical, as if a giant hand was trying to pull him back inside the cabin. The conflict raged within. His guilt over abandoning the Lord's words fought against his fear of not being able to ride out. He finally spurred the mule weakly down the valley path. He had little awareness of his trek to the main trail.

Tenny opened his eyes to see two angels hovering over him and speaking softly. It was heaven, and the Lord had not abandoned him but had brought him home.

When he finally regained consciousness, he was alone, but it was not the same room in the old cabin, and he was not cold. He sensed the odors and noises of the house and knew it was not familiar. It had a warm strangeness that was not unpleasant.

"You are awake. We didn't know if you would be."

The woman speaking these words to Tenny was a stranger.

"You have been asleep for two days since my husband and son found you on the trail and brought you to our home."

Tenny closed his eyes tight, pressing his eyelids close together, trying to clear his brain. When he opened them again, it was Rachel bending over him. Slowly her image faded and that of Gladys appeared.

"You are dead," Tenny cried out in fear. The frightened woman backed away from his bedside.

Tenny's cry brought the woman's husband into the room.

"What is wrong with the Preacher?" he asked his wife.

"I don't know," she replied. "He doesn't seem to be quite right in his head. We had better let him rest some more. Did you send one of the boys upriver to find his home and fetch someone to come and get him?"

"I sent John up a couple of hours ago. He should be home soon," the man replied.

Scud arrived the next day with the wagon. The young man had told Rachel and Scud that his folks had found the Preacher almost frozen to death on the trail. He had been acting strange ever since they brought him home. They wanted someone to come and get him right away.

Scud didn't know what to expect. In the back of his mind, the unsettling thoughts he had over the past year made him realize that Tenny was unstable. This feeling caused him more and more concern about his sister's welfare and protection.

When Scud came into the room, Tenny had no idea who he was and refused to climb into the wagon for the ride home.

Finally with the help of the men at the farm, Scud had to wrestle him to the ground, bind him firmly, and toss him into the wagon while listening to Tenny's threats of calling the wrath of God down on them.

By the time they had reached the store, he had calmed down, and Scud had stopped and untied him. He had been silent for the last hour, but as soon as they arrived home he jumped out of the wagon and ran into the house. He ignored Rachel and Melissa and shut himself in the bedroom. Rachel didn't know what to do. She had never seen him like this, so she did nothing. She just waited.

It was well after dark when Tenny emerged. He was obviously agitated as he paced back and forth across the room. Rachel had given up her vigil and bedded down with Melissa earlier in the evening. Only Scud remained in the room, sitting quietly at the table. Suddenly aware of his presence, Tenny stopped and sat down across from him, staring intently into Scud's eyes.

"I have to go back," he mumbled. "He's telling me I must go back and get my Bible. I can't go on without it. He won't let me."

Scud had no idea what he was talking about, but he was becoming more and more uneasy with Tenny's intensity and strange talk.

"You have to take me back to the cabin. I have to get my book and my notes. We have to go now."

"Not now. Too dark. We go morning."

"No, we go now," Tenny yelled, pounding the table.

Scud grabbed him as he headed for the door, holding him firmly as Tenny struggled to get free. He carried him back and set him down in a chair.

"We go morning," the big man repeated.

The next morning broke clear and cold as Scud saddled up the two horses. Tenny was anxious to get going. After they had set off down the trail, Scud asked, "Where cabin?"

When he received no answer, he asked again, but again there was silence.

Tenny was somewhere else, listening to a greater voice.

"You are failing me. You are no good. I believed in you to do my work, and you are failing me."

"No! No!" Tenny cried out then slumped forward in the saddle.

Scud reached over quickly and grabbed him before he fell off the horse. He stopped, got off, and roped Tenny firmly to the saddle.

Scud had very little idea where he was supposed to go. He knew from Tenny's ramblings that it was a cabin, but where it was, he had no idea. He could see that Tenny wasn't going to be much help. He considered just taking him back home, but he suspected they would be doing this all over again tomorrow. Without any plan in mind, he rode on with the unconscious Tenny and his horse trailing behind.

By mid-afternoon they arrived at the farmhouse where he had come to get Tenny the previous day. The man that had found Tenny met them at the door. Haltingly Scud explained their problem. The Preacher needed to find that cabin to retrieve his Bible.

The man thought for a moment then replied, "We found him a mile or two back down the road to Downieville. He was never conscious enough to tell us how he got there. You say he is looking for a nearby cabin. The only one I know of is the old Houghton cabin back up Slate Castle Creek. Houghton and his wife found a pocket of gold back in 50 and built their cabin near the diggings. He died the next winter, broke his leg while out hunting and froze to death. She waited all winter and finally found what was left of his body in the spring. Lost her mind, she did. She wouldn't let anyone go up there, claiming they were after her gold. She shot at anybody that got too close. Finally a group from around here went up last fall and found her body stretched out on the ground. She had starved to death. As far as I know, no one has been up there since. Folks claim her spirit is still around."

.

THE DESERTED CABIN.   Source. Hunting for Gold - Wm. Downie. 1898

"Must be cabin," Scud replied.

He was reluctant to find out and face the old woman's spirit, but Tenny had come awake and heard the last part of the tale.

"We must go there now," he announced, and before Scud could hold him back he had spurred his horse down the road.

As they watched Tenny ride off, the man said, "I'll take you down to the creek crossing where we found him. After that, you are on your own. I'm guessing he came down the old creek trail that leads up to the Houghton cabin. I've got no desire to go up there. It's kind of spooky. Just be careful."

The creek trail was partly overgrown and almost impossible to follow, but Tenny didn't seem to notice. He just crashed his horse through the brush and pockets of snow.

The cabin had suffered further from the winter storm. One sidewall had become detached and leaned precariously over the bank, and that part of the roof it had supported was caved to the ground. The door had come off, and the doorway was filled with snow.

Tenny jumped off his horse, clawed his way through the drift, and squeezed his slim body through a hole in the collapsed entrance. Scud watched with concern as he disappeared inside.

"I found them," he screamed, as he scratched around on the dirt floor in the fading light, frantically picking up scraps of paper and stuffing them into his pocket. He tore apart nests that pack rats had lined with pieces from his Bible. He was too intent to answer Scud's calls until he had searched every inch of the floor that he could reach. Only then did he slither back out through the small doorway.

"See! It's all here. I am forgiven," he said as he pointed to his treasures.

All Scud could see when Tenny emptied his pockets were bits and pieces of torn paper, some with writing, some with print. It was very puzzling for the big man, but he said nothing. He was steadily becoming more wary and confused by Tenny's strange ways.

Suddenly without a word, Tenny slumped to the ground unconscious. Scud tried to rouse him, but when Tenny showed no response, he gave up. He lifted his limp body and lashed him firmly into the saddle. Then he tied Tenny's horse behind his and led them down to the main trail. Tenny was still unconscious and shivering with the cold when they reached their cabin. Scud carried him into the bed, where he slept through to the next evening.

Throughout the spring of 1851, Tenny hung around the cabin but showed little interest in the store, the mining, or his companions. Every evening he stared at his treasure of paper scraps and prayed. The rest of the time he wandered up and down the river trail talking intently to everyone and to no one.

By summer, he was ready. The Lord had visited him during the night and told him it was time to go out and do His work. Tenny was filled with joy when he left before dawn the next morning without a word to anyone.

His followers in the old camps warmly welcomed him, at least for the first couple of days. They soon found that this was not the same man that had so inspired them only a few months before. He mumbled, he ranted, and he made sounds that no one could understand. Much of what he said made no sense. Those who came searching for some guidance in their lives left sadly disappointed and didn't return. Curiosity brought a few back for a second evening, but after that his followers stayed home, confused by the changes in the man they had admired.

As he traveled farther south there were brief stretches of time during which his mind was clear. He began to understand what had happened, and as he did, these periods of sanity became longer and more frequent. The realization that the voices were actually in his head was the ultimate shock. He was becoming slowly aware that the Lord had not talked to him and that these fantasies were the product of the physical and emotional traumas that he had suffered in the cabin during the storm. This made him question his mission for the first time. His convictions had been so strong, but now there was doubt.

He moved on further to the south, stopping at more of the camps that had welcomed him with enthusiasm in the past. To each group he preached a brief sermon, but it was uninspiring, and his followers left disappointed at the end of the service.

By the time he reached Mokelumne Hill he knew he had to be alone and take some time to sort it all out. It was a wild camp, but it was home to some of his more avid followers.

At his request, Tenny was offered lodging in return for private consultations and words of guidance. Even this was difficult as he was now beginning to feel that he was the one that needed guidance. He seriously doubted the validity and worth of his perceived mission. He was gradually losing his faith as late summer stretched into fall. He settled into a comfortable routine. His days were spent in discussions with his followers as well as with non-religious members of the community. Meetings were also arranged with the occasional itinerant preacher that passed through the area. All points of view were listened to and discussed. Everything he heard was food for his thoughts during the many hours he spent alone.

By October he felt physically strong and mentally confident enough to travel home.

However, the first snows had come to the valley. His friends warned him that he was not prepared or equipped for a trip of that distance this late in the year. He readily accepted their advice and stayed for the winter.

That winter of 1851 was a period of revelation for Tenny Woods. A number of unrelated remarks from the many discussions began to fit together and make sense. He had kept notes on most of his talks. At first he rejected any ideas or views with which he disagreed, but there were so many of them that the seeds of doubt in his mind continued to germinate.

One evening he met with another traveling preacher that he had briefly encountered on his previous visit to the area. Pastor Joe was a local character and a fire-and-brimstone interpreter of God's word. Tenny had talked with him before when the Pastor was sober and fired up about his mission in much the same way Tenny had been the previous year. Tonight, however, he was suffering the effects of an afternoon of sampling some homemade cider. He was very drunk. Sitting across from Tenny in his small room, he began to cry.

"I'm a fake," he sobbed. "I have been cheating these fine people. They have treated me with goodness and respect right from the day I arrived in town, and I have been lying to them and taking their money. I can't do it any longer without guilt."

Tenny was shocked by these words. His first reaction was to put it all down to the ravings of a drunkard, but some of Joe's remarks struck a familiar chord in Tenny's mind.

After he passed out, Tenny wrapped the young man in his bedroll and laid him out on the floor of the cabin to sleep it off. The next morning the Pastor apologized for his behavior.

"I guess I said some things last night that gave you concern. Maybe it was the drink or just that I had to voice these thoughts that have been bothering me for some time. I feel that I am losing my faith. I keep preaching, saying the same words, but I don't believe them anymore."

Tenny was quiet for a moment then asked, "How can you delude these people if you don't believe what you are telling them?"

"I tell them what they want to hear. Most of them come to us because they are looking for some meaning to their lives. They want to believe there is some divine reason for the things that happen and that some greater power is up there looking after them. So I get up and tell them it's all part of God's plan, and he is in control of their lives. This makes them feel better about themselves and their lives in general. They don't have to feel responsible for what they do if God is in control of their lives. If I feel I am doing some good in this manner, I can justify to myself continuing my ministry."

Tenny sat outside in the crisp air thinking about Pastor Joe's words. They made sense and mirrored what Tenny was beginning to believe. He was relieved he could go on with his work.

4

Tenny didn't leave Mokelumne Hill until
early in the spring of 1852. In the low areas that
far south, the snow was melting quickly, and
patches of green grass for the mules were in
abundance. It wasn't the best traveling weather,
but he was anxious to be on the move again. As
he proceeded north, the final traces of winter
were still very evident, but the roads and trails
were open. He kept a leisurely pace, traveling
from camp to camp, where some of his more
loyal followers asked him to conduct services.
However, he didn't feel ready or at ease
speaking to a large congregation again. He
knew that they had no desire to hear about the
doubts that had plagued him all winter. All
these thoughts had eaten away at his confidence.
It didn't feel right to preach his old sermons, as
they no longer had any meaning for him.
Instead, he offered personal guidance to small
groups in their homes. When he observed the

apparent benefit they were receiving from his talks, he became more encouraged. Those whom he counseled found this calm, concerned preacher very different from the intense young man they were used to or the raving maniac that had appeared briefly the previous year. He was quieter, talked more slowly and softly, and left the impression with each one that he was genuinely interested in them and their problems.

DOWNIEVILLE IN THE EARLY FIFTIES.   Source: Hunting for Gold - Wm. Downie, 1898

When he arrived in Downieville, he could see evidence of the rapid growth of the small town. Solidly built cabins and houses were replacing the tents and shanties that had lined the streets the previous year. A number of adobe houses reflected the influx of a small Mexican population.

As a result of all these stops to counsel his friends, his trip home was slow. In spite of an exceptionally severe winter, spring flowers were bursting through, and the tree buds were unfolding in the valley. Along the trail, he came to the spot where it joined the path to the old Houghton cabin. Jumbled flashes of memories flooded his mind, but they seemed to be happening to someone else in another time period so long ago. The more he tried to remember that time, the more it became hidden in the darkness of his mind. What was vivid in his memory was the extreme cold, his hunger, and the anger.

As he rode along, he tried to examine his feelings toward his family. He felt in his heart that all the love he once had for Rachel had been lost the night of the Indian attack. His mind knew that it wasn't her fault, but his heart couldn't forgive the feeling that she somehow enjoyed the assault. He did care for Melissa and longed to see her again. She was the only one he missed while he was away. As he searched deeper into his mind, he knew there was something else. He needed his family more than they needed him. In fact, he had come to realize that they really had no further need for his presence. When he was out on his missions and believed so strongly in what he was doing, he needed nothing or no one. He'd had his faith, but now that was gone, and he felt like a lost wanderer. He wondered if his home and his family were his only anchors.

They were all surprised to see him. Rachel

and Scud had come to the conclusion that he probably was still deranged, or dead, and they felt quite sure they would not see him again. However, the homecoming was stilted. Tenny was genuinely happy to see Melissa, but as he had expected, when he looked at Rachel and saw Joaquin beside her, memories of that night on the trail flashed through his mind again, and all longing for her disappeared.

He still did not feel ready to cover his circuit again. He mostly stayed around home with the occasional short visit to former followers in the nearby settlements. He made repairs to the cabin and store and took over the task of hauling supplies in from Downieville, but his efforts were halfhearted.

For the past couple of years most of the major creeks in the area had been producing less gold. Many prospectors were abandoning their worked-out claims and concentrating instead on searching for the quartz veins that were the sources of the placer gold in the creeks. Miners were leaving the larger camps and coming together in temporary settlements near smaller creeks, where some of the poorer deposits that had been overlooked before were now in demand. The Yuba district was no exception. Most of the newcomers were hard rock miners looking for a rich lode farther up the valley.

As soon as the ice had gone out of the creek, Scud began prospecting the claims he had staked above Tenny's original discovery. The water was still high, and there wasn't much to find. He panned a few colors here and there, but most of it produced no results. When Tenny returned, they worked his claim and found more than enough gold to make up for the loss of business from the store.

During the previous fall, the Reilly brothers and some other miners working higher up the creek had constructed a dam to divert the waters so that they could mine the original streambed. This had been a benefit to Scud as the water beside the store now flowed along a shallow channel to the east, opening up more of their rich claim area. With the early spring runoff from the snow pack, part of the dam had been dismantled to let the excess water run down the original channel. When the water level was low enough, the dam had been rebuilt, and their rich ground was again available to Tenny and Scud. Most of the recovery was flour gold with the occasional pinhead nugget.

"From what I've observed and learned in the other camps, this could be just the top of a rich zone," Tenny remarked. "As they dig down deeper, the gold is more abundant and coarser with the best values sitting in streaks on top of the rock below. We need to go deeper."

Laboriously they dug a three-foot deep channel along the length of the pay streak, panning out the gold as they went. The gravel was slightly richer with a few more nuggets. They agreed they had to go still deeper, but as yet there was too much water moving along the original creek bed. As they dug deeper their channels filled within minutes.

"Summer come, creek dry. We go deeper," Scud suggested.

Tenny agreed.

One morning in May a tall man drove his team of oxen and wagon up to the store. He got out and slowly stretched as if recovering from a long uncomfortable ride. He tied his team to the rail and walked in. He was over six feet tall and had to duck under the doorframe. He had a slim, wiry, muscular build. No one would call him a handsome man, but his shoulder-length raven black hair and hawkish features lent interest to his appearance. Rachel was tending the store and was immediately attracted to the stranger. She made her interest obvious, but it was essentially ignored.

"My name is Henry Madsen, and I'm looking for the Preacher."

Rachel sent Melissa outside to find her father.

When Tenny arrived, Madsen stated the reason for his visit.

"I'm looking to pick up some gold claims that show promise. Some folks I met farther down the valley near Downieville said you might have some good ground for sale."

Tenny thought for a minute then said, "We have a couple of claims above where we've been mining, but so far we've only been able to get a few scattered colors from them. We sort of gave up on it to concentrate on our more profitable part of the creek."

"Is it on the same creek?" Henry asked.

"It covers the bed of where the creek used to be before they built that dam farther up the valley. There's not much water in it now."

"I'd like to have a look at it," Henry replied.

The two men walked along the creek bed to the upper limit of the claims that Scud had staked. Henry climbed on a fallen log, sat down, and lit his pipe.

"I've had success over the past year down south finding pockets of gold in small creeks that others had given up on. I set out to study what was similar about the areas where the successful prospectors had made strikes. Then I used what I had learned to test some creeks that weren't being mined and found some gold. In the process, I've learned a lot about how and where the gold occurs. Just this brief look at your ground tells me it could have some potential. This creek bed along here shows a number of places where gold can concentrate. The watercourse is not straight, which is good. There are a series of bends where the water has changed speed. Also, these large boulders and the partially buried logs slow the water flow and are good potential spots for gold particles to accumulate. It doesn't appear to me that you folks have seriously tested this ground."

Scud had come along and was listening intently to Henry's words.

"Why we not find gold here?" He asked.

"I'm guessing you didn't go deep enough, or you looked in the wrong places."

"I can see that," Tenny observed, "but how come I found gold nuggets right on the surface on our main claim?"

"I don't know. Show me where you made the discovery."

The three men walked down to Tenny's original find.

"This is about what I figured," Henry announced. "You've got less than a foot of gravel over bedrock, and over here the rock is right to the surface. This is easy ground to work, where you don't have to move a lot of barren gravel to reach the solid rock on bottom. Gold is heavy and as the water moves it around, it tends to sink, but once it reaches bedrock, it can't go any deeper and lodges in or against anything on the bottom that stops it from moving farther downstream."

"Do you want to test your ideas on that ground of ours above the cabin?" Tenny asked.

"I think it's worth a try, depending on what kind of deal you are prepared to offer."

"The price is $10,000," Tenny replied.

Henry Madsen didn't answer immediately. He walked up the creek to the top end of the claims again, stopped, crossed over to the other side, and walked back.

He sat down on the log next to Tenny.

"I'll pay your price, but it will come from gold that I recover from the claim. We can write that into a simple agreement between us. When I've paid your price, you transfer the title to me."

Tenny thought for a minute and replied, "I can go along with that, but what happens if you don't recover enough to pay me in full?"

"Then I walk away, and the ground is yours. I won't have any part of the ownership until you have all your money."

At this point Scud spoke up, " You leave with gold. We get nothing."

"Well, that is not something I would do, but you don't know me. So I can understand your concern."

Henry's final offer was to pay Tenny half the gold he recovered each week, and he invited him to be present each time he collected the trapped gold from the sluice or pans. Henry wrote a simple agreement, and Tenny signed it.

That afternoon Henry purchased some provisions from their store before he set to work building a small cabin at one of the few level spots within the claims area. It took him four days to put it up, and it was not a thing of beauty. The four walls were built with unpeeled logs that had been washed up during flood times. A pitched roof composed of green saplings tied together with moss stuffed in between the cracks completed the structure.

"Cabin no good for winter," was Scuds only observation.

"I don't intend to live here in the winter. If the weather gets so bad that I can't mine the gold, I'll go live in Sacramento until the snow goes," Henry replied.

The next day he started his preparations for mining the claims. The first task was to draw an accurate map of the old path of the creek, the present course of the water flow, and surrounding banks. On it he located all large boulders and stumps that would have slowed the water and acted as spots for the gold to accumulate.

He dug an old rope harness out of the wagon. One end was tied around the yoke between his two oxen, and the other end was looped around a large boulder in the old streambed. The oxen easily moved the rock and deposited it on the shore. The rest of the boulders were systematically pulled out of the channel in the same manner.

During the second week Henry dug a series of test pits at the spots he had located on the map. Bedrock was only two to three feet below the surface except at the upper end where he had to go down over five feet. As he expected, the gold values were higher near the bottom. To this point Henry was using only a pan to test the pit material. By mid-July he had taken out over $5,000 of the yellow metal, half of which was paid to Tenny. Now that he was reasonably assured that the claims would produce, it was obvious he would have to speed up his operation in order to complete payment for the claims and make some money for himself before winter.

Scud had paid special attention to Henry's work. He and Tenny had panned out only the upper layer of sand on most of Tenny's claim. Though they had recovered a considerable amount of gold from the channels they had dug, it became clear to Scud that they had only scratched the surface.

During the third week in July, Henry took a trip into Downieville and returned with materials to build a rocker box and a sluice. With diagrams, he showed Scud the steps in constructing these devices and how they worked to extract gold from the gravels and sand.

"My one problem," Henry observed, "is getting enough water from the main creek. The only way I can see to do this is by digging a channel to divert part of its flow. However, there won't be enough for your sluice. I think you are going to have to build a pipe to bring water down from that beaver pond above the trail to have a steady supply."

The next day the two men dug a small trench from the creek to Henry's diggings, bringing just enough water to do the job. The small amount of excess water was directed down to Tenny's claim, where Scud used a sluice they had built to process the deeper deposits. By the end of August, Henry had recovered enough gold to pay the purchase price in full for his claims. He wrote out a bill of sale and Tenny signed it.

"I guess you two won't have to keep an eye on how much gold I pull out of here now," he laughed.

On the fourth of July everyone except Rachel went to Downieville for the celebrations. Most of the miners in the valleys put down their tools to celebrate the event in the various saloons that had recently opened. Traveling shows provided other entertainment. Rachel had gone the previous year with Scud and witnessed the hanging of a beautiful Mexican woman who had been accused of murdering a drunken miner. The unfair verdict and the brutality of the event had profoundly affected her, making her realize the danger to women living in this hostile environment. More than ever, she appreciated the protection of her brother, who was devoted to her.

As Henry continued to extract gold from the spots he had tested, he found that, although the pay streaks were rich, they were very limited in extent and were usually mined out in a day or two. By the end of September, he had run the sand and gravel through the sluice and rocker from all the locations that he had test pitted, and he had recovered an additional twenty thousand dollars in gold dust and nuggets.

One evening, just as he was about to dump out the larger pieces of gravel from the top of the screen on the rocker box, he noticed a tiny glint from a piece of hard clay that had not been broken. As he tapped away the covering, a nugget emerged that was larger than anything he had found so far. But what was more interesting than its size, was its shape. It had almost a human form, with two arms branching out from the base of a circular mass at one end and a wedge-shaped form at the other. The nugget was just over an inch long.

Henry was fascinated.

WORKING THE ROCKER Source: Hunting for Gold, Wm. Downie 1898

"I've seen a symbol very much like that shape before," he thought. "I just can't remember where I saw it or what it represents."

It was late, but he wandered down to the store to show the nugget to Tenny, who examined it closely.

"It looks much like one of the false idols that are described in the scriptures as being worshipped by those who are not Christians. I think it is some kind of a pagan symbol."

Rachel had been listening with interest. She took the nugget, held it in her hand, and examined it closely. With a shriek, she dropped it then backed away quickly with fear in her eyes.

"Please take this out of our house. I can feel forces coming from it. I don't know if it is good or evil, but I believe it will have a strong hold on the person that possesses it. Please take it away."

Henry was puzzled by her reaction but did as she requested.

As he walked back to his cabin he thought, "She may be right. I'll just have to wait and see, but it's too beautiful to get rid of."

During the days that followed he became even more puzzled by Rachel's newly developed fear of him. All summer she had been very friendly, even to the point that Henry felt she was trying to establish a romantic relationship. Although he considered her a very attractive woman, he had never felt comfortable in the company of non-whites. He was not an abolitionist, an attitude that had caused serious rifts between him and his brothers back in St. Louis. It was one of the factors that had prompted him to seek his fortune out west. He also felt and acted superior to the natives and Mexicans he encountered. Rachel had been unable to understand why he had spurned her interest in him. Now this strange nugget was solving the problem. He no longer needed to discourage her advances. He had purchased a gold chain in town and had a hole drilled in the nugget to attach it. As long as he continued to wear it around his neck, Rachel kept as far away from him as possible.

Henry believed he had recovered most of the easily accessible gold on his claims and that there was little point in returning the following year. Payback for time spent in prospecting new deposits would obviously not be as lucrative and besides, by the middle of October, the days were getting colder.

With this in mind, he decided to leave his equipment for Scud to use and spend the winter in Sacramento, where he could sort out his plans for the coming year. Going there would also increase the value of his gold from the sixteen dollars an ounce he could get locally, to twenty-two dollars an ounce in the larger city.

The morning before he left he decided to pass on some observations he had made on a part of their claim that Tenny and Scud had not prospected. He called them over and they walked a few yards below the store, where Henry stopped.

"You told me when I first arrived that the gold in this old stream bed was not continuous, and you pointed out that it stopped here at the trail and didn't show up again until down there near your original find. That has bothered me, as I could see no obvious reason for the gold values to be missing between these two areas. I've walked it a number of times, and I think I can see what has happened. If you look across the trail, there is a slight U-shaped depression extending from where the gold stops until where it picks up again. It looks like the old streambed, at one time, crossed over and back to where the trail is now. It is hard to see that part of the old channel because of the dirt that has filled in over the years as the trail got more use. I think that if you put some pits in around the outside of that bend, you'll find gold. You'll need to get down below the dirt that has filled in from the trail."

What they had not noticed before became obvious to Tenny and Scud as Henry traced it out.

"You help test?" Scud asked.

"No, I've had enough. I'm getting out of the walley and going to the city for the winter."

Henry loaded his wagon with his few possessions the next morning and said his goodbyes.

"When you come back?" Scud asked.

"Í don't know, certainly not before the snow has gone and the creeks are down. The chances are that I probably won't be back. I don't think there is much gold left on my land."

.

HANGING OF THE MEXICAN WOMAN.

It took Henry most of the day to reach Sacramento. He was surprised at how much the city had grown since his last visit earlier that year. He booked into the Orleans hotel, where he had stayed the previous May. The next day he swapped his dust for currency at the Mills Bank but decided to keep his nuggets. The next stop was to Bailey Brothers Jewelry to have a heavier gold neck chain made for his special nugget. The jeweler remarked on its unusual shape and informed Henry that it looked to him like the ancient symbol the Egyptians called an ankh.

"I thought it reminded me of something I had seen before."

"Do you wish to sell it?" The jeweler asked.

"No. I think I'll keep it, but I am interested in learning more about it."

"Give me a few minutes and let me look it up."

The jeweler went into the back of the shop but returned shortly with a dusty old book.

"It says here that the ankh represented divine or eternal existence to the ancient Egyptians. They wore amulets in this shape because they believed them to possess unusual powers. They even included them in the linen wrappings of their mummies in hopes of protecting the dead and ensuring eternal life."

"That is interesting. I know I had a good feeling when I found it, and I have certainly had good fortune working my claim."

"Well, it sounds like this is a strong symbol that will bring its owner good fortune and a long life. You are wise to keep it close to your body and wear it at all times. Consider it your talisman."

By the end of the month Henry had definitely decided not to go back to his claim. He now planned to return to St. Louis and his family. He had no trouble selling his wagon and team to a group of newcomers, who were setting out to spend the winter in the goldfields. He then purchased two fine horses and a Concord buggy with harnesses, which he kept at a nearby stable.

1852 was an election year. Henry had always taken an interest in politics and made a special effort to vote, no matter where he was. Although he was not a supporter of the Democratic candidate, Franklin Pearce, he was strongly opposed to the anti-slavery views of the Whig candidate, Winfield Scott. On the evening of election day, Tuesday, November 2,

Henry was one of a crowd of people outside a millinery shop that evening, where the local votes were being counted.

Fire broke out at 11:30 in the shop and spread quickly to the adjoining and nearby wood buildings. Henry's hotel was a few blocks away. The fire was moving so fast that he ran to his room and quickly gathered his clothes and possessions. He took it all to the livery stable, loaded everything into the buggy, hitched up the horses, and drove quickly out of the city. Behind him he could see the rapidly moving flames engulfing entire city blocks. When he felt he was a safe distance from the conflagration, he tied the horses to a tree, rolled up in his bedroll, and tried to get some sleep under the stars.

By morning the fire was under control, but not before most of the city was destroyed. Although only a half dozen people had been killed, many had suffered burns and lost their homes and possessions. Henry fingered his talisman, vividly aware of his good fortune in escaping without harm.

The remainder of the winter was uneventful. He found lodging at a boarding house in San Francisco and joined a group traveling east in the spring.

5

Jonathan Sarsfield, to those who took the trouble to get to know him, was considered a bit strange. Had he been rich, they would probably have made an effort to get to know him a little better and then considered him interesting or somewhat eccentric, but Jonathan was not rich so he was just thought of as strange.

He worked as a carpenter. This occupational talent used judiciously in the growing city of St. Louis of the 1840's should have provided Jonathan and his family with a comfortable living. Jonathan was more than a carpenter, he was a craftsman, but the fact was they often skirted the boundaries of poverty. He was happiest when he was able to ply his craft constructing intricate items of fine furniture from exotic woods or design unique pieces of molding and trim. Unfortunately these commissions were few and far between. The demand was for builders of houses, stores, and warehouses, who could work quickly. Jonathan had no trouble constructing fine buildings. It was the 'quickly' part that required more concentration than he could muster for extended periods. Hence, by completion date the owners would generally find an unfinished structure with Jonathan totally absorbed in the intricate carving of some obscure cornice or pillar. At times when his economic situation would become desperate and his wife Mary particularly difficult to placate, he would bear down, become single-minded, and actually complete a commission in the allotted time. A period of financial stability would then generally ensue as word spread among potential clients about the quality of his work. This would last until Jonathan transcended from the pragmatic to the fanciful and once more became engrossed in the artistic facets of his craft.

The beauty of composition and form continually fascinated him, whether expressed in a work of art, the human body, or the natural landscape. His attention could be totally absorbed by a master's painting, a beautiful woman, or an autumn sunset.

Hence, it was somewhat of a shock to his friends and acquaintances when he married Mary. Jonathan's love of beauty had attached him to more than a few of St. Louis' attractive young ladies during the years prior to his marriage. His muscular six-foot frame topped by curly black hair and finely chiseled features had provided a complimenting escort to many of the belles of the local social scene. It was wondered by some in passing why these liaisons never seemed to last very long, but in due time he would appear with another beautiful girl on his arm. What Mary lacked in beauty, she made up for in doggedness. She refused to let Jonathan escape. And he felt extremely fortunate to have found such an understanding and attentive young lady. Where Jonathan's previous paramours had been attracted by his good looks but were subsequently driven away by his strange ideas and outlook on life, Mary appeared to listen with interest and acceptance. It was only after they were married that Jonathan determined that she was partially deaf and had probably heard very little of what he had told her during the courtship. This was a devastating discovery, and Jonathan set out to ascertain if she, in fact, really knew who he was and what he believed. Painstakingly, he drew her into discourses about life, beauty, their marriage, and their lives. It was a slow process, but Mary became increasingly aware that this man for whom she had worked so hard to marry was, indeed, strange. The years that passed with this evolution of Mary's awareness produced two offspring. Joshua was born in 1838, nine months and a few days, from the day of nuptials. Elizabeth appeared three years later during the latter stages of the period of awareness.

Jonathan and Mary drifted slowly apart. Their marriage soon existed only by nature of their physical presence in the same house and their love for their children.

An event in 1848 in a far removed territory was to have a profound effect on the lives of the Sarsfields. Gold was discovered in January of that year at Sutter's Mill in California. When the news reached St. Louis, most of the people put it down to some more of the wild stories dreamed up by speculators to lure decent folk to this wild, untamed land. It was not until later, when gold nugget samples that had been sent east were put on display that people started to listen to the stories. Since St. Louis was a gateway to the western frontier, hordes of emigrants poured in, and the city entered a boom period beyond the wildest dreams of the local merchants. As a result, the demand for new construction was insatiable. Jonathan got caught up in the frenzy, working long hours every day. For the first time in their marriage, Mary was able to cast off her worries about money for an extended period of time. To Jonathan his life was that of a leaf being carried rapidly along on a raging river, oblivious to its surroundings. He wasn't happy, nor was he unhappy. He did, however, miss his time to contemplate the beauty around him, which he felt was rapidly diminishing.

As more news and samples of the discovered gold began to filter east, some of the most outstanding collections of nuggets were put on display by relatives and friends of the gold-seekers in attempts to raise money for their own passages to the Promised Land. Jonathan went to see some of the displays and was captivated by the beauty of these natural jewels. He knew he must possess such a thing of beauty and enquired as to the prices of the samples he particularly favored. To his chagrin, he discovered that their value was based not just on the amount of gold contained but on each sample's uniqueness of size, shape, and form.

Someone with an eye as keen as Jonathan's had used beauty as an additional yardstick for pricing. Consequently the nuggets that Jonathan favored were, of course, the most expensive and beyond his reach.

The gold-seekers brought disease as well as prosperity to the city. During the second week of April, Mary and Elizabeth became suddenly bed-ridden with fits of vomiting and diarrhea. Jonathan went immediately in search of a doctor; whose diagnosis was that cholera had invaded the Sarsfield household. Mother and daughter appeared to age rapidly as the disease ravished their bodies. Mercifully, Mary died on the third day of her confinement with Jonathan and Josh by her bedside. Elizabeth lingered on. Jonathan's heart was torn when he gazed down on the small wrinkled face and looked into the dark, sunken eyes of his daughter. He was only able to work when someone could be found to stay with Elizabeth and Josh a few hours each day. But Elizabeth hung on to life, and soon her body began to respond to the care and take on a healthier appearance.

Now Jonathan was the sole supporter and caregiver to his small family. It was a sobering realization. He felt the added burden of his children's welfare during his normal working hours on one hand, but he experienced a sense of freedom that had been dormant since the dawn of his marriage. His mourning for Mary had been short-lived, as they had become only minor actors on each other's stage during the last years. Jonathan was impatient to get on with his life and dreams.

The problem of what to do with Josh and

Elizabeth while he was working became a major concern. It was difficult to find anyone to look after them. For a portion of each day, they were in school. At other times he had taken them to the worksites to play, but this had proven unsatisfactory for a number of reasons.

For several weeks the gold-seekers and their wagons had been passing through the city, heading westward to Independence and St. Joseph to join up with the groups that were setting off for the western territory. The spring rains provided a building slowdown and a temporary solution to Jonathan's problems. Intrigued by the stories from these outpost towns along the Missouri River, he decided to take a short holiday and booked passage for the three of them on a river steamer for the St. Louis to Independence run. The trip generally took two or three days, but with the Missouri river swollen to near flood level, their progress was painfully slow. The steamer was crowded to overflowing with people and freight headed to the goldfields. The discomfort of confined quarters, the noise, and the continual threat of cholera was finally dispelled eight days later when they landed at Lower Independence Landing. The wild frontier atmosphere of Independence was more than Jonathan had bargained for. Masses of humanity poised to begin their western adventure took full advantage of the saloons and gambling houses. The rains, which had delayed many departures, had turned the streets of Independence into a sea of mud with people, animals, and wagons contesting for a right of way. The adventurers were mostly waiting for the prairie grass to grow tall enough to provide feed for the oxen and mules. Jonathan saw the town as a squalid, unruly site of discord and was ready to return almost immediately. The children found all this excitement fascinating.

What did interest Jonathan were the wagons and their variety of forms and construction methods. Generally they were small and light, about four feet wide and ten feet long, with hardwood bows bent over the top to which canvas covers were attached. Water barrels and extra wheels were hung along the sides. Examining them closely, he was surprised to discover that very few of the wagons sported any method of slowing their speed on descent or any kind of springs to soften the ride. They were ideally suited for the long trek across the flat prairies, but Jonathan suspected that the rougher passages through the mountains would be their downfall. Slowly a vision formed in his mind of a wagon designed to deal with all kinds of terrain, light enough to pull easily yet strong and comfortable enough to carry more than a ton of people and provisions. It would have a braking system and would be waterproofed for fording the rivers and streams without soaking everything within. He would build these wagons at home with the children and make a good living to boot. It was a chance to craft an object of his own design that he hoped would be in demand for some time.

Back home in St. Louis, Jonathan was anxious to get started. The design was clear in his head, and it took only a few days to draft it to paper. His only puzzlement was wheel construction. He had observed a variety of forms ranging from solid wooden slabs to spoked types. Most of these he felt would not stand up to such a long arduous journey even though, in many cases, extra wheels were strapped to the sides of the wagons. There was a design with wooden spokes radiating from a hardwood hub to a circular wooden rim encased by a metal band that appealed to Jonathan. The wooden part of the construction posed no problem, but he had no idea how to encircle the rim so tightly with a metal band that it could not be easily dislodged.

He went in search of a wheelwright. His quest led him to two establishments where exactly the right type of wheel was being made. Josman and Sons was a large foundry employing a few craftsmen and many Negro slaves. Although Missouri was a slave state, Jonathan was a confirmed abolitionist, another characteristic that often made him unpopular with his contemporaries. He had lived with a policy of neither doing business with nor using the products of those who owned slaves. Hence, his decision regarding a source of wheels fell to a small family establishment of three brothers, the Madsens. Richard, the youngest, was like Jonathan, a carpenter. However, his expertise was limited to producing strong, interlocking assemblages of hardwoods to form the wheel. Samuel, who was two years his senior was an ironmonger. He used their small kiln and forge to fashion the iron bars into bands, which were hammered into shape with the ends riveted to form a circle. The rim was allowed to partially cool to the point where it could be placed around the wheel. The entire assemblage was then plunged into cold water to contract the iron band and tighten it about the wood rim. Edward, the older brother, who managed the business end of the operations, also supervised the entire process. It was to Edward that Jonathan presented his request.

"Your drawings of this wagon are good. It looks to be better built than most of the ones we see rolling through the city. I like this system for slowing it down on all four wheels. Most of the ones we see don't have brakes. I do see one change I'd make. This extra width that you've designed for carrying more load could be a problem. You have it extended out from the main box. That would be fine traveling over the grasslands, but it won't be any good once you get into the forests or the mountains."

"On what do you base that?" Jonathan questioned, somewhat irritated.

"Well, we have another brother who went out to California a few years back. Henry wasn't much for working in the business here. He just wanted to hunt and fish and be out of the city, so he packed up everything and headed out west with a bunch of people. We get a letter, maybe once a year, telling us about his life out there. His trip was rough, and one thing I remember him telling about was how narrow the trails were in the mountains and the trouble they had getting their wagons through. That's why I say you need to make your wagon a bit narrower."

Jonathan thought about it then agreed, "That makes sense. Is your brother living in the area where they are finding the gold?"

"We don't know for sure. We ain't had no

letter for a while. Close as we can figure from the last time he wrote, he was somewhere north of a place called Sacramento City. It must be near the ocean as Henry described some good-sized ships going up-river there."

Jonathan and Edward continued most of the afternoon to discuss minor modifications to the wagon design. Although the two men differed widely in their approach to the problem, the combination of their talents was effective. Jonathan's eye to form and beauty was tempered successfully by Edward's more practical approach.

"I don't care how pretty it is. If it don't work right, it ain't worth making."

This was a sobering approach to Jonathan. His enthusiasm was somewhat deflated, but he could appreciate the value in the suggestions Edward was making.

Jonathan's mind was puzzled as he walked home. He had set out with the simple task of buying some wheels and arranging future additional purchases. He was returning empty-handed. He had become so engrossed in his deliberations with Edward on the wagon design that he had forgotten the original purpose of his trip.

That evening after Josh and Elizabeth had gone to bed, he set about reworking his drawings. He toiled well into the small hours of the morning trying to compromise his desire for beauty of form with Edward's more workable suggestions. Morning found him asleep at his small table, the unfinished drawings in disarray. A knock at the door broke through his slumber, and as he came slowly awake, Josh welcomed

Edward Madsen into the parlor.

"I've come to offer you a deal," Edward announced as Jonathan shook the last cobwebs of sleep from his mind. "Me and my brothers, we had a long talk about what you're wanting to do. We figured we would like to work with you if we can all get together on how to do it."

Jonathan was cautious, but interested. "What did you have in mind?"

"Well, we see it as all of us going into business together. We make the wheels and look after selling the wagons. You build the wagons. We split everything into three parts. You get one part and we get two. We can build the wagons down at our place where there's more room, and your kids can come stay with my family while you're working. Richard can work as your helper and learn the craft."

Jonathan was excited with the proposal, but he remembered the many other times when he had gotten himself into problems by being too enthusiastic. He responded calmly to Edward's offer, telling him he'd think about it for a day before he decided.

The next afternoon Jonathan took his children to meet the Madsen family. Seeing Josh and Elizabeth enjoying themselves with the other children finalized his decision to accept the offer.

Over the next four years the emigrants continued to use St. Louis as the starting point for their westward journeys. As a result, the wagon business flourished. They had expected most of their wagons would be heading west with the gold seekers, but the great migration of 1849 tapered off. Wagon sales, however, continued to increase as local farmers and merchants became aware of the superior vehicles being assembled at the Madsen yard.

For the first time in his working life, Jonathan was doing what he wanted, and he was prospering. In the first six months he was able to move his family into a larger house nearer the Yard and provide them with a better standard of living.

One morning in October of 1853, Jonathan showed up at work at 7 AM as usual. What was not usual was that the Madsen brothers did not arrive until well after nine. Richard was the first to appear, the obvious victim of a late evening and too much to drink. This surprised Jonathan, since the youngest Madsen brother, although a bit slow of wit, had proven to be the most reliable.

"We had a party last night. Henry came back from out west. He rode right up to the door about suppertime. We had no idea he was coming. We all got talking and drinking and kind of forgot about bedtime. I reckon Edward and Samuel will be along soon."

Jonathan met Henry the following Sunday at the Madsen home, where he and his family and other friends had been invited for a homecoming celebration. The two men took to each other immediately. Although Jonathan had worked daily with the younger brothers, he had felt no kinship with them. It had been a profitable arrangement of convenience but nothing more. To Jonathan, the three brothers were simply unimaginative men, the type he had always been able to work with, but with whom there were seldom any meaningful words exchanged. The brothers had mentioned that Henry was different from them, a bit odd, chasing off to California looking for gold instead of staying with the family business. Jonathan could see in a different light what set Henry apart from his younger siblings. He was more intelligent and interested in everything around him and was always looking for some new form of excitement. He was a tall man, over six feet, with little extra weight on a lean wiry frame. In certain poses he appeared gangly with thin extra-long arms and fingers. At other times as he moved, he seemed to flow across the floor with surprising quickness. A large black bushy moustache muted his hawkish nose, and the thick hair of his head fell to his shoulders in a style that had become popular with men of the frontier. Henry was not what would generally be considered a handsome man, but the intensity of his manner often had a mesmerizing effect on those around him.

He informed Jonathan that he had just come home for a visit and was considering returning west the following year. For the past seven years in California he had tried just about everything there was to do to survive. Most of the time he had lived off the land, working a while in one spot then moving on. That all changed when gold was discovered. He had been running a few cattle just north of Sutter's Mill when he heard about the find and got caught up in the excitement. That spring he set out to learn as much as he could about gold, but he soon discovered that most of the people were as uninformed as he was about where to look and how to recover it. So he just decided to go do it, figuring he had as much chance as anyone to strike it rich. He sold his cattle, bought some supplies, and went prospecting. He worked the creeks nearby, steadily moving north. He found lots of gold mostly in small rich pockets that petered out after a few days of panning. He kept moving, hoping the next patch of ground would be a little bigger and rich enough to allow him to settle in one spot for a while. All the time he was learning. It became a fascinating study, often more exciting than actually digging up the yellow metal. Soon he became able to predict with more and more success where the gold had been laid down before even taking a shovel-full of earth or a pan of gravel. Eventually he bought a claim on Lost Miner Creek in the north part of the gold belt, and in a year he had pulled out over $30,000 in dust and nuggets. Now he could get out of the cold wet winter of the Northern California Mountains and come home and take it easy for a while.

During the months that followed, Henry would often drop in on Jonathan and watch with interest his precision and craftsmanship in building the wagons. Jonathan welcomed the visits as an opportunity to ply Henry with questions about California, the frontier life, and his methods of finding and mining the gold.

On one such visit Henry remarked, "I understand from Joshua that you are interested in gold nuggets. He told me of your trips to see the exhibits when they come to town."

"That's true," Jonathan replied. "I am continually amazed at the beauty of some of the forms that nature has created with this metal."

"Then you might enjoy seeing a very

special nugget I dug from my claim last year." Henry slowly pulled a chain from his watch pocket. Jonathan had always assumed there was a timepiece at the other end of the chain, but a rounded fragment of pure gold appeared.

"This has a very special shape," Henry went on. "Although moulded gradually over the centuries by natural forces, it has taken on almost a human form. I have shown it to a jeweler in Sacramento and people here at the museum, and they tell me it resembles an ancient Egyptian symbol for life, known as an ankh. See how the rounded top appears as a head with two arms projecting outward below. The claim that produced this was the most lucrative I had worked. Finding this nugget was a natural sign of my good fortune. It is my talisman."

It was the most beautiful gold nugget that Jonathan had ever seen. None of the pieces he had observed in the exhibits had such well-defined form. As he held it in his hand, it seemed to radiate warmth throughout his body. He longed to possess it. "Would you consider selling me this nugget?"

"I am afraid not," Henry replied. "I need it with me when I return to California in the spring. I feel it must be close to my body in order for me to be successful and stay out of danger."

Jonathan thought about the nugget long after Henry had taken his leave. Its perfection of form had captivated him. The more he thought about it, the more obsessed he became with finding a way to convince Henry to part with it. In the days that followed, many proposals floated through his mind only to be sunk by Henry's adamant refusal to discuss any kind of a deal.

During the winter months the demand for wagons dropped off, and the partners were able to shorten their working days. Jonathan saw less of Henry. He had a vague feeling their friendship had cooled somewhat, but he was uncertain as to the cause if, in fact, that was the case. The truth of the matter was that Henry had found Jonathan's single-minded crusade to obtain his nugget somewhat tiresome. He regretted the passing of their previously stimulating discussions on a wide range of topics, but he felt Jonathan was becoming a bore.

Even with his lack of sensitivity, Jonathan began to sense the reason for the rift in their friendship, but this was secondary to the disappointment he was experiencing in the failure of his quest. It took an unrelated event to drastically alter the flow of their lives. Henry fell in love.

A few months previous, Jonathan had introduced Henry to one of his lady friends that they accidentally met on the street. Before Mary had entered his life, Jonathan and Clarissa Monteau had occupied a season of each other's lives. Clarissa was a tall striking brunette and a very independent lady of the fifties. Jonathan had been attracted and held by her beauty but had been unable to deal with her uncanny habit of finding weaknesses and inconsistencies in his ideas and views of the world. Normally Jonathan's lady companions would not go to the trouble of disagreeing, they would just cease

117

spending time with him. This time it had been Jonathan that had ended the relationship, but he had the lingering suspicion that much of what Clarissa had said might possibly have held some grains of truth. Before he had been able to fully analyze these thoughts, he had met Mary, and the suspicions were allayed by her apparent acceptance of all he said.

Clarissa and Henry were well matched. They were intellectual equals and found each other's company stimulating. As winter wore on, they became inseparable. To Henry, Clarissa was perfect in every way except for one. She refused to leave St. Louis, much less travel to the unsettled wilds of California and live in a log shack. She had taken over her father's thriving retail business on his death, and through the incorporation of new ideas and hard work she had guided it to greater prosperity. In addition, she was the sole support and companion of her ailing mother. Running off to California with Henry, no matter how much she loved him, was totally out of the question.

Henry spent many sleepless nights attempting to solve the dilemma. He had tentatively made up his mind to return to the goldfields and build on the small fortune he had accumulated, but the desire to marry and settle down with this special woman that had come into his life was too strong. In the end, love prevailed.

Jonathan knew nothing of Henry's torment. They had spent very little time together, and Henry had been loath to confide in Jonathan about his feelings for Clarissa. Consequently it was a surprise to Jonathan when Henry came to call one morning in the new year. He welcomed his old friend heartily into his home.

"Jonathan, I have come to discuss a business proposition with you. I think you might find it interesting."

Henry continued to tell of his former plans of returning to California, but now his impending marriage had changed it all.

"I have been trying to decide what to do with my claim. There are some friends in the valley, the Preacher and his wife, who might be interested in taking it over, but there should still be more gold out there in the gravels, and I do not want to just let it go without receiving something of value in return. Then I thought about all our conversations, and it came to me that you might be interested in a new adventure of taking your family out there and making your fortune. If this appeals to you, I know we can come to an arrangement beneficial to both of us. It may seem like a crazy idea to you now, but all I ask is that you give it some thought."

The idea did not sound at all crazy to Jonathan. Since holding Henry's nugget, wanting it so desperately, and then being unable to obtain it, he was beginning to convince himself that maybe there were lots of nuggets, even more beautiful than Henry's just lying around waiting for him to pick them up. The thought quickened his pulse, and a plan began to form in his mind.

Jonathan brooded and fussed over his decision for days. He took long walks by himself and often spent extended periods of time seemingly staring into space. Josh and Elizabeth were becoming a bit frightened of his behavior until one evening he sat them down and explained his dilemma. They listened quietly as he described what Henry had related about the journey and what life was like in this far-off land. The children were captivated by the tale and excited that they might have a chance to go. Jonathan was aware that he may have glossed over the dangers and hardships they might encounter, but he did not want the children to suspect that he was anything but totally enthusiastic about the venture.

It was late February by the time Jonathan got around to returning Henry's visit. As he planned his strategy, he thoroughly convinced himself that his enthusiasm for the adventure had not clouded his thinking. He knew what he wanted, but he had no idea of Henry's thoughts other than what he had been told. Henry was at home with Clarissa, and they both greeted Jonathan warmly. After the pleasantries, Clarissa retired to her own interests, and the men abandoned their small talk and sipped their wine in silence.

"Henry, I've come to tell you that I am somewhat interested in further details regarding your proposition. I have given the idea considerable thought and am not entirely convinced that uprooting my family to rush off to California is a sensible thing to do. I need to know much more about the life out there and how it may affect my children."

"What I propose, Jonathan, is a trade. I will put up my gold claim for your share of the business with my brothers. In addition, I will swap my gear, supplies, horses, buggy, and my cabin on the claim for your house. The offer is a straight across deal with no money involved. We can have a lawyer draw up the agreement as soon as you wish."

Although he knew he was being less than truthful about the condition of his cabin and the potential for becoming rich from the gold on the claim, he pushed this to the back of his mind in his eagerness to complete the transaction. Since he had no first hand knowledge of what Henry was offering, Jonathan was wary. Henry's offer was about what he had expected. He felt the values were near to equal only if Henry's claim still had as much gold as he described. Jonathan felt more confident in the fact that he had anticipated Henry's offer.

"That seems reasonable," Jonathan replied, "but there are a couple of other things to consider. You may keep your buggy, as I would prefer to build a wagon of my own design. In return, I would ask your indulgence in teaching me and my children what you know about finding and extracting the gold."

"That seems fair," Henry replied, "I would ask you then for your instruction on wagon-making. What is the other item?"

"I want the nugget, or there is no deal."

The effect on Henry was immediately visible. He had only half expected this demand, but now he could see he should have focused more on Jonathan's desire for the nugget and used it as the prize to get a better deal. He had been careless and was now forced into a bargaining position of which he had little control. Frantically he searched his mind for a counter proposal, but he could tell by the look on Jonathan face that his last words were the ultimatum. The decision was inevitable.

"I shall pass the nugget to you as the ink of your signature dries on our agreement."

Jonathan could not savor his victory. Now that the deal had been made, the reality of his situation began to set in. His excitement for the adventure and the chance to acquire the nugget had foreshadowed rational thought and carried him to this point. Now he must make the plans that would take him from the comfortable life he had known and cast him and the children into a life and land that existed only in the stories they had been told. Jonathan was flooded with self-doubt. That evening he told Josh and Elizabeth. This time he took care to include the dangers and deprivations they might face. He honestly voiced his fears and concerns, half hoping that the children would plead with him not to take them away from their home and friends. But such was not the case. Josh and Elizabeth listened quietly until he had finished his narration and looked questioningly into their eyes.

Josh replied slowly, picking his words with care. "Father, Elizabeth and I have talked about it since you told us we might be taking this trip. We are both afraid, but we don't want to stay here if you go to California. We want to stay together as a family."

Jonathan put his arms around them as they buried their heads in his chest, and the tears slowly and quietly flowed down his cheeks.

The days that followed would be remembered only as a blur in Jonathan's mind. His agreement with Henry was drawn up and duly signed within a few weeks, and the nugget he had cherished for so long was finally his. He immediately commissioned a local goldsmith to fashion a new and stronger chain so that he could wear his prized possession around his neck without fear of losing it.

Although many other things were on his mind, Jonathan was true to his word and proceeded to teach Henry his art of wagon making. Richard was included in the lessons but continued to show little aptitude for the fine points of the craft. Henry, on the other hand, was an apt and very competent student and soon excelled his younger brother in the construction process. As the land warmed with the longer days of spring, Henry took the Sarsfield family to a small creek outside the city to learn the techniques of panning. At first their efforts were clumsy. Josh, however, soon learned a gentler approach and was able to concentrate a tail of heavy black sand in the bottom of his pan. Elizabeth and her father showed little progress and were much less successful.

The wagon-building and gold-panning lessons continued through the month of March. On one trip, Henry decided to put a few colors of gold in the pans to give his pupils a taste of the real thing. Elizabeth managed to lose half the gold in the creek and gave up in disgust. Jonathan fared somewhat better in managing to keep all the gold in the pan, but with his concern for not losing any, he was unable to concentrate the sand enough to pick out the colors. Josh, on the other hand, managed to wash the contents of his pan down to the thin streak of black sand glistening with the planted gold.

By the middle of March they were ready to go. Jonathan had completed his new wagon, harnessed four mules he had purchased, and they had excitedly taken a few practice trips through the countryside. In order to make up for her failures as a gold miner, Elizabeth learned to drive the team. Apart from the mules and all the equipment necessary to live on the trail, Henry's outfit included two horses, a ten-year old gray gelding named Chief that served primarily as a packhorse and Henry's riding horse, a spirited three-year old stallion called Lobo. Jonathan's riding lessons met with intermittent success and some painful falls. Eventually he was able to remain in the saddle for extended periods of time on a regular basis, but the training period was enjoyed neither by horse nor rider. As a consequence, Josh's requests to try and ride Lobo were accepted.

Henry cautioned Jonathan not to set out until the spring grass on the prairie was tall enough to sustain the animals and, what was most important, travel with others as a group. Jonathan could see the wisdom of the advice but was anxious to get under way.

They had planned to leave the middle of April, but the heavy rains forced them to postpone their departure. Everything was loaded on the steamer for the 400 mile trip upriver to Independence, and on a bright sunny morning in early May, amid the farewells and good wishes of their friends, they took their last look at the St. Louis skyline.

Jonathan had planned to hook up with a wagon train in Independence, but during the long steamer trip he became acquainted with a group of Michigan farmers and their families that were traveling to California, not for the gold but to farm the rich valley lands that were being settled. They agreed to accept him as part of their group. By the middle of the month the small wagon train was stretching its way across the prairie toward the western ocean.

Jonathan would not remember the long trip west with fondness. The small group of emigrants had been beset by continual bad luck. The grass had been in short supply as a result of little rain. As a consequence, a number of mules and horses had starved. In addition, many of the expected water sources had dried up. Because the train was smaller than normal, they were subject to Indian attacks on a regular basis. Animals were stolen and a number of deaths resulted from sickness and Indian arrows. Wild game was scarce, and hunters from the group had to range over greater distances to procure food. Jonathan had purchased a musket and pistols before they left, but he was such a poor shot that others in the group suggested he would be most useful in applying his skills to making the many repairs needed by the wagons. By the time the wagon train finally reached the Sierra Nevada Mountains, winter had set in. Jonathan was totally disillusioned with the venture and greatly regretted leaving his home. Elizabeth tried to cheer him up, but she had never totally recovered from the cholera, and the trip had further weakened her. Only Josh had flourished. He had grown stronger and more competent and began take on more of his father's duties. He had learned to shoot both the musket and the pistols and had developed into an excellent marksman. One of the men in the group had taught him about knives and how to throw accurately, a skill, which he continued to improve on throughout the winter. The leaders of the wagon train were advised that any attempts to cross the mountains would be futile, so they were forced to return to Salt Lake City and wait for spring.

SUTTER'S MILL, COLOMA, CAL.—WHERE MARSHALL FIRST DISCOVERED GOLD.

Source: Hunting for Gold, Wm. Downie 1898

6

Horse and rider moved casually down the hill, weaving their way around the mud holes and ruts. They appeared to move as one being, the rhythmic motions of the young man blending with those of his mount. At the bottom of the hill the trail swung sharply to cross a small creek. A sturdy log bridge had once covered the crossing, but now the spring flood had left only a few pieces of wood thrown up on the bank.

With a gentle touch, the rider stopped the horse at the edge of the water. He turned in the saddle and looked expectantly back up the trail. Horse and rider were motionless until a wagon appeared over the brow of the hill. Then the young man spoke softly to the horse and slid from the saddle as the horse wandered into a patch of fresh grass and began to eat.

"Father, I can see Josh and Lobo down by the creek."

This announcement brought Jonathan from the back of the wagon to sit with his daughter, who kept a steady hold on the reins as the mules bounced the wagon over the ruts.

The first thing that Jonathan noticed was the length of the shadows on the trail.

"You should not have let me sleep so long. We might be lost or on the wrong road again."

"It's alright. Josh talked to some people in a cabin back a ways, and they gave us better directions than this old map we got from Mr. Madsen. According to them, this will take us to the main road. Then all we need to do is find that Preacher and our gold claim."

Jonathan slumped back on the seat. He kept telling himself to keep his spirits up if only for the sake of his children, but it was tough. He was completely disillusioned. It had taken almost a year of bad luck, breakdowns, injuries, and sickness to get this far, and now that they were almost there he had serious doubts about what awaited them. The bright new wagon they had loaded on the riverboat back in St. Louis was now a broken wreck. Almost every day some part of it had to be repaired or replaced. For a long time Jonathan had doubted if they would ever reach their destination.

Elizabeth pulled back with all her strength on the reins as they moved the wagon up beside Josh.

"There's another spoke broke on that back wheel," Josh observed. "Another fixing job tonight. Anyway, this is a good place to camp. There's water and grass for the animals, and maybe I can catch us a fish or two."

Josh and Elizabeth set camp. The fishing was good, and Elizabeth prepared the trout in the way she had learned from the other women in the wagon train.

After dinner Jonathan and Josh replaced the broken spoke and then sat about the dwindling glow of the fire as Elizabeth arranged the beds for the night.

"From what those folks told me this morning, we'll probably reach the Preacher's place some time tomorrow afternoon. Right away they knew who I was talking about. I guess everybody in this valley knows the Preacher. I asked them about Henry Madsen, and they weren't sure who he was until I described him. They knew he had gone back east, but they weren't surprised that he wasn't returning."

With mention of Henry, Jonathan automatically fingered the talisman. Throughout everything that had happened, he continued to believe this beautiful gem would eventually bring him good luck.

The next morning broke with a late spring chill in the air. Jonathan had spent another night of little sleep. His worrying over their plight had heightened as they drew closer to their destination. The cheerful and secure young father that had journeyed from St. Louis with his little brood had deteriorated into a depressed and frightened man.

"Did you hear all that ruckus early this morning?" Josh asked, as Jonathan and Elizabeth piled out of the wagon, rubbing the sleep from their eyes. "Lobo was real excited, and there was a lot of growling. I went out to have a look just as this big cat was heading out across the creek. It took a long time to get Lobo quieted down, but he wasn't hurt or nothing. It got me thinking about how those wolves got old Chief back on the trail last winter. It was a good thing Lobo wasn't tied up, or he might not have been so lucky."

Jonathan took the reins as they headed across the creek and up the other side after breakfast. As usual, Josh rode ahead to make sure the trail was good enough to get the wagon through. The track was narrow, rough, and potholed, making for slow progress. In many places it had been simply cut into the steep hillside. Washouts forced Jonathan to get down from the wagon and carefully lead the mules over the debris. They moved steadily upward.

Josh had been gone from sight for a couple of hours as the sun moved up to its zenith. Suddenly he appeared coming up the trail behind them.

CATCHING BREAKFAST ON THE YUBA. Source: Hunting for Gold
Wm. Downie: 1898

"This isn't the main trail. There's another track over in that next valley beside a small creek. We should have turned off about a mile back there. We can get down to it on another trail over the next rise, but it's real steep. I think we had better go back."

Much as Jonathan wanted to forge ahead, he had learned as the trip progressed to trust the judgment of his son. They turned the wagon around at the next wide spot and headed back the way they had come. The branch trail took them up over a sharp knoll and down into another valley. At the top the dense growth of fir opened up to reveal a panoramic view up Lost Miner valley.

"It's beautiful!"

Jonathan pulled back on the reins, and the mules came to a stop. All of a sudden the beauty of this new world began to work its magic on him. The strokes of nature's paintbrush sparked his appreciation of the colors and symmetry of this land to which he had attributed his misfortunes of the past months. The only noises were the labored breathing of the mules and the dim roar of the cascading water in the valley far below. Father, son, and daughter quietly absorbed the peace of this strange land.

"I think we've finally found our home."

The tears came to Jonathan's eyes as he put his arms around his children.

"Our claim should be just about a mile or so up that valley," Josh observed. "We should be there by dark."

When they reached the valley bottom they pulled onto a trail, which more or less followed the creek as it wound its way through the rough terrain. After a mile or so of slow going through a large grove of fir, their path became more level as the valley widened. All along the watercourse they had observed the work of the gold seekers. There were cabins and tents dotted throughout the valleys. The smell of wood smoke carried on the breeze, along with human voices.

Looking closely at Henry Madsen's map, it appeared to Jonathan that his claim and cabin should be around the next major bend in the creek. The trail skirted a wide beach area where a group of men were busy shoveling gravel into crudely built equipment designed to capture the gold. Jonathan stopped the wagon as Josh rode over to the men to ask directions to the Preacher's claim.

"It's around the bend and up a piece. You can't miss it. The Preacher's got the only cabin with two floors in this part of the valley."

Josh rode on ahead but was back just as they were urging the mules through another rough stretch.

"I found the Preacher's cabin. It is just like Mr. Madsen described it. Our cabin should be just a little way beyond. I didn't go looking for it."

They passed the two-story structure just as dusk was settling. A bit farther down the trail Jonathan stopped the wagon, got out, and he and Elizabeth made their way along an overgrown path toward the sound of the creek. When they reached the shore, Josh was sitting slumped over on Lobo, his gaze focused on a small clearing by the water.

"I think that's what's left of our cabin."

Three walls of the log structure were standing, but the roof had caved in, and the front wall had fallen and evidently washed away, as none of the logs were to be seen.

Jonathan walked slowly around the ruins a few times shaking his head. It offended his sense of craftsmanship to see something so poorly built with unskinned, mismatched logs and with no evident attempt made to fit the joints.

By now it was dark, and Elizabeth announced, "We can't stay in that tonight. We had better find a place for the wagon and set up camp. Maybe this will look better in the light tomorrow."

"It ain't never going to look any better than what you see."

The words came from a man who had ridden up along the shore. He was about Jonathan's age but shorter, with a slim, wiry build. His clothing was a mixture. The pants were deerskin, carefully hand stitched, while the coarse cotton shirt was typical of those available at most of the trading posts. A rich head of black hair flowed to his shoulders capping his delicate facial features. But it was his eyes that held their attention. His gaze was the most intense that Jonathan had ever experienced, and it unnerved him.

"What are you folks looking for around here?"

"It appears that we have come all the way from St. Louis to take up residence here, although we expected something quite different."

"Wait, this here is Henry's place, least it

was when he left, but he never said for sure whether he was coming back. Henry Madsen is the owner of this claim and what's left of the cabin. You know Henry?"

"Yes, I purchased the property from him. I have a copy of his claim title and a bill of sale. I would be glad to get them and show you if you wish."

"No. I believe you. I wasn't really expecting to see him come back. What are you folks planning to do here?"

"Why, mine the gold from this claim after we build a cabin that will stay together."

The man smiled.

"I think we need to talk more about this. You are welcome to bring your wagon back to our place. We have an extra room that you can stay in tonight. My name is Tenny Woods, but most of the folks around here call me the Preacher, as I hold regular counseling sessions up and down the valley."

Jonathan introduced himself, Josh, and Elizabeth and then returned to the wagon to drive to Tenny's cabin.

What appeared from the outside to be a two-story cabin was actually a main floor with a loft, which was accessed by a wide split-log stairway up one side of the main room. Jonathan noticed two doors at the back of the room, which he suspected led to two smaller bedrooms. The main room was bright and cheery with a fire blazing in the large stone fireplace, which covered half of one wall. The feeling of spaciousness came from the open ceiling of large hewn rafters. Oil lamps that hung from the rafters bathed the room in their yellow glow.

A large burly man, two children, and one of the most beautiful women Jonathan had ever seen were seated around a large table finishing their evening meal as Tenny and Jonathan's family entered the room.

"This is my wife Rachel, her brother Scud, our daughter Melissa, and this is Joachim," Tenny announced.

Scud stood and silently shook his hand, while Rachel smiled and held his eye contact a bit longer than he expected. Melissa and Elizabeth eyed each other suspiciously until, at her father's urging, Elizabeth made an attempt at friendship. Melissa immediately recoiled from the gesture.

Josh walked over to the big man and held out his hand.

"I'm Josh," he said.

"Scud," the big man replied, smiling at Josh.

"I'm afraid Henry Madsen was not entirely truthful with you," Tenny began as Rachel set steaming bowls of stew in front of their guests. "He certainly worked for the gold he was carrying, but in my opinion he cleaned out most of what was there. He had a system for finding the gold and worked it from one end of his ground to the other. We learned a lot from Henry. It looks like the last thing he's teaching us is that when the gold is gone, you go home and sell your claim. Originally I was having some success with my claim until the course of the creek was changed. After that our gold production improved."

"How did that happen?" Jonathan asked.

"Well, before last year the water used to run through that low spot between the house and the road. In fact, our house was at that time on the other side of the creek. Then last year a bunch of miners upstream got together and dug a big ditch to divert the flow of the creek so they could work the old bed. That moved our portion of the creek to where it is now. Fortunately the old stream course also passed through Henry's claim. Scud and I are working my new diggings and finding lots of gold, but as I feel I have been chosen to offer guidance to the folks in this valley, I am anxious to get back to my mission."

"So you're saying this claim we got from Henry Madsen is worthless, and we were cheated."

"You can't say that for sure, but I think he got most of what was there. You're not going to know until you work the ground yourself. Whether you got gypped depends on what you had to give up. You didn't just buy into a cabin and a gold claim, you took on a new way of life. Whether it pays off is up to you and the Lord."

Jonathan had nothing to say. He got up, walked to the fireplace, and stared at the flames. He then turned and looked across the table at Tenny.

"It seems I've run out of choices. We're sick of traveling and just about out of money and supplies."

Tenny thought for a moment then said, "I'm willing to offer you a deal. If you can't find any more gold on your ground, you can come and help Scud get our gold out. I'll go for a three-way split, with you getting a third and

Scud and I each taking a third."

Jonathan looked back into the fire. The day had become a major disappointment. His hopes and dreams had begun to crumble like the tumbledown cabin and were now being completely destroyed by the word that there was little chance of any gold left on his claim. They had used up most of their money and supplies making this trip, and the thought of moving on was totally discouraging. Jonathan could see no solution to their situation other than to take Tenny's offer.

"We will do it. Josh and I will work the claim with Scud. We thank you for your offer. This has been a disappointment to discover the true value of our property, but we must make the best of this. We will also need to take time to build a cabin for ourselves before winter."

It was clear and cold when Josh awoke the next morning. He had chosen to sleep in the wagon, while Jonathan and Elizabeth shared a small bedroom in Tenny's house.

"I have a bunch of meetings down near Rose's Bar this week, so Scud will help you put up a cabin, show you to the diggings, and explain how we're set up to get the gold out."

Running down the center of the dry creek bed was a ditch about ten feet deep extending for close to 500 feet between the cabin and the main trail. Beside the deepest part of the ditch was a well-constructed sluice box, below which a shallow trench sloped gently to the creek.

"Water come from pond up there," Scud announced to Jonathan and Josh, pointing along the suspended waterline that coursed down the hillside, crossed the road, and ended with its outlet suspended above the sluice.

Jonathan climbed the hillside along the trace of the pipe that had been crudely slapped together from slabs of rough sawn logs. It was mostly a gentle climb up to the edge of a small body of water. Here a beaver dam blocked the outlet. The pipe penetrated the center of the dam, leaking water along the full length of its course. Although there was no wind, Jonathan could see a continual disturbance of the water at the upper end. Puzzled, he skirted along the grassy knoll that bordered the pond to the source of the disturbance. He noted that a silty soup was bubbling up from the bottom, replacing the clear water above. As the water flowed outward, it cleared. It was warm, almost hot, to the touch. He turned to Scud, who had trudged up the slope behind him.

"That pipe is in need of repair if we want to get good water pressure. We are losing far too much water through leakage. Who built it?"

"We did," Scud replied.

"Well, it has to be fixed before we work that sluice any more. We need to shut the water off, find a lot of pine gum and moss, and patch the seams."

The repair of the water pipe took the better part of the next two weeks. Scud and Josh did most of the work while Jonathan divided his time between supervising their efforts and building the cabin.

He was able to salvage almost all the logs from Henry's old cabin. His respect for Henry decreased considerably as he became more aware of the extent to which he had been cheated. He went to work trying to make something livable from the remnants of Henry's poorly built cabin. After the bark came off and the logs were trimmed for a snug fit, the walls went up quickly. By the end of the month Jonathan and his family were able to move into their new home. Rachel rounded up enough furniture and decorating materials from other settlers to turn this simple house into a comfortable home.

Tenny was gone all this time. The day he returned he brought a wagonload of supplies and gifts. That night Rachel prepared a banquet for all to share.

"I had good meetings. The Lord was in the tent every night giving me the words to bring all these souls to salvation. They were most thankful, as you can see. It was good, and it's going to get better. There are so many out there that need me to light their way to Christ, but there is so little time."

Tenny and Jonathan talked long into the evening with Tenny doing most of the talking. Jonathan sat back, listening, and taking the measure of the man. He heard the words of a saint, but he also sensed the anger and the touch of madness of a mortal. This man of contrasts that, by chance, had become an integral part of his life, fascinated Jonathan.

VARIOUS METHODS OF MINING IN THE EARLY DAYS.

Source: Hunting for Gold - Wm. Downie, 1898

Josh and Scud had wandered up the main creek to where a bunch of miners were playing music and telling stories. After an hour Scud returned, but Josh stayed until the stories were over and the last miner had wandered off to bed. It was a bright night. The moon was full and had climbed to its zenith lighting his return. When he neared the big house he saw a dim light flickering from a rear window. As he approached he could hear muffled sounds from the room. He moved silently to the small window and carefully peered in. Tenny was sitting beside a desk with an open Bible in his hand and was speaking rapidly, gesturing wildly, and occasionally pointing at Rachel, who was seated on the floor at his feet. She was completely naked and sobbing softly. Tears trickled down her face and dripped onto the bronze surface of her breasts. The light from the candle picked up every curve of her body as she moved toward Tenny with her arms outstretched to embrace him. Tenny suddenly drew back his arm and slapped her sharply across the face. The sound was like the crack of a rifle causing Josh to almost lose his balance. A thin line of blood appeared at the corner of Rachel's mouth as she moved quickly away from her husband. Josh felt the anger boil up inside. He had to move away from the house to gain control. He trudged slowly over the trail to their cabin, his mind racing with questions about the scene he had witnessed. By the time he had climbed into bed he had decided to tell no one what had happened and try and sort it out on his own.

With the cabin completed, Jonathan devoted his time to gold mining. His patched pipe was holding, providing a substantial increase in water pressure for the sluice. The only problem was that the gold values were decreasing as they mined their way along the old creek bed.

"We're running out of gold," Jonathan announced to Tenny on one of his infrequent visits home. "At this rate we'll be washing barren gravel in a couple of weeks. We tried going deeper, but the side walls keep caving in."

"There's a claim being worked farther up this creek where they're pulling gravel up from about thirty feet down," Tenny replied. "They dig pits then enclose them around the sides with logs. This allows them to dig the pits deeper as long as they keep lining them. Some of these shafts go down over thirty feet. They claim the gold colors increase, and the nuggets get larger as you go deeper. You should take a trip over there and see how they do it. Maybe it would work for us."

The next morning Jonathan, Josh, and Scud hitched the wagon and took off up the trail to have a look at the diggings Tenny had described. The trail ran along the narrow valley beside the creek. The signs of early summer brightened their trip. As they gained altitude, they found the hillsides covered with a profusion of brightly colored alpine flowers. The air was cooler as it blew off the snow-capped peaks to the east.

At midday they reached the confluence of two major tributaries, the site of a major mining operation. Both valleys were dotted with groups of men working their diggings. Water from both creeks was being diverted through a single sluice box, and multiple boxes attached in a line along the banks. Much of the gravel appeared to be mined from the terraced hillsides. The three travelers stood and watched this beehive of activity in silence.

Josh was the first to speak.

"Over on that far hillside, that looks like what Tenny was talking about."

Shading his eyes from the sun, Jonathan could make out two men turning a crank on a barrel, which was winding rope from a hole directly below. All at once, a bucket full of gravel appeared, which was unfastened from the rope. An empty bucket was put in its place and lowered back down. The bucket of gravel was dumped into a sluice box through which ran a steady stream of water. The three moved closer and watched as the ritual of raising and lowering the buckets was continuously repeated.

"Someone in hole fillin buckets," Scud announced.

"Yes," Jonathan replied. "I think we need to have a closer look."

As they walked up the hill the two men at the shaft greeted them. Scud recognized them but said nothing.

"Hello. My name is Jonathan, and this is Scud and my son Josh. We're working a claim down the valley and are at the point where we need to be doing something like this. I guess we could use some advice on how to do it."

"I'm Bill Reilly and this is my brother Tom, and you're welcome to have a look around as long as you're not from the government or the army."

"You can be sure of that."

"Well, we're down about thirty-five feet and still in gravel. Younger brother Michael is doing all the work down there. He's the smallest of us and able to get around easier. We'll haul him up if one of you want to go down and have a look."

"Yes, I would like that," Jonathan replied. "The Preacher told us about you and sent us up here."

"Everyone knows the Preacher, but how come he sent you?"

"We're working his claim."

"I hope you're getting paid."

"We're working on shares, but I sense a warning in your words."

"Forget it. It's just talk. But time's a wasting. Let's have Michael come up, he's due for a rest and some sun. One of you can descend into our golden hell and find out what life is like down below."

Jonathan was apprehensive as he descended into the shaft. Sunlight was quickly replaced by the eerie flickering glow from the lantern at the bottom. On the way down he felt better when he saw the opening was bounded by a double thickness of logs spaced so close that the ends alternately overlapped for increased strength. At the bottom, his nervousness returned. It was just a feeling lurking in the back of his mind, which he put down to simply being confined in this small space.

The bottom three feet of the shaft was not completed, and gravel was spilling out from behind the logs. Along the exposed part he could see that the column of gravel was naturally arranged in layers according to particle size. He grabbed a handful of sand, examined it closely, and was surprised to see the tiny flecks of yellow. None of their gravel had run this rich. For the first time Jonathan felt excited about the possibilities of going deeper on Tenny's claim.

"We were beginning to think you were going to stay down there all day," Bill Reilly remarked as Jonathan climbed up the ladder. "We thought about sending Michael down to rescue you."

"It's quite a world down there," Jonathan replied.

That afternoon Jonathan decided to return, leaving Scud and Josh to learn more about the Reillys' operation. He rode Lobo back through the twilight, reaching the cabin after midnight.

A few days later Jonathan awoke early to a bright, warm summer morning. On impulse, he decided to hike up to the lake and check the water line. They had shut off all but a trickle of water before they left, giving him a chance to have a look for major leaks before opening the gate. A small tree that had fallen across the line caused the only major damage he encountered. This was easily fixed. He walked around the lake to the beach area near the hot spring. He sat down on a log by the water and let his gaze wander along the shore without really seeing anything. His mind journeyed back over the past few months and the changes that had impacted on his life. He relived the hardships suffered on the trip across the country and the disappointment in finding nothing at the end of his rainbow. Now for the first time in so long, he was optimistic about the future.

The morning heat made a swim in the lake

look inviting, so Jonathan shed his clothes, slipped into the water, and swam lazily away from the heat generated by the spring. He floated into the cooler water and then dove to the chilling layer near the bottom. As he surfaced he heard a rustling noise and saw the foliage move at the edge of the beach. Expecting a wild animal, he stayed afloat with as little motion as possible, carefully watching the shore. Suddenly the branches parted and Rachel emerged from the trail. Jonathan started to call out but stopped as she walked to the water's edge slowly unbuttoning her dress, which fell away as she stepped into the water. She picked it up and tossed it back on the shore. The beauty of her naked body took Jonathan's breath away. He couldn't take his eyes away from her. Never had he seen such perfection. It appealed to all his senses. The desire to possess such beauty was overwhelming, a feeling he had not experienced since the first sight of his talisman.

He became aware of his own exposed position and looked frantically around for a place to hide. But there was none, and Rachel was now swimming slowly toward him. He backed into the shallows, where he could stand on bottom and stood facing her. She came smiling to him. Jonathan felt powerless. It had been too long since he had been with a woman, and now this beautiful creature was within his reach. Her breasts seemed to float on the surface making tiny ripples as she moved. No words were spoken as she reached out, took his hands, and cupped them around her breasts. He could feel the nipples harden as he squeezed slightly.

She moved closer and kissed him full on the lips as he wrapped his arms around her slender body. When she reached down to grasp him, his desire became overwhelming, and he pulled her body firmly to him. He started to lead her to shore, but she stopped him, wrapped her arms around his neck, and lifted herself so that he could enter her with ease. Penetration was immediate and complete and Rachel's scream became a whimper as they reached the point of no return together.

Afterward they swam back to the beach, spread out their clothes on the sand, and stretched out to soak in the sun.

Jonathan must have fallen asleep, for when he awoke Rachel was propped up on one elbow looking down into his face.

"I think we should…," he started.

"Shhh! Don't talk, just love me."

And so they made love again, this time more slowly, exploring all of each other's sensitive areas.

"I will go back first before anyone comes looking for me," Rachel said as she slipped from Jonathan's embrace.

"When will we be together again?" Jonathan asked.

"Don't worry. I will arrange it, but we must be careful."

Jonathan wandered back to the cabin hardly able to believe what had happened. It seemed like a dream.

Elizabeth looked questioningly at her father as he entered the room.

"I didn't think you were coming back for breakfast when I saw you had taken your talisman. Scud came for Josh about an hour ago."

Jonathan dug greedily into the pancakes that she had kept warm on the stove. He explained how they hoped to deepen the shaft down to the old creek bed to find more gold.

"Isn't it dangerous? What happens if the creek starts to flow again? Won't the hole fill up with water?"

"No, you have to understand, the creek has been dammed by the miners working upstream and now flows over there," he said, pointing toward the front of the cabin. "So we don't have to worry, although there may be some underground flow. If there is, we will find it with the shaft."

Elizabeth wasn't convinced. "What happens if the dam doesn't hold the water or something causes it to break? Won't the water flow back down its old path?"

"I don't think so," Jonathan replied. "We had a look at the dam. It's well built with lots of support and bracing. Many of the men that helped build it are working downstream. You can be sure that they're going to build it well. They don't want to get washed out."

Jonathan walked down to the dry creek bed fingering the talisman. Elizabeth's questions had made him uneasy. It was ridiculous to be worried. He knew that, but Elizabeth had a habit of undermining even his strongest convictions.

Scud and Josh had the shaft down and supported to a depth where a ladder was needed to get in and out.

"We need rope and pulley," Scud announced.

"I came down to build it," Jonathan replied. "We'll cut down some of these firs for a frame and a good sturdy round log for a windlass. That short rope we have will last us for about a week until Tenny gets back. He promised to find us more rope to go deeper."

They worked all afternoon building the hoist according to the sketches Jonathan had made of the system the miners were using upstream. By evening they had it in operation. Jonathan used the ladder to go to the bottom of the shaft, filled the bucket with gravel, jerked on the rope, and Scud hauled the bucket to the surface, where the contents were dumped into the sluice. By dark they realized they could haul up five buckets of gravel for every one they had managed before by climbing up and down the ladder.

As Elizabeth prepared the evening meal, Scud and the Sarsfields discussed how they would proceed with their new mining system. They finally decided that Jonathan would work underground extracting the gravel and filling the buckets. Scud would operate the windlass and empty the buckets into the sluice, which Josh would operate, collecting the gold. They would drive the shaft until they reached a rich streak, or bedrock, or they ran out of rope.

As Jonathan drifted off to sleep that night, for the first time in many months he looked forward to the coming days, especially as he became aware of Rachel sliding under the covers and pressing her warm body against his.

They were twenty feet down with no sign of bedrock or any gold when they ran out of rope, which was, in fact, becoming too worn and frayed to be trusted any longer. They waited through a week of perfect working weather for Tenny to come back.

"I got all they had in the store in Downieville," Tenny announced that evening when he returned. "The storekeeper there told me this was the best kind you can get for this type of work."

Scud and Jonathan looked it over carefully and agreed that it would do. Tenny also brought the rains with his return. It started that evening and just kept coming down, often as showers, sometimes as hail, but most of the time as a steady downpour. Tenny was planning to leave to set up some more meetings over in the next valley, but he was forced to wait until impatience got the better of him, and he set off at the first brief sign of sunshine. Jonathan, however, refused to let the rain force him to delay their project and talked Scud and Josh into helping him deepen the shaft.

Fifteen feet, twenty feet, and then thirty feet and the rains continued. Finally at thirty-two feet they hit bedrock, which was a black slate zone striking across the direction of the creek bed. At that depth the water was seeping in. It was not enough to fill the shaft, but it was sufficient to make working at the bottom very uncomfortable.

After Jonathan sent up the first bucket of gravel that he scraped off bedrock, he signaled Scud that he was coming up. Josh washed the gravel and sand down the sluice revealing a handful of nuggets, some as big as peas.

"We hit it," Jonathan yelled as the three danced around the sluice.

7

The autumn of 1854 passed quickly. More and more rich streaks of gold-bearing gravel were encountered sitting on top of the bedrock. Jonathan drove side tunnels exploring a few of these but found they mostly occurred as streaks that disappeared after a few feet. More logs were required for support, so Jonathan taught Elizabeth how to identify the type and size of the trees they needed. He tried to interest Melissa in helping, but it was clear that she wanted as little contact with the Sarsfields as possible. She had become moody since their arrival and spent most of her time by herself. It was only when her father was home that she came out of her shell. Consequently each morning when the chores were finished, Elizabeth would hike through the forests alone seeking out and marking the trees to be cut.

The daily output of gold increased steadily. Josh was becoming an expert at recovering the fine gold from the sluice, losing only a small fraction of the precious metal.

Jonathan wore the talisman around his neck every day just as Henry had done. Henry had assured him that the nugget had brought him good luck, and Jonathan believed it had carried him through the dangers and adversities of the trip to the goldfields. Every evening just before he retired for the night, he held it to his forehead for a few minutes then placed it gently in a cigar box he kept solely for that purpose. Each morning he would remove it from the box and place it around his neck before beginning the day's activities. Rachel had initially reacted to it as she had when Henry showed it, but as she and Jonathan became lovers she took it to be a symbol of their bond. With Jonathan she no longer felt lonely and unwanted. Each day she looked forward eagerly for the time they could be together. Initially she was concerned that Tenny would find them out, but she soon came to the realization that he was either not aware or didn't care.

By late October the second shaft hit bedrock at thirty feet. As Jonathan angled the shaft down to the main channel, an increasing amount of the gold was found as small nuggets. One morning he literally flew up the ladders clutching a nugget the size of a small egg.

"Look at this," he yelled. "We've finally hit a rich streak. This was sitting right on the bottom in a crack."

Now the problem was to determine how far they could dig and reinforce a tunnel safely on this streak. They knew that progress would be much slower as the heavier logs had to be lowered down the shaft, dragged along the tunnel, and driven in firmly to support the weight of the load of gravel above.

"I don't want to be very far from the shaft if the tunnel starts to cave," Jonathan announced. "We'll go about twenty feet in each direction and then we will have to dig another shaft down from the surface and connect the tunnels that way."

Tenny spent more time away from home. His counseling took him farther afield as his popularity started to increase again. Every two weeks he would show up for a day, check on the mining and then disappear the next day.

Melissa begged her father to take her with him. She was becoming more jealous of the attention her mother was showing Elizabeth and distanced herself from both of them.

Rachel and Jonathan continued their frantic lovemaking, taking more chances as they became confident and trusting in each other.

Only once had their secret been revealed, when Josh discovered their bodies intertwined on the grassy bank by the pond, which was their favorite spot. Josh was fascinated and hid in the bushes by the side of the trail watching until the danger of being discovered pulled him away. Ever since the evening he had watched Rachel and Tenny through their back window, he had been unable to get the image of her body out of his mind. Now this new vision was taking over. He was beginning to understand what was going on, but there was no one he could ask. It wasn't the sex act that confused him, it was the relationships of Rachel and Tenny, and Rachel and his father that was puzzling. He was tempted to talk to Elizabeth. She probably knew what was happening and could explain it, but he didn't want to take the chance in case she didn't know.

One evening Tenny returned with the news that the Reilly brothers were bringing in some new equipment to mine the gold from the high banks on either side of the creek. The next day they watched as wagonloads of lumber, canvas hose, barrels of gunpowder, and other materials and equipment were transported up the old trail past the store.

By the end of the week, Jonathan had run a tunnel along the bedrock surface as far as he felt safe. He had dropped about two more feet in depth to the end of the tunnel, where he calculated he was under about thirty feet of gravel. He was loading the bucket at the low point in the old creek bed when he felt a slight tremor beneath his feet. The water trickling down had suddenly increased to a steady drizzle, washing a considerable amount of sand onto the tunnel floor and covering his feet with water. The tremors increased in number, and as the shaking got stronger, more and more material sifted down. Clutching the talisman, he knew he could go no farther and hurried to get to the surface right away. He couldn't understand the source of the tremors, but they felt very real. As he moved to the top of the ladder he saw Scud and Josh looking at a depression slowly forming on the surface over the end of the tunnel.

"Did you feel that shaking? Our tunnel is starting to collapse, and I don't think there is any way we can save it. We are going to have to start over at another spot."

As Jonathan, Scud, and Josh watched the surface material slowly sift down into their underground workings, Tenny rode down the creek trail toward them.

"I came to warn you to get up on the surface. That bunch up there are setting charges in small holes along the hillside to break up the clays and gravels so that they can wash it down into the sluices."

"So that is what is making the ground shake," Jonathan observed.

The next day they walked up the creek trail to where all the activity was taking place. The scene was vastly different from the last time they had visited the Reillys. Above the dam they could see a long canvas hose snaking its way up the valley. At the lower end was a wooden nozzle from which a stream of water was being ejected under considerable pressure at the sides of the valley.

"I wondered when you fellows were going to come up and have a look."

It was Michael Reilly that approached them on the trail. Scud had seen the youngest of three brothers only once since he had thrown him against the store wall after his attack on Rachel. He tensed, ready for another encounter, but the young man showed no animosity.

"We are getting everything ready to wash down those high bank gravels above the dam. That stuff isn't as rich as what we been mining down here, but we've got this lower stuff pretty well mined out. Besides, we can run a lot more sand and gravel through this series of sluices. This thing is called a Long Tom, but it is just a bunch of sluice boxes joined end to end. The whole camp up here is working as a group on this, and we all get an equal share of the gold."

"Where is the water going after you run it through that string of sluices?" Jonathan asked.

"We collect it in a pool behind the dam then let it out slowly into the creek below the dam so it won't interfere with the work downstream."

The next day Jonathan, Tenny, and Scud had to decide what course of action to take to extract the gold from the rich streak Jonathan had found at the low point in the buried channel. Since the tunnel they were using was now completely caved, they decided to sink a new shaft straight down over this low spot and then tunnel along the deep part of the channel.

"We need to line this shaft with stronger timbers," Jonathan observed. "And another thing, we need to make some arrangement with the Reillys as to when they plan to do their blasting. I don't want any of us down in that shaft when the ground starts shaking again."

Tenny agreed to go up the valley and talk to the miners. That evening he informed them that the folks farther up the valley had agreed to do their blasting only after mid-day.

For the next ten days the two men and Josh drove the shaft to the base of the channel. The gold values and size of the nuggets increased steadily as they went deeper.

The next morning when Jonathan opened the box to take out the talisman, he found that it was missing. He was positive he had placed it there the previous evening, as was his custom. He had made it a strict habit to put it in the box every night before he went to bed, but this morning there was no sign of it. Frantically he searched every inch of the small cabin and through all the bedding, but it was nowhere to be found. Neither Josh nor Elizabeth had seen it.

"Maybe it came off while you were down in the shaft," Josh suggested.

Jonathan and his children searched all around the workings but to no avail. He took the lantern down so as to be able to see better at the bottom of the shaft. The talisman was gone and with it much of Jonathan's confidence of success.

Running the tunnels from the base of the shaft went more slowly. Jonathan felt the need to come to the safety of the surface much more often, to the point that Josh took over more of the underground work. Jonathan's moods darkened as the days progressed. He lost interest in Rachel and spent much of his time brooding about his lost treasure. Work was slowing down so much that, with Josh's encouragement, Scud suggested that Jonathan do more to carry his share of the load.

By early September the upstream portion of the tunnel had been extended for fifteen feet, which they all agreed was a safe limit. The gold values, although spotty, had been encouraging. Throughout the previous month the amount of water running in the creek bed and seeping into the workings had slowly increased. This was the result of the continued operations upstream, which involved using more water under pressure to wash down the gravels and sand.

A blast above the dam one afternoon near the end of the month loosened an entire hillside of earth, driving it down into the holding pond. The force of this extra load was too great for the dam. Tons of material and water broke through and cascaded rapidly down the valley floor, sweeping away everything in its path. Trees were uprooted, cabins destroyed, and workings obliterated.

Jonathan was underground when his companions on the surface heard the roar of the flood descending upon them. Frantically they yelled down to Jonathan to get out. He could barely hear them but scrambled to the bottom of the shaft and up the ladder. Firmly he grabbed Scud's hand just as the wall of water and debris hit. Scud and Josh were picked up like sticks and carried rapidly downstream on the surge. Jonathan could not make it to the surface and was driven back into the shaft and buried under tons of sand and gravel.

The flood swept away the Sarsfield cabin along with Tenny and Rachel's home and store. Fortunately for Rachel and Elizabeth, they were on the hillside above the cabins picking berries, and Melissa was perched on a rock higher up. They could only watch helplessly as their homes and possessions were swept away.

Scud had been knocked out when the torrent hit and was carried unconscious until being deposited onshore half a mile downstream. As he slowly came to, the whole terrible scene played back in his mind. At first he had no idea where he was. He finally recognized a few landmarks, but most of it was unfamiliar. Where there had been cabins and a well-marked trail, there was now only piles of rock and mud. The receding water had washed out much of the path, limiting his progress as he plodded his way back upstream. The only buildings remaining were the few that had been located higher up the hillside or on the nearby flats. No one was mining, as most of the workings had been destroyed. He encountered a few exhausted men that had been fortunate enough to drag themselves from the flood. He could only be sure he had returned to their property when he saw his sister and the two girls sitting on a large rock on the opposite shore.

"Everything is gone," Rachel sobbed, "everything, our home, our clothes, everything."

By now the flow of water had decreased to the point that Scud could easily make his way across the creek. He climbed up on the rock, put his arm around his sister, and held her while she wept. Later he climbed down off the rock and knelt down in front of Elizabeth and took her hand.

"Your father buried and Josh gone."

Elizabeth said nothing as a single tear trickled down her cheek.

Melissa had been quietly observing with a smile starting to form. She turned to Elizabeth.

"Josh is dead too. Now you're all alone with no one left."

Scud looked at her in dismay and interrupted her before she could say more.

"Don't know Josh dead. Go look tomorrow."

"I want to go now," Elizabeth replied. "We must find him. He may be hurt."

"Too late. We go morning."

Rachel agreed.

"We need to go up to the meadow to see about the animals and find some sacks or something to keep us warm tonight. It will be cold, but we can sleep in the wagon or the shed."

They spent a chilly night nestled in the straw under the shed roof. At dawn Scud and Elizabeth saddled two of the mules and took a third one along with necessary supplies in case they found Josh. The flow of water was now reduced to a trickle that snaked its way through the debris that littered the valley floor. Most of the trail was gone, but the surefooted mules were able to move safely along the course of the creek. About a mile down, past the point where Scud had been dumped onshore, the valley took a sharp bend around a large rock. Just beyond, they could see a ribbon of smoke rising through the morning mist. Two men were brewing tea over a fire. Josh was seated, leaning against a nearby tree.

"We been wondering if anybody was going to come looking for this young fellow," one of the men said. "We pulled him out of the water last night. He is banged up awful bad and don't seem to be able to stay awake very long at a time. We can't get him up on his feet to walk."

Elizabeth explained to them that he was her brother and that he had been working in the creek when the water hit. She thanked them for rescuing him. Scud lifted the unconscious Josh onto one of the mules and tied him securely to the animal. The small procession made its way slowly back upstream.

When they finally returned to what was left of their camp, they laid Josh out in the straw bed. His body was covered with cuts and bruises, and both ankles were badly swollen. However, no bones appeared to be broken.

Tenny arrived late in the afternoon. He had

heard the news of the flood in Downieville. To prepare for the worst, he had rounded up a tent, some bedrolls and enough supplies for a few days.

"I didn't expect it to be this bad," he observed. "It is a good thing we buried the gold up here by the shed. We're going to need it to get back on our feet after this."

The next morning Tenny and Scud took stock of what was left. They still had eight mules and three horses, plus two mules and Lobo that now belonged to Josh and Elizabeth. The shed Scud had built for the animals was undamaged, but the only clothes they had left was what they were wearing.

When Elizabeth went to dig up the sacks containing their share of the gold that they had hidden near their cabin, she found that the blue canvas bag belonging to her father was missing. Since she and Josh were the only ones who knew where he had buried it, she considered it pointless to ask the others, but she did have her suspicions as to who had taken it. Surprisingly Josh's and her small bags of nuggets were still in their hiding spots.

After they had eaten their meager breakfast of biscuits and tea, Tenny told them of his plan.

"There is lodging for us in town until we can build another cabin out here if you decide you want to stay in this valley. Our gold mining may be done, but we have this rich land up here on the flats to grow crops and raise beef."

"I stay here and build," Scud responded.

Melissa said with anger as she pointed to Elizabeth and Josh, "Do they have to come with us? They are not part of our family. Can't they just stay here or go away?"

Rachel looked sharply at her daughter and replied, "We will look after Josh and Elizabeth until Josh is well. We are their family until they decide what they want to do. They do own their father's portion of this land, and it is good land."

They loaded their few possessions on the mules and left that afternoon for Downieville to find a temporary home. They were able to rent rooms in one of the new houses that had been built after the devastating fire of 1852.

After a week confined to bed Josh was able to walk, although unsteadily at first and with considerable pain.

Elizabeth's and Melissa's relationship continued to deteriorate during the course of the month, culminating in the discovery by Elizabeth of her father's gold talisman and his sack of gold tucked away in Melissa's pile of clothes. She immediately snatched them away from the younger girl.

"They are mine," Melissa cried. "I found them."

"You mean you stole them. You watched where my father hid the gold and the nugget he wore around his neck, and you stole them."

On hearing these words, Melissa flew at her accuser and was grabbed and held just in time by Tenny to prevent a battle between the two girls.

Rachel sternly addressed her daughter. "We all know that these were Jonathan's possessions. He wore this nugget around his neck every day. You know that. Even if you did find it, you knew it was his. They now belong to Josh and

Elizabeth."

Tenny was at odds. He knew his wife was right, but he was loathe to alienate his daughter. Softly he spoke to her, "You must give up what is not yours. God and I want you to be a good Christian. I will give you some money of your own to spend."

Melissa was somewhat mollified, but any fragile harmony that had existed in the small group was gone.

The next morning Tenny announced that he would take Melissa with him as he visited a few of the nearby camps before winter set in.

Josh mended quickly, and by the time Tenny and Melissa returned, he was more than ready to leave. He and Elizabeth were well aware of the continued resentment by Tenny and Melissa to their presence. It was obvious that only Rachel wanted them to stay. The next day they loaded the two mules with their few possessions and a tent Josh had purchased. He saddled Lobo and they left for the claims where Scud was building a cabin. Only Rachel bid them goodbye and wished them well.

Scud had the log cabin half finished by the time they arrived. It was now late October and he was working dawn to dusk in order to get the building enclosed and the roof on before the heavy snows came. He was happy to see them, as he now needed help with the roof.

"You help build cabin. We build rooms for you and Elizabeth," he said to Josh.

"I'll help you," Josh replied, "but we want a separate cabin on our own land." He could see no point in telling Scud they didn't want to live with his family.

Working together, they had the buildings finished late in December just as the first serious snowfall arrived. Both buildings were constructed of logs, carefully hewn to fit, with few gaps between. Any spaces were chinked with a mixture of moss and pine gum. With the trail washed out in many places, the wagon was of no use for bringing in supplies, especially sawn boards for the roof. The only choice was to fit saplings close together with a pitch steep enough for the snow to slide off.

After the storm had passed Scud rode into town to bring back his family. Josh and Elizabeth had been dreading their return, but when Scud came back the next day only Rachel and Joachim were with him.

When they were settled in, Rachel sat down with the Sarsfields and explained that Tenny had decided to remain in Downieville for the winter, and Melissa was staying with him.

"Neither one of them will talk to us or even want us there, so I decided to come out here and live. Tenny spends all his time visiting the camps and preaching at a church in town. Melissa has learned his ways and is talking to groups of the children. My son and I are not welcome there."

The winter was tough. With the trail still in no shape for travel by wagon, Scud and Josh took turns taking the four mules into town for supplies, often being forced to return the next day because of the sudden storms that hit the valley. Neither made any attempt to contact Tenny. Only once did he come out to the valley during a mild spell in January. In spite of being invited to stay, he simply walked around, looked the place over, and rode back to town.

February was extremely cold with an unusual amount of snow. No work could be done outside with the exception of tending to the animals. Keeping warm was a continual battle. Josh and Elizabeth moved into the big building to share the heat from the wood stove that Scud had salvaged from the remains of the old house.

A severe storm just after Christmas forced them to stay inside for a week. When they finally emerged into their world of white, the snow was up to the edge of the roof. Scud and Josh cleared a path to the shed and discovered that two of the mules were missing.

"Why would they leave the shed to go out in the storm, and why just your two? Our mules are still back there in the corner," Josh wondered.

"They go look for food."

"Well, they must have gone at least a couple of days ago. There's no sign of any tracks anywhere around the shed. We need to find them. I'll saddle Lobo tomorrow and try to make my way down what's left of the creek trail. I think they'd go that way. They know it, and it would be easier than plowing through these drifts."

Much of the snow on the trail was melted by noon of the next day. It was partly sheltered by the tall firs and pines that had not been washed away by the flood. This made Josh's journey easier than if he had tried to travel over the higher ground where the drifts were much deeper. The biggest difficulty was dodging the low branches laden with snow, which dumped on him if he was unable to avoid brushing them.

Along a wind-cleared section, he picked up a set of tracks that looked familiar. He wasn't sure, but he followed them until any further traces were covered. By now he was about a mile from the cabin, and the sun had slipped under the bank of clouds that were quickly gathering to the west.

"I think I had better get back to the cabin before it gets dark," he thought as he turned Lobo around on the narrow trail.

He didn't see the flash of flying fur, but he heard the snarl as the big cat leaped from the tree and landed on him, knocking him off his horse and into the deep snow. The cougar momentarily lost its grip as Josh rolled down the slope. He was able to pull his knife out of the sheath just before the big cat was on him again, digging into his flesh with its claws. Josh's arm was free enough to slash weakly at its throat, raising a thin stream of blood. The animal seemed momentarily confused. When he tried to get away, they rolled further down with Josh ending up on top of the cat. As it came at his throat, Josh quickly pulled back, and with one motion sunk the knife through the ribcage and into the animal's heart. Within seconds the creature went limp and died. Josh lay there until the evening shadows started to creep along the bank. He retrieved his knife and slowly and painfully crawled back up to the trail. He realized he had lost a lot of blood and was very weak. He just wanted to curl up and sleep, but he knew from stories he had heard that falling asleep was the worst thing he could do. He had to get back to the cabin if he was going to survive. Lobo had taken off right away and was probably not coming back to the smell of the cat. Josh tried to walk, but he was getting weaker and kept falling down from the weight of his water and blood soaked clothes. Finally he gave up and resorted to crawling back along the trail.

There was no moon, and darkness had quickly closed in around him, making retracing his tracks even more difficult. Progress was slowed further as his wet clothes began to freeze. Every ten yards or so he had to stop and rest, keeping the danger of sleep in the forefront of his mind. As the cold penetrated his body, staying in motion became increasingly more difficult. When he saw a familiar bend in the trail, he suddenly realized he was still far from home, and he was so tired and weak he didn't know if he could keep going. He tried to get up on his feet using a small tree by the trail as support, but his legs wouldn't hold him, and he plunged headlong into a deep drift. This time he was unable to get up.

The next thing he knew he was being shaken awake by Scud, who had him by the shoulders and was pulling him out on the trail. He lifted Josh onto Lobo's back and led them back to the cabin.

Rachel immediately heated some water and, with Scud's help, stripped the bloody clothes from Josh's body and lowered him gently into the tub. Most of his cuts had stopped bleeding, but there was still enough oozing out to color the water. Josh was slipping in and out of consciousness but was able to tell them a disjointed story of what had happened.

"I get cat tomorrow," Scud announced, "and

skin for hide."

In the meanwhile Elizabeth had been preparing bandages by tearing up strips of linen and smearing them with tallow. They lifted Josh's body carefully onto the bed and applied the bandages to his wounds.

Josh's recovery was slow. The effects of two serious accidents in such a brief period of time had robbed his body of much of its ability to heal. Two weeks saw him out of bed and stumbling around, anxious to be outside and active, but he was still too weak.

Scud had found the bodies of the two mules after much of the snow pack had melted. They had worked their way down into a small draw near the shed and were unable to climb back up out of the deep snow. As a result they had become prey to the wolves and cougars that hunted the area. All that was left were pieces of hide and bones.

The spring of 1855 came late. As soon as the snow had melted, those who had remained in the valley got together and decided to rebuild the washed-out sections of the trail. They needed to use their wagons to bring in supplies rather than just depend on the mules. At the same time the miners farther up the creek were busy rebuilding the dam so that their operations could be resumed. As the weather warmed, more and more miners came back to the valley to clear the debris from their claims and resume their work. Josh and Scud considered reworking the old areas but decided they had gotten most of the surface gold and were unwilling to attempt any more underground work. Josh tried panning from the bank below his cabin and

170

recovered a few gold flecks. It was not rich enough to get him excited, but it was sufficient to keep his interest. Scrounging around the valley, he found enough boards to build a rough rocker box, and with Elizabeth's help, their gold recovery improved. Soon they had enough to purchase a milk cow, two steers for beef, and enough lumber to build a separate shed for their own animals.

Living in close proximity to Rachel was having a troubling effect on Josh. Since the night he had seen her naked body through the cabin window and then watched her with his father by the pond, she occupied his thoughts and haunted his dreams. His feelings were mixed. Part of him wanted to be around her all the time, but he also felt he had to be away from the temptations of her beauty. His mind was increasingly in turmoil as his desire to be with her increased. As a result, when he was well enough, he moved back to the small cabin and spent most of his time there or with Scud. Elizabeth remained living in the big house, where she helped Rachel plant and tend a garden and look after Joachim. Josh had purchased a new throwing knife, much superior and better balanced than his old one. Each evening he practiced with it, becoming more accurate as he steadily increased the throwing distance.

Scud prospected their claim with little success. Since it was Tenny's ground, he had little incentive to make it pay. The bed of sand that produced the colors that Josh was finding did not extend past their claim. Scud decided his time could be better spent upgrading the cabin and shed for next winter. This type of work he enjoyed much more than mining, especially after the previous year's disaster. He repaired their wagons and purchased four more mules with the idea of resuming the freighting business now that the trail had been rebuilt.

When Scud or Josh made one of their infrequent brief trips to town for supplies or materials, they made no effort to contact Tenny. With Tenny and Melissa away, the small group was able to pass through the spring in peace, unaware of the turmoil awaiting them.

8

In 1856 Melissa was fourteen years old, but most of the people she met assumed she was much older, probably in her twenties. She gave them no reasons to alter their assumptions. In one year she had been transformed from a thin gangly child into an attractive and desirable young woman. She was tall and had her mother's beauty with slight olive skin coloration and dark, soulful eyes. Her raven-black hair had been allowed to grow halfway to her waist and was carefully groomed each day. She made herself aware of the current ladies fashions in San Francisco and Sacramento and wisely used the money she earned or that Tenny had given her to purchase garments that promoted the illusion of maturity and accented her beauty. All this attention and care, which she lavished on herself was done with a purpose, a very strong purpose, to eventually seek fame and riches. She had definite plans to use her beauty and brains to get what she wanted in life.

Fortunately she had inherited her father's determination and strength of will. She also had his temper, which at times was uncontrollable.

During the July 4th celebration of the previous year, a dynamic woman, Sarah Pellet, had been a featured speaker at the Independence Day celebrations. Miss Pellet, who had recently arrived in California from New York, was an active force in the temperance and women's rights movements wherever she traveled. Melissa and Tenny had joined with the rest of the crowd to hear her and the other orators speak. Melissa was mesmerized by the intelligence and confidence of this beautiful lady. She had witnessed her father's ability to captivate an audience, and she had experienced it in a small way herself in guiding the younger children, but this woman on the platform had a powerful effect on everyone within the sound of her voice. She was encouraging the men to put away their alcoholic drink and join her group advocating temperance. What was even more mystifying to Melissa was the number of known drinkers that were agreeing to change their ways.

Melissa knew that she wanted to have this kind of power. She cared not whether people drank, believed in God, or led a good life. She just wanted to learn how to have the ability to sway people to whatever message she was delivering at the moment.

After the last speaker had his say, and the crowd was drifting away, Melissa sought out Sarah Pellet. She waited until all the well wishers had bid the lady goodbye before she approached her. She had thought out carefully what she wanted to say. She desired to convey her interest without revealing her true purpose, and she needed to know what she must do to pursue her goals.

Sarah was impressed that a young girl would be interested in promoting temperance and was more than willing to advise her.

"Come and see me this evening, and we will talk. I am staying at the Metropolis Hotel, but I have to leave for Sacramento in the morning."

Melissa waited until after the dinner hour to visit Sarah. She was greeted at the door and welcomed into the room.

"I have heard that your father is a preacher in this valley and that you have been talking to children about worship. Is this what you wish to do with your life?"

"Something like this," Melissa replied, "but I want to speak to people about all kinds of things that will help them live a good life, just as you are doing."

"Well, you must study hard. You have a lot to learn. I have been fortunate to graduate from college back East and had excellent schooling before that. It doesn't appear that you will have these opportunities here. Have you been to school?"

"No," Melissa admitted. "I have learned much from traveling with my father, but in listening to you today, I realized there is much more that I need to know. That is why I came to see you. I need your advice on how to prepare for the work I wish to do."

Sarah sighed and thought for a few minutes.

"First you need to grow and develop as a woman. To convince people to listen to your message, you must have the appearance and self-confidence of an adult. Hopefully that will come as you grow older. Next you must learn to speak correctly. You must study the language. Listen to people who can speak convincingly, and keep track of what they say and how they say it. You need to be able to project your voice so that when you are in front of a group even the folks at the back can hear you. Lastly, be sincere. If you don't believe and feel passionate about your topic, your audience will sense this and not be convinced."

"That is much to learn," Melissa observed quietly.

"It is, and that is why you must be certain this is the path in life you want to take."

"I am sure of that, but what I don't know is how I'm to learn, or who can teach me what I need to know."

"I would like to help you, but I have a busy schedule and must leave tomorrow, however, I am acquainted with Mr. Calvin MacDonald. He publishes the Sierra Citizen and is a fine writer with an excellent command of the English language. I will talk to him in the morning on your behalf. Possibly he knows someone that would be willing to tutor you."

The next morning at the hotel Melissa was informed that Miss Pellet had gone out but would return soon. Waiting in the lobby she could not help but notice the number of men that already had too much to drink so early in the day. One particularly inebriated young man staggered over, sat down on the bench next to Melissa, and put his arm around her.

"Give me a kiss," he slobbered, "and come

on up to my room for some fun."

Melissa was startled and momentarily in shock. Then with anger, she got up quickly, slapped him hard across the face, and walked away just as Sarah Pellet came in through the front door. Sarah observed the event and rushed over to Melissa just as the young man started after her. Before he could grab Melissa, Sarah quickly placed herself between them, facing the young man.

Calmly, she warned him, "Leave this young woman alone and go sober up. If you do not leave immediately, I will call the authorities and have them take you away and lock you up. Now, go!"

At no point in the confrontation did Sarah Pellet raise her voice or take on a harsh manner, but it had the desired effect. The young man sheepishly slunk away.

Melissa was amazed at the level of calmness with which Sarah handled the situation.

"That was a first lesson, Melissa. You need to learn to take control of your anger and face unpleasant situations without losing your temper. If you follow my path, you will encounter many conflicts and insults. You need to learn to meet these situations without reacting violently."

"I guess I have much to learn," Melissa replied.

"Come, and we will have tea, and I will tell you about my meeting with Mr. MacDonald. He has offered to make arrangements for you. There is a lady in town, a Mrs. Johnson, a banker's wife. Mr. MacDonald has agreed to talk to her on your behalf to see if she would tutor you. She is a graduate of Oberlin College, the same school I attended."

By the end of the week Melissa had begun her quest. Sally Johnson was a plain woman in her thirties with a lively six-month-old child that demanded full time attention. She was happy with the diversion of instructing Melissa but was unable to devote much time to her until Melissa offered to help with the child. As a result, Melissa moved in with the Johnson family, trading her help around the home for her much-needed training.

The first month of this new arrangement went well. Melissa learned quickly how to read, write, and speak correctly with conviction. However, her lack of social manners was a challenge and the major target of Mrs. Johnson's instruction. Melissa found it tiresome but accepted it as part of the process necessary for her to achieve her goals. Her teacher was relentless, encouraging Melissa to practice all aspects of her training until she got it right. In spite of this pressure to be perfect, Melissa appreciated her teacher's efforts and slowly learned to consider her a friend.

As the summer progressed, Melissa became more and more aware of the changes taking place in her body as she transformed from girl to young woman.

Mrs. Johnson sat her down one day in September with a copy of an Eastern fashion magazine that she received regularly by mail.

"It is time you acquired some appropriate clothes. You are changing rapidly, and you must learn to dress like the woman you wish to become. We will go through these magazines and identify suitable attire for you."

Melissa leafed through the pages fascinated by the beautiful clothing.

"These look like they cost a lot of money, but I have very little. I can't afford any of them," she observed.

"Maybe your father can help pay for one nice outfit."

"I will ask him," Melissa replied.

Since leaving Lost Miner Creek, Tenny had been making the rounds locally, visiting his followers and perfecting the messages he was delivering. He also filled in as an assistant to the pastor at a small local church.

Only one incident that had occurred during the previous month had broken the tranquility of his new life. A series of violent robberies on the trails had plagued the area for months. In each case the bandits attacked late in the day and focused on people traveling alone. They were always masked and had yet to be caught or even identified. Many blamed a group of Mexicans that had moved into the area. Others thought a band of natives were coming down from the high country to strike and run. Tenny's friends warned him about traveling between the camps alone in the evenings and offered to accompany him on his rounds. He was concerned, especially after brutal robberies had taken place on successive nights, but his pride prevented him from accepting help. It was suggested that he carry his musket for protection, but he felt he would be sending a message contrary to his teachings if he was packing a firearm.

The attack came on a soft August evening as he was returning to Downieville. He had been traveling all day from a group of camps to the south and was hurrying to make town before dark. As he rounded a bend in the trail, two men wearing masks blocked his progress.

"Hand over your gold and lay down on your belly in the ditch."

Tenny decided quickly to try and make a run for it, but just as he moved behind the mules, a third man came out of the shadows and hit him on the side of the head with his gun butt. Before he passed out, he felt the bandit going through the pockets of his great coat looking for his small sack of gold dust. There was just enough light from the moon for Tenny to see the dagger tattoo on the man's arm.

When he returned to consciousness, the moon had passed beyond the horizon, and it was dark. His gold and mules were gone, and he felt a sharp pain in his head every time he moved. More than mourning his losses, Tenny was mad. He was even angrier than when he had killed the Cheyenne warrior that night on the Oregon Trail. In his mind, he vowed revenge.

His walk to town took all night, each step punctuated by a stab of pain. The farther he walked, the angrier he became. Daylight was beginning to filter through the bank of clouds when he reached his rooms.

Tenny slept all day, and by evening the pain had subsided to the point of being tolerable. The next day his first trip was to the doctor to have his injury bandaged. His second task was to report the attack and buy shot for his musket and pistol. Tenny's experience with using the guns was confined to hunting game on their trip from back east. He knew he had to get some shooting practice before he went looking for the men that had robbed him. Forgiveness was no longer an option. He wanted vengeance. In the afternoon he visited a number of his friends, relating the story of the attack and tried to get some idea as to the identity of the bandits. All that he learned was that the robberies had been going on all summer. On a chance visit to the editor of the Sierra Citizen, he learned that a group of men was being assembled and supplied by town merchants to hunt these bandits. McDonald had information that the band was made up of remnants of the Joachim Murietta gang that had been broken up in '53 by the California Rangers. Murietta was supposed to have been killed and his head taken as proof, but there was doubt about the identity of the head, and many felt he had returned to terrorize the valley. Captain Love and the Rangers refuted these claims and were unwilling to hunt for him again.

"We don't know for sure who it is, but these attacks have to stop. From what I've heard, you are lucky to be alive," McDonald observed.

"I need to go on the hunt," Tenny replied. "I want to get that man that beat me, and I won't let up until I find him."

"Those are harsh words coming from a preacher."

"That is probably true," Tenny replied, "but this is personal. I doubt if my faith will ever be strong enough to turn the other cheek to this."

"Well, it's your decision to make. The group is assembling at the hotel the day after tomorrow, first thing in the morning. Make sure you've got a good horse or mule, enough supplies, and warm clothes. They're going to the high country to the east to look for them."

Tenny spent the rest of the day replacing his mules and getting equipped for the trip. That evening he went to see Melissa to tell her he would be gone for a few days.

"I want to go with you," she announced.

"Not this time. I'm going into the mountains to hunt for some murderers. It is not a place that you should go."

Reluctantly, in spite of her desire for more excitement in her life, she accepted his reply.

"You don't seem to be happy," he observed. "Is something wrong?"

"I don't know," she replied hesitantly. "I may want to come home while you are gone. May I have your key?"

Her reply troubled him, but he gave her the key.

"If we are successful, I will be back in a week," he concluded.

The next morning Tenny left early and rode to the miners' camp where he had been offered instruction on the effective use of his firearms.

When his friend heard about the mission, he was concerned about Tenny's safety.

"Those are very dangerous men if they were part of Murrieta's gang, and they know the high country. You need more than this Colt. It is a single shot and only good for about eighty yards. If you get that close, they will have the advantage unless you can surprise them. If your posse is a bunch of miners, I don't think you will surprise anyone. Your musket is the most useful. You have one that is accurate and can be reloaded rapidly."

He handed Tenny back his Colt.

"Do you know how to load and shoot this thing quickly?"

When Tenny shook his head, his friend retrieved the gun and spent most of the day teaching him how to handle his weapons effectively and with ease. Tenny learned how to reload, however, hitting targets accurately was a challenge.

"You need a lot of shooting practice. Try and stay out of gun fights is all I can advise you now."

Somewhat bewildered by the experience, Tenny was still firm in his resolve to take vengeance on the man who had beaten him.

The next morning he showed up at the hotel just after dawn. Five men were standing around the lobby. All except McDonald, the editor, were outfitted for travel. McDonald introduced Tenny to this strange crew.

Joe Bajor was a big man, well over six feet. McDonald described him as a former soldier and member of the California Rangers. Tenny's first impression was the aura of strength radiating from the man. His bushy hair and chest-length beard added to the fierceness of his gaze as he stared at Tenny.

"What are we going to do with a preacher on this trip? Is he here to pray that we find these crooks and say a few words over their bodies before we throw them in a hole?"

Tenny looked the big man in the eye and replied, "I intend to find the man that robbed me and settle with him in my own way."

"Well, just don't get in our way. We're not going to look after you or wait for you if you can't keep up," Bajor replied.

Sensing a potential confrontation, McDonald quickly continued his introductions.

"This is Quintarro," he said, referring to a younger man apparently of mixed Mexican and Indian heritage. "He has been hired as a scout and tracker."

"And he's one of the best in these parts," Bajor interrupted. "If anyone can find these men, it will be Quintarro. He worked with the Rangers and was partly responsible in finding that bastard Murietta."

McDonald ignored the interruption and continued, "These other two gentlemen are the Reilly brothers, William and Michael. I believe you know them."

Tenny nodded. Since he had never been told of the altercation in the store over Rachel, he had no reason to harbor bad feelings toward the brothers.

"These men killed our brother Tom while we were in town. They came right into the cabin, grabbed him, slit his throat, and left him there to die alone. They took about twenty thousand dollars in gold dust," William responded.

The last man of the group stepped forward and extended his hand to Tenny.

"My name's Jim Calcon, but most folks call me Calico. I just want to see these men captured and pay for their crimes. I spent some time as a Justice of the Peace down in the southern counties where they started their wave of terror, and I've been working as a deputy sheriff in a couple of other places. I've seen too much evidence of their brutality. We have to stop it."

The words were spoken so intently that

Tenny could immediately sense his sincerity.

"Enough of this. We're wasting time. I want to get on the road by noon," Bajor added.

"We got word last night that a small farm on Shady Flats was attacked the day before. No one was killed, but the man and his two sons were tied up and robbed. I'm hoping they can give you some information to help your search. All of the recent attacks have taken place along the North Fork. I think the bandits are holed up somewhere north of Sierra City. Anyway, I feel that's the way you should be headed," McDonald advised.

Tenny spent the next couple of hours packing his mules for the trip and taking some target practice. He was ready to go when the posse rode out of town.

Bajor and Quintarro rode spirited horses, while the rest of the crew plodded along on mules. The trip to Shady Flats took the rest of the afternoon. They camped at the farm. They questioned the father and sons that evening and learned, as they had expected, that the robbers were three Mexicans. They were big, brutal men that spoke very little. The boys described them in detail even down to the dagger tattooed on the arm of one of the bandits.

"What did they steal from you?" Tenny asked.

"My Colt Dragoon pistol and about $3,000 in gold dust," the father answered.

"Did any of you see what direction they went when they left?" Bajor asked.

One of the boys pointed to the east.

They left the farm the next morning and made their way along the North Fork trail, talking to miners and farmers in the area. Only one man they encountered had seen three men fitting the general description heading up the trail to Quartzite Peak the previous evening.

The mood among the group had been relaxed until they began their journey up the Quartzite Peak trail. Believing that their prey was somewhere up in the reaches of this narrow canyon produced a level of fear, especially with the Reilly brothers. William, in particular, was reluctant to face the dangers that might be in their path. Voicing his concerns to the group, he was immediately shouted down by Bajor telling him to turn back if he was a coward. Acting the peacemaker, Tenny suggested they send Quintarro ahead to scout out the situation and look for evidence of their prey. Even Bajor agreed.

Quintarro was gone only a few minutes.

"There's a wagon turned over off the trail up ahead," he reported.

The group rode up to the spot where the scout pointed down into the bush. Only a wheel could be seen from their vantage point, but when they climbed down and turned the wagon over, the body of a man slid out.

"His throat has been cut just like my brother's was," Michael Reilly sobbed.

Searching around the wagon they found mining tools, cooking utensils, some moldy food, and two satchels containing clothes.

"There's dresses in this one," Calico noted. "There was at least one woman with him, maybe two. The clothes in here are different sizes. We need to take a longer look around here. Someone could have gotten away and is injured."

"There's no time," Bajor shouted. "If they're here, they're dead, and we can't do anything for them. The more time we waste here, the more time these crooks have to escape."

They moved cautiously up the trail in single file as Quintarro scouted ahead. By dusk they had progressed over a mile up the sinuous valley trail that was rapidly deteriorating into a boulder-strewn footpath.

Calico got down from his mule and carefully examined a muddy stretch of the trail.

"There's been a fair amount of travel up and down this path since that last rain a week ago, but the most recent prints are of horses and mules going up."

At a wide spot in the trail bordered by a stretch of grass, they decided to make camp. Darkness was descending rapidly. Quintarro had been scouting ahead most of the afternoon and had not returned by nightfall, causing considerable apprehension among the group.

"We better post guards tonight," Calico suggested. "We just don't know how close these fellows are. I'm sure they know we're here and looking for them. They may decide to attack us at night."

"That was to be my next order," Bajor cut in. "You two brothers take the first watch. Calico and the Preacher will relieve you during the night."

The moon was high overhead when Tenny awoke. He climbed out of his bedroll, splashed water on his face, and shook Calico awake. They were not surprised to find both Reillys sound asleep. After they sent the brothers back into camp to finish their naps, they sat on a log at the edge of the trail.

"Good thing those fellows didn't show up last night. They could have danced right into camp and got us all."

"I kinda expected the brothers wouldn't be too alert so I slept light and checked them out a couple of times," Calico said. "There wouldn't have been much we could have done anyway if they came in here with guns blazing."

"I know that," Tenny replied, "and besides, I'm not confident in our leader if we do get in trouble."

Calico nodded in agreement.

"Yeh, I've been thinking that you and I are going to have to look after each other. I'm starting to get a bad feeling about this hunt."

"What do you mean?" Tenny asked.

"I've heard a few stories about Bajor. Evidently he was drummed out of the military and wasn't that popular with the Rangers. A friend of mine that served with him told me his cruelty was just too much for those in charge. His enjoyment of killing was more than they could stomach."

"So how do we deal with him?"

"We keep an eye on him and make sure we don't get caught in something we can't get out of."

"Do you think we should warn the Reillys?" Tenny asked.

"I don't know," Calico replied. "I'm surprised they are still with us. I thought they'd be running for home by now."

The morning broke clear and cold. Calico and Tenny slept in shifts and were ready to face the day at dawn. Quintarro still had not returned.

Tenny asked no one in particular, "What do you think happened to our scout?"

"That damn breed probably just got scared and ran off. Nothing we can do about it. Just grab some food and saddle up. Time is wasting," Bajor barked as he headed up the trail.

Progress was slow and difficult as the path was overgrown along many stretches. They had to cut their way through these patches, while continually keeping watch for any danger. Calico was in the lead. As he broke through a particularly dense thicket, a shot rang out chipping a rock a couple of feet from his head. His reaction was immediate as he jumped back into the thicket. He wormed his way slowly through the underbrush and up onto the south bank toward the source of the shot. The remainder of the group, with the exception of Bajor, also sought cover in the dense foliage. Bajor was off his horse, walking along beside it on the opposite side.

The second shot came when Bajor and his mount were in the clear, smacking into a tree beside them. Bajor dove for the north bank. By now Calico had moved far enough up the other side to have a clear view of the rifleman when he got off his second shot. At the same instant Calico reached for his revolver, but the holster was empty. Crawling through the brush had ripped it loose. He could see it lying on a rock below him, out of reach. The gunman picked up the movement from the corner of his eye and quickly pulled his gun from the holster and fired just as Calico threw his knife. The ball caught

Calico in the shoulder, spinning him around and causing him to slide down the slope. When he came to rest beside the trail and looked up, he saw the bandit splayed against a rock with the knife sticking in his neck. Blood was spurting from the wound, and the man wasn't moving.

As Tenny helped his friend get back on the trail, retrieved his gun, and stretched him out on a blanket, Bajor climbed up to have a look at the gunman.

"He's dead," he shouted down to the rest of the group as they emerged from cover.

"I need to have a look at him," Tenny replied, as he started to climb up the slope. When he reached the dead man, he tore off his shirt, but there was no dagger tattoo on his arm.

When they had assembled again on the trail, Bajor tossed the bandit's rifle to Michael Reilly, with balls and a bag of powder.

"You better learn how to shoot this thing."

"Let's go," he continued. "They can't be too far from here."

"I'm not going anywhere until we take care of Calico," Tenny replied. "He needs to be bandaged before he can move. You can take off without us if you're in that much of a hurry to get shot at again."

Calico's wound was clean. The ball had gone through but had broken his upper arm. Tenny poured some whisky into the wound, eliciting a scream of pain from the injured man. Bandages and sling were made from the bandit's shirt. The Reillys helped him up on the mule.

"Let's go," he shouted, grimacing with pain.

As they moved higher, progress continued to be slow. The undergrowth was just as thick and the path became more difficult to follow. It was obvious that this portion, so far from the main trail, had much less use. Whenever they broke through the brush they could see the snow-covered spires in the distance. Dusk found them only a few hundred yards from the site of the ambush.

All the men were desperately tired and fearful of what lay ahead. The Reillys again suggested they turn around and go back, but the rest of the group felt they had gone too far to quit. Even Calico, who was in constant pain, was determined to finish the hunt.

The night air was cold at this elevation, but Bajor decided not to risk detection by starting a fire.

"I don't think it matters," Calico observed. "They know where we are, and they can come and get us any time they want, but if the folks back at Shady Flat are right, there are only two of them left. We need to go back to that last patch of thick bush, tie the animals up, and bed down in the densest part with at least two of us staying awake and guarding both ends. Maybe that way we can spot them before they get to us."

Agreeing to this, Bajor took the first watch with Michael Reilly to make sure the young man stayed awake. Tenny took the older Reilly for the second watch but sent him back an hour later when Calico found he couldn't sleep because of the pain and came out and found William asleep again. Fortunately the night passed without an attack.

A cold gray dawn with threats of rain or snow greeted the group the next morning. No one had dressed or brought enough clothes for these conditions, and discomfort was widespread. Food supplies were running low, and their bedding was soaked with dew. Thoughts of turning back were getting stronger.

Tenny voiced their concern.

"If we don't find some trace of these men by nightfall, I think we need to end this tomorrow. We don't have enough food for us or the animals to go much farther."

This time there was no disagreement from Bajor.

From the edge of the thicket, where they had camped, the hillside was clear of brush for a few hundred feet before the forest closed in. As they moved to the edge of the woods, a large pine blocked their path. Hanging by his neck from a thick branch was the body of Quintarro.

.

9

Nobody moved. No one had considered that Quintarro could be captured. They had conceded that he had run off on them.

"We can't leave him like that," William announced. "I'll cut him down."

Without hearing or paying attention to warnings from the others, he rode toward the tree, stood up in the saddle, and started to cut the rope. When the shot caught him in the chest, it drove him off the mule onto the trail. He was dead before he hit the ground. His brother ran to his side and dragged his body into the woods out of sight. The rest of the group scanned the side of the hill looking for the gunman. By the time they spotted him scurrying along the upper slope, he was well out of musket range. Tenny and Calico gathered beside Michael and attempted to offer support, while Bajor cut the scout's body down from the tree.

Michael gained control of his emotions after a few minutes and said calmly, "This is as far as I'm going. I'm taking my brother's body back to our home and bury him. We will all be killed if we keep after these men. I've had enough."

Tenny helped him load and tie his brother's body onto the mule. They watched as he headed back down the valley.

"I'm beginning to think he may be the smartest one of us," Calico observed.

"You want to give up and go back with him, go ahead, and take the Preacher with you," Bajor snorted.

Neither man replied. They spurred their mules on and continued their journey deeper into the forest. As they rounded a sharp bend in the valley, they could see a thin wisp of smoke curling through the trees on the opposite side. A faint trail wound its way up the slope toward the source of the smoke.

"Well, we know where they are, and I'm sure they can see us," Calico went on. "If we ride up that trail and try to rush them, we'll all get shot. Any ideas?"

Bajor thought for a minute then replied, "We wait until dark and then walk up the trail and get in positions to surround their cabin before dawn. Then we go in."

Tenny and Calico agreed that was about the only way they could see it being done.

"Let's get some rest," Tenny added. "It's going to be a long night."

It was also a dark night. Any chance of moonlight to guide them was blocked by a heavy cloud cover. They trudged slowly up the path. It was difficult to follow, and a number of times they found themselves floundering through the bush. They had decided to leave the animals tied up in the woods at the bottom as it would give them a better chance to move in noiselessly. Halfway up the path, the mature fir trees gave way to a scrubby second growth. From this point they could see a dim light ahead. The brush had been cleared on all sides for a hundred yards around a small log cabin. This gave anyone inside a clear view in all directions. They stopped at the edge of the clearing, where Bajor laid out his plan.

"We stay out here in the bush until dawn then I'll sneak up on the front side of the cabin and bust in, taking them by surprise. You two station yourselves on either side and take out anyone that tries to go out the back. There should be only two of them, but we don't know for sure, so keep your eyes open."

As light began to filter through the leaden sky, a sudden clatter of pots and pans broke the stillness.

"Damn," Calico thought. "They had a trip wire set at the edge of the clearing, and that fool Bajor just set it off."

Immediately, a man rushed out the front door with his arm locked around a half-naked middle-aged woman. He was holding her in front of him as a shield.

"Let the woman go and drop your gun," Bajor yelled.

The man wheeled around and fired toward the source of the voice. The ball struck a tree beside Bajor. He stepped out in the clearing and raised his guns.

Calico yelled, "Don't shoot. You'll hit the woman."

Bajor heard him but fired anyway, his shot hitting the woman in the chest. She fell immediately, breaking the man's grip on her. Bajor's second shot caught the man in the face. By the time Bajor and Calico reached them, they were both dead.

"I'm going in after the other one," Bajor announced and walked toward the door.

Tenny was lying in the bushes on the west side of the cabin. He was about to join the others when he saw movement on the path leading up to the building from the back. He lay still and watched as a man forcibly led a young woman around his side. When he heard the shots the man stopped, looked around, and moved along toward Tenny. He stopped again within feet of Tenny's hiding spot, frantically searching the area. He continued to have a firm grip on the struggling girl with his arm across her throat. Tenny could clearly see the dagger tattoo on the man's arm. Tenny slowly withdrew his gun from the holster and moved it to point at the man. He had only one shot, but the girl blocked his line of sight. As she turned her head, she caught sight of Tenny and held his gaze. He moved his free arm slowly to his mouth and made the motion as if he was biting it. The girl smiled and quickly bit down hard on the bandit's arm. He screamed and let her go at the same instant as Tenny's shot caught him in the belly. He doubled over and lay on the ground in agony. Tenny walked over to him, turned him over, and said, "Remember me? I don't suppose you do."

Tenny carefully reloaded his gun. As the man tried to scramble away, Tenny shot him in the head. He looked up to see Bajor standing at the corner of the building.

"That's too bad. I thought he was going to save me the trouble of killing you."

"What are you talking about?"

"Do you think I'm stupid enough to pack all that gold back to town and hand it over. I'm taking it and going over the pass and out of this country, and I'll take this little lady to keep my bed warm. Maybe someone will find your bones up here someday."

Bajor had his Colt pointed at Tenny. As he pulled the hammer back, Tenny dove to the side just as he heard the shot. He felt nothing. He peered through the foliage just in time to see Bajor pitch forward with half his head blown away. The girl was screaming, and Calico was leaning unsteadily against the side of the cabin, cradling his musket.

Tenny got to his feet and walked over to their dead leader.

"I thought I was done. I started to pray then realized that would do no good if this man was going to shoot me, so I just got out of the way. It was the only thing I could think of. Thank you for saving my life. How did you get there without him hearing you?"

"I heard the first shot and wanted to see what happened. There was no sign of Bajor inside the cabin. When I came around the corner, I could see he was going to shoot you but was too busy bragging about what he was going to do with the girl and the money. I got kind of interested in what he was saying, or I would have shot him sooner, but it's done. We set out to get the bandits, and we did. Anyways, where's the girl?"

The two men walked around to the front of

the cabin to find the girl bent over her mother, her body shaking with deep sobs.

"Bajor didn't have to shoot the woman," Calico said. "I yelled at him, but he didn't care. He just shot her. Maybe that's why it wasn't so hard to blow him away, although I had a hell of a job holding this gun steady."

As they walked over to the girl and stood beside her, Tenny asked, "What do we do about her and all these bodies? We can't leave her here. It looks like her whole family is dead."

"I don't know. My guess is we take her into town and turn her over to someone. Maybe McDonald will know what to do, or possibly she's old enough to look after herself. As for the bodies, I say we tie them to the mules and load them all into the girl's wagon when we get down to the main road."

They waited until the girl was composed then sat her down to talk. They learned that her name was Rebecca and that she, her parents, and younger brother had come from Ohio two weeks before. They were on their way to the high country to pan for gold on the claim they'd purchased, when they had been attacked.

"We found your father's body and the wagon, but we didn't see your brother," Calico said. "Where did he go?"

"They killed him too," she sobbed. "We were all so excited about our new life, and now it's over for them. It's not fair. They never had a chance. I don't know what I will do, but I will go on."

By the time Tenny had gone down and fetched the four mules and Bajor's horse, and they had the bodies securely tied on to the mules, it was dusk. Calico was of little help in loading the bodies, but the girl proved more than capable of helping Tenny with the task. They learned that she was seventeen and came to the conclusion that she was definitely capable of looking after herself. The men were impressed by the way she handled the animals, especially Bajor's big, high-spirited horse. They agreed the horse, saddle, and his guns were to be hers.

It was a bitter cold night. Tenny and Calico spread their bedrolls on the dirt floor. Rebecca wrapped herself in all the clothing she could find and then cut a bunch of pine branches for a bed. The men took turns during the night keeping the fire burning in the small woodstove. They all welcomed the dawn and the meager amount of heat the sun rationed to the hillside. They systematically searched through the cabin and around the outside, collecting guns, small bags of gold, and some of the valuables the bandits had taken. Rebecca had seen one of the robbers open a hole that had been dug under the cabin and covered by a large rock. When they rolled the rock away they found a number of large bags of gold dust and nuggets.

The trip down the slope was slow. The dew had frozen on the shaded stretches of the path, leaving a thin coat of ice that made travel treacherous even for the sure-footed mules. Rebecca, on horseback, led the column keeping her animal under complete control. Tenny rode at the rear of the group to prevent the mules from straying into the bush.

When they reached the wagon, they left Rebecca alone with her father's body until she reappeared on the trail.

"I have to find my brother," she announced.

After they turned the wagon upright, harnessed two mules to it, and pulled it back on the trail, Calico and the girl went to look for her brother. Tenny untied the bodies from the mules and loaded them into the wagon. By mid-afternoon they had found the boy's body. He had not died right away but had crawled along the slope until he passed out just below the trail. They retrieved his body and loaded it into the wagon with the others. They waited a little longer until Rebecca got herself under control before they continued their journey.

It was after dark when they arrived at the Shady Flats farmhouse, where the bandits had tied and robbed the farmer and his two sons. They were overjoyed to hear the bandits had been found and killed and were fascinated by the story, especially when it was narrated by this beautiful young blonde lady.

"These are the guns we found," Tenny said, as he opened a canvas bag and dumped a number of firearms onto the table.

The farmer immediately identified his Colt.

He asked, "Did you find the gold they took? Our nuggets were in a cloth sack with our brand on it."

Calico rummaged around in one of the saddlebags and finally came up with it.

"You folks were lucky," he said. "You got your stuff back and you're all still alive. Rebecca has lost everything, including her whole family."

That night Rebecca got the spare bedroom, while Tenny and Calico bunked in the hayshed.

The next morning after they had thanked their hosts and set off down the road to town, Rebecca announced, "I would like to arrange for a funeral for my family and have them buried on our claim. We were going there when we were attacked. I don't know exactly where it is, but I believe it is somewhere in this valley. I have the map my father was given."

They stopped at noon at a wide part of the road, where there was water and grass for the animals. Tenny and Calico took the opportunity to examine her map.

"This is a bad map," Calico observed. "You'd be lucky to find anything using this. Where did your father get it?"

"He got it from the man in Marysville that sold him the claim."

"At least, you were in the right valley. From the markings it looks like your ground is somewhere up in the high country beyond where you were attacked. It might be tough to find unless the claim posts can be located."

"I will conduct the funerals at the church where I have been working in Downieville," Tenny said. "We can seal the bodies in boxes until we can locate someone to help you find your claim, where the bodies can be buried. I won't have the time to go with you, and Calico will need a chance for his shoulder and arm to heal, but I will try to get my wife's brother and their neighbor to help you."

The first stop in town was at the undertaker, who was given instructions to seal the bodies of Rebecca's family in boxes for later transport. He was to wait on instructions for the others. The next stop was the office of the Sierra

Citizen, where the rest of the afternoon was taken up describing the week's events to McDonald and the local Justice of the Peace. It was decided that the bodies of the bandits should be buried locally without ceremony. Bajor's body would be held for a short time until the Rangers and the military could be contacted to see if anyone would claim the remains. McDonald agreed to publish their story with an announcement of services for this unfortunate young family that had come to California to seek a better life, only to have it ended so abruptly. Local residents were invited to attend.

By the time Tenny, Calico, and Rebecca reached Tenny's rooms it was evening. He was surprised to discover his daughter had moved back.

While Rebecca and Calico were settling in, Tenny took Melissa into another room.

"What happened? Why did you leave the Johnson's? I thought you were happy there."

"I haven't left. I just go over there in the daytime after Mr. Johnson leaves for work. I don't want to be in the house when he's there."

"What happened?"

"For a while I've been very nervous in that house at night, especially while undressing for bed. I always felt like someone was watching me. At first I thought it was just my imagination, but then I found a small hole in the wall one night after I had put out my lamp. Light from the other room was coming through the hole. Then I did get scared. One night last week, when I was just about asleep, I heard my door open slowly and her husband came into the room. I lay very still, hoping he would leave, but he took off his clothing and got into bed with me. I knew what he wanted, so I kicked him as hard as I could where it would really hurt. I got out of bed quickly, grabbed my clothes, and ran here. Thankfully you had given me the key."

"I think I had better go see him," Tenny replied angrily.

"No, please don't. I know Sally knows nothing about what happened. It would hurt her very deeply to find out what kind of a man she is married to. I like her and don't want to cause her pain. I have been going over there each morning for instruction and to help her with the baby, but I leave before he returns from work. I just tell her that I have to come home and help you. Yesterday I went down to the bank and told him that if he ever tried anything like that again, I would let the bank owners and the newspaper know and would post notices all over town."

Tenny was impressed as to how his daughter had handled the problem and decided it would probably not help to go after Johnson, much as he would like to.

"Who is this girl, and why is she here?"

Tenny related the events of the past week and how Rebecca was now alone without her family.

"Rebecca and Calico will probably only be here for a few days."

"Well, she's to stay out of my room. She can sleep somewhere else," Melissa replied.

The next morning Calico walked over to see the local doctor to have his arm and shoulder treated. After a very painful examination, the doctor informed him that it was too damaged for him to repair. He recommended a surgeon in Sacramento.

Calico stayed in town just long enough to attend the service for Rebecca's family. Tenny was surprised at the number of people that turned out as a result of McDonald's story in the Citizen. Even the farmer and his two sons from Shady Flats had made the trip. After the service, some of the women offered Rebecca room and board until she got settled, but she was adamant about wanting to proceed with the burials as soon as possible. Tenny decided to postpone his trip to the surrounding camps long enough to get her started on her venture. That afternoon Calico said his goodbyes and left for Sacramento.

As he had promised, Tenny decided to take Rebecca out to Lost Miner Creek and arrange with Scud and Joshua to take her to her claim in the high country for the burials. When he asked Melissa if she wanted to go with them, she replied, "I don't ever want to go out there again and see any of those people, especially my mother."

Rebecca was up early the next morning and had the mules hitched to the wagon and her horse saddled by the time Tenny arrived at the stable.

"You don't seem to have any trouble with that horse, which is strange," Tenny observed. "Bajor was always fighting to keep him under control."

"I can see marks where he beat this horse. It's no wonder he had trouble with him," she replied.

It was a hot, dusty ride out to the cabin. Tenny didn't know what kind of greeting to expect, and he really didn't care. He had felt for some time that that part of his life was over, and he was ready to turn the claim and the land over to Rachel and Scud. The more he thought about it, the more he liked the idea. It would put some pressure on them to take Rebecca off his hands and help her fulfill her mission. He had no desire to return, and Melissa had left no doubts about her strong feelings.

They arrived in mid-afternoon. When they pulled up to the cabin, Rachel greeted him coolly at the door. Tenny was a bit taken aback by Rachel's appearance. She seemed to have let herself go, become more matronly with occasional streaks of gray in her hair. However, he still found her attractive until Joachim appeared by her side. The boy showed all the racial characteristics of his parentage. At seven he was now old enough to remember the hurt and gazed at Tenny with a look of pure hatred.

When Scud came over, Tenny introduced Rebecca and told them her story, ending with his request for Scud and Joshua.

"Will you take her and the bodies of her family up the North Fork to her claim and help her bury them? She has a map that shows where the claim is located."

"We do that," Scud replied.

Rachel added, "Josh and Elizabeth went to town for supplies, but I am sure he would be willing to help. Are you planning to stay and have dinner with us?" It was clear she was hoping he would refuse.

"No," Tenny replied. "I won't be coming back, and Melissa has chosen to stay with me."

Rachel had no reply, and no emotion showed on her face.

"I have had a paper made out assigning the gold claim and the land to you. It is all yours to do with what you want. I will have no further connection with you or anything out here. I'm leaving the wagon with the bodies. It is Rebecca's wagon. You don't have to return it."

With those words, he unhitched his two mules and headed back to town. He was surprised that this final unburdening was providing such a strong feeling of relief.

The three sat around the big table in silence.

Finally Rebecca turned to Rachel and said, "I don't want to stay if you don't feel good with your husband leaving me here. I see that you and he are not like a normal husband and wife, and that there is trouble between you. I don't want to remain if it will make it worse."

The words brought tears to Rachel's eyes, and she walked over and hugged the girl.

"I don't want you to leave. Our troubles started a long time ago and we no longer live as husband and wife. You are welcome to stay with us as long as you like."

It was close to midnight when Josh and Elizabeth returned. Rachel and Rebecca were still awake.

"We had company while you were gone," Rachel said, and went on to explain about Tenny's visit and their new guest.

"Rebecca will be staying with us. The coffins in that wagon are all her family. She wants to bury them on their claim, and Scud has agreed that you and he would take her there. I told Tenny you would help."

"Where is the claim?"

Rebecca pulled her map out of a pocket and gave it to Josh.

"Calico said he thought it was somewhere up in the high country above the North Yuba River valley. That is where my family was headed when we were attacked."

Josh studied the drawing for a minute then said, "It looks right. I was up there on Lobo this spring. That is rough country."

"Will you and Scud take me there?"

"If Scud said we'll do it then we'll do it. I hope you have some warm clothes. We can easily be in snow that high up this time of year."

"All I have are the clothes I am wearing," she replied.

"Elizabeth and I will find you warm things to wear," Rachel offered.

That night as Josh lay in his bed trying to sleep, the arrival of this young woman and the events of the summer took control of his mind. His attraction to her and his nervousness around her puzzled him, especially in relation to the girls he knew. Elizabeth was his sister and probably his best friend. They talked about everything in their lives and made their plans together. Ever since their father's death, her cautious attitude toward life had saved him from potential danger and embarrassment on a number of occasions. Melissa was an enemy. She had stolen the talisman and their small sack of gold after the flood, and only through Rachel's efforts had she returned them. Then her treatment of Elizabeth had further alienated him. It was a happy day for the Sarsfields when Tenny and his daughter moved into town.

Then there was Rachel. Josh's mind traveled back over the events of the past few months. When did it really start? It seemed sometimes that it was always there since that first day they had arrived. There was that night he had walked back from the miners' party and, without thinking of any consequences, looked through their window and saw her without clothes. He remembered the strange sensations in his body, those feelings he had never had before and couldn't explain. During the years that followed, he always tried to be near her without being obvious, but she knew. He felt now that she had always known, but she had never said anything or gave any sign that she was aware of his interest until one night last winter. They had been alone in the big cabin. Elizabeth and Scud had each gone to their own rooms.

"You have been watching me," she said. "I have felt your eyes on me more than usual this past month."

"I am sorry," Josh stammered, "I didn't mean to embarrass you."

"No, no, you don't embarrass me. It pleases me that you like to watch me and spend time with me. It has been very lonely, and I need you to be my friend."

That simple disclosure had changed their relationship. Because he felt needed by this beautiful woman, it dissolved his guilt. He felt more comfortable being with her and was seldom at a loss for words when they talked, which was often. He became aware of the changes in her. She was happier, often singing while she worked in the cabin. She started paying more attention to her appearance.

That warm day in March when the trail opened up and they went to town together was special. They quickly picked up the necessary supplies and then had lunch at the hotel. They visited all the general merchants as Rachel searched for a new dress.

They laughed at some of the creations she tried on. It was a happy afternoon for them, and they returned to Lost Miner Creek with a deeper bond.

Later that month winter came back with a two-day blizzard that clogged the trails and drove everyone inside. When it blew itself out, Josh and Scud dug their way out to the barn to spread feed for the livestock. They found the shed door partly open and Lobo missing. Josh was frantic. The ties between Josh and his horse had grown strong over the years. He had trained Lobo to come on his call, but this time there was no sign of his horse. He slogged his way upslope calling as he went. As he came over a low ridge, he heard an answering whinny. It came from a small valley running off to the east. The area was packed with snow that had been driven in by the strong westerly winds. Lobo was buried up to his shoulders and was trying to force his way through the frozen mass. Josh could see he was exhausted. The more he struggled, the deeper he worked himself in. Josh ploughed his way down and secured a halter on him. With Josh pulling on the halter rope and Lobo struggling to gain footing, they slowly

worked their way down to the main valley,
where the snow had either melted or been blown
away. By then it was dusk. The wind had picked
up, and the temperature continued to drop.
When Lobo reached firm ground, Josh pulled
himself up onto his back, and hanging firmly
onto the rope, he urged his horse home. It was
dark when they reached the cabin. By then Josh
was almost unconscious. He had no idea where
he was until Scud helped him off. He carried
Josh into the cabin and then led Lobo back to
the barn. Josh lay on the small bed shaking
violently with cold as Rachel stoked the fire to
boil water. Elizabeth wrapped her brother in
blankets and led him to sit closer to the stove
and absorb its heat. When the water boiled,
Rachel mixed it with just enough cold so he
could stand it. They stripped his wet clothes off
and got him into the tub. It took half an hour for
Josh to stop shaking.

"You'd better stay here tonight," Rachel
said. "Your cabin is too cold."

Josh wrapped himself in the blankets,
curled up in the small bed and was asleep
immediately.

Sometime in the deep part of the night, he
came suddenly awake. He was aware of a
presence in the room. It was in total darkness,
but he sensed a soft movement toward him. The
blankets were moved aside, and Rachel slid in
next to him. The sudden warmth of her body
and her fragrance was intoxicating. He could
feel his body swelling with desire. He didn't
totally understand it, but it was overwhelming.

"Shh," she said, "just try to relax and go
back to sleep. I only want to stay here beside

you and keep you warm."

She kissed him then turned his body over, away from her.

The next morning, when he awoke he wasn't sure if he had been dreaming until she moved closer and kissed him again.

Josh smiled as he brought back those wonderful memories. It all began the following night. He had moved back into his own cabin. He lay awake thinking he should go and be with her, when his door opened slowly and she glided into his room. He had never seen that look in her eyes as she stood by his bed. Slowly she loosened the sash on her robe and let it slide away to reveal all the beauty of her body.

"Do you still find me desirable?"

"Yes, always," he replied. He pulled away the covers and opened his arms to hold her as she moved in beside him. She kissed him with a passion that matched his desire. Gently she pulled him closer and straddled his body grasping his manhood as it swelled and began to throb. Lifting her body slightly, she guided him inside her until he felt totally immersed. She began to move back and forth with a rhythm that heightened his desire until he could contain it no longer. She let out a whimper as he exploded inside her.

They made love again more slowly that night, the next morning, and almost every day after. They made no attempt to hide it from Scud or Elizabeth, and soon it became a normal and acceptable part of their lives.

Tenny's brief visit had cast a shadow. Rachel was still his wife, a fact they had put out of their minds, but even though Tenny had declared he was not coming back, Josh could detect the slight change in her, or maybe it was a change in him. The presence of Rebecca, now within the confines of their small family had created even more confusion in Josh's mind. He found her very attractive and desirable in a manner much different from Rachel, but almost as strong.

Somehow, it was important to him that she should not find out about his relationship with Rachel.

10

By the time Josh and Scud had eaten their morning meal, Rebecca had the mules harnessed to the wagon, her horse saddled, and was ready to go. They waited just long enough for Josh to put the saddle on Lobo before they took off.

Rebecca was somewhat apprehensive traveling with these two men that she had just met for the first time the previous day. Tenny had assured her she would be safe, and she had sufficient trust in him to undertake the journey. She immediately felt comfortable around Scud. His gentle and kind nature was reassuring. Josh was another matter. She found him attractive but remote and a bit mysterious. She had been used to young men showing a keen interest in her, but Josh seemed to be unmoved by her presence. Besides, the important thing now was to get the bodies of her family to their final resting place.

With Rebecca and Josh on their horses, they were able to easily outdistance Scud driving the wagon. Toward dusk, Rebecca located the farm at Shady Flats, where she had stayed with Tenny and Calico. The farmer again welcomed her and her companions to spend the night.

The next day was cold, giving the three travelers a taste of what to expect in the high country. The four mules pulling the loaded wagon set the pace giving Rebecca time to think back over the past few months and examine her life. She and her mother had resisted leaving their home and moving to this unknown western land for over two years. Their small farm in Ohio was familiar and provided most of their needs. They were not rich, but except for her father, they were content. He was persistent in wanting to seek his fortune in the goldfields and had finally worn down their resistance. They arrived in California without incident. Although the trip was long, stretching over four months, the trails were well worn and marked by the passage of so many before them. In Sacramento her father had met a man who was tired of the lonely life of a miner and was preparing to return to his home in Missouri. He had a claim to sell and a pouch full of gold, which he assured her father had been taken from his claim. Her father bought it on the spot along with some tools and was given a piece of paper with a crude map on one side and a hand-written claim transfer on the back. Rebecca questioned the validity of the document and convinced her father to have it verified, which he did. By noon the next day they were off for the goldfields. Forty-eight hours later all her family were dead.

Seeing the tears on her face, Josh rode up beside her to find out what was wrong.

"I was thinking about my family and how my father was so excited to finally be chasing his dream, only to have it destroyed. It was so futile, leaving our home and coming out here to this."

"My father had the same dream, and it also ended with his death," Josh replied and went on to tell her of Jonathan getting trapped in the tunnel when the dam broke.

"That is sad, but at least you have your sister going through it with you. I feel so alone with all of them gone. I don't know whether to go back home or try and make a life out here. It's so confusing. I still have family back there who would welcome me, but it's such a long hard trip."

"You have the winter to decide," Josh observed. "There isn't enough time to make it through the mountains safely before the bad weather comes."

Evening found them in a small grassy meadow about a mile past the trail to Quartzite Peak. Rebecca had led them up the creek trail to show them the place where her family had been attacked.

"Why you on this trail?" Scud asked.

"My father thought our claim was up here. When he got to this point he realized he was wrong and was trying to turn the team around when the robbers showed up."

"I can see how he would make that mistake," Josh said, looking again at the map.

"But it seems to me it has to be closer to Sierra City, and we are still at least three miles from there."

Sleeping arrangements were primitive that night. Rebecca wrapped herself in her bedroll and curled up under the wagon. Scud and Josh set their bedrolls out under a canvas strung between two trees for cover.

The next morning started with cold biscuits and hot coffee for breakfast. Travel to the east was slow. About a mile down the road, they came across a small three-man mining operation. These men were washing gravel down from the bank on the opposite side of the creek and running it through a small sluice at the bottom. After examining their map, one of the men pointed up the road and said, "The claim looks to be on a small creek that flows through Charcoal Flats, just this side of Loganville. It's about a mile up there."

They had no trouble locating the creek where it passed under the small bridge. The water was low, but the valley sides were steep enough that only a narrow, overgrown trail gave access to the upper reaches. It was barely wide enough for Josh and Rebecca to ride the horses through. They were forced to go along the creek bed to avoid occasional washed-out stretches. There was no room for the wagon.

"We should be able to find the posts if they are here, and we are on the right creek," Josh observed.

In her excitement, Rebecca spurred her horse up the path, and Josh soon lost sight of her through the underbrush. When he heard her yell, he quickly rushed to the spot to find her standing by a rough-cut post.

"I found it," she announced happily. "It is right where the map shows it to be."

They rode back down to the road, where Scud was parked with the wagon, to announce their discovery.

"How you bury your people there? Wagon not go."

"I was thinking about that," Josh agreed. "From the looks of the ground we covered, there's probably not enough gravel or soil to dig a hole anywhere in that canyon. We should stay in town tonight and come back in the morning. We need to go up to the other end of the claim and see if there's a place we can dig."

It took the rest of the afternoon to make their way into Sierra City. The town was quiet, and they were able to get a meal and lodging for the night.

The next morning they left the wagon with the bodies in town, and Scud took one of the mules to ride to the claim.

"I learned in town last night from an old miner that lode claims up here are usually two hundred feet long and that a discovery post should be set up on the original vein discovery. That post we found yesterday probably marks the centerline or one of the corners of the claim. We need to go farther up the canyon to find the original discovery," Josh reported.

It was a tough climb up the narrow, overgrown path, but finally they emerged into a small glade in a slight widening of the valley. Partly upslope to the west was a pile of rocks at the edge of a small open pit. Most of the rocks around the pit showed tiny quartz-filled fissures.

The discovery post was beside the pit. It showed the location of the Charcoal claim staked by John Walters on June 24, 1854. It extended seventy-five feet to the north, one hundred twenty-five feet south, fifty feet east, and fifty feet west.

"Is that the name on your claim transfer paper?" Josh asked.

"Yes," Rebecca replied, showing him the document.

In the meantime, Scud had been busy breaking open rocks and examining the pit, which was half-filled with water.

"Don't look like much," he observed. "Veins small. No gold."

"Not only that, but the pit is too shallow for burying," Josh observed as he sat down beside Rebecca. "I don't see any way we can bury your folks on this claim unless there's some better spots farther up."

"I know," she replied. "I guess I'll have to accept it and figure out something else. We should go back to town and find someone who knows what to do."

"I would still like to prospect the rest of your claim to see if there are any other veins, but we have to find someplace where we can get the bodies buried soon," Josh said.

Scud gathered up a few of the more promising rock samples, and they made their way back down the path. As they came to the bridge on the main trail, they saw an old man sitting on a log holding the halter of an overloaded mule. The animal was lying on its side. It was desperately thin with nothing but skin covering its ribs, and it was obviously sick.

The man didn't look much better. He was small and very thin with a tangled mass of dirty gray hair. His clothes were tattered and ripped with the original colors and patterns hidden by layers of dirt and stains.

He hailed them as they came off the path.

"What are you folks doing up on old John's claim?"

"I own it now," Rebecca answered. "Mr. Walters sold it to my father."

The old man was silent for a moment then replied, "I hope your father didn't pay much for it. There's nothing left up there. Old John mined out that small lode and then took off. He said he was going home. He'd had enough of this life. I was planning to do the same thing before winter gets its grip on this land, but my poor old mule gave out."

"Is your mule dead?" Rebecca asked.

"She might as well be," he answered. "She decided she can't go any further and just laid down on the road. I've been trying to get her up, but she's done."

"Maybe if you unload her, she might try to make it," Josh observed.

"Ain't no use. She's done."

"So what are you going to do?" Josh asked.

"I figured I'd sit here until someone came along that could give me a ride. It's either that or walk out with nothing."

"We will be leaving in a few days. We can take you then if you are still here," Rebecca said.

"Yes, I can wait for you at my cabin. It's on my claim just up the road beyond that bend. You could stop and get me there when you go."

Josh got down off Lobo and proceeded to unload the old man's possessions from the back of his mule. Scud lifted the front of the mule until it had its feet planted then heaved up the back end. The poor animal staggered around but managed to stay on its feet.

"We'll take you to your cabin," Rebecca announced as Scud lifted the old man up on the horse behind her.

They tied his possessions on Lobo behind Josh and set out for the old man's cabin, his mule stumbling along behind them.

Around the bend in the road was a small grassy flat bordered by steep volcanic cliffs. A trail veered off to the right, and in the distance they could see it led to a small log cabin, partly hidden in the trees.

"That's my cabin, and right here is the edge of my claim," Old Dan announced as they left the main road.

"How deep is the dirt here on the flats?" Josh asked.

"Only a foot or so. It is just the sand and silt left when the floodwaters drain off. I dug pits all over here looking for gold colors, but it's mostly barren."

"Where is discovery post?" Scud asked.

"Up behind the cabin by the tunnel."

"Why did you dig a tunnel?" Rebecca asked.

"I found this big quartz vein on the side of the cliff. On the surface it showed a few flecks of gold so I figured it might get richer back into the fresher rock. I drove the tunnel for twenty feet. The vein was just as wide and just as barren. I finally gave up on it."

They reached the cabin and dismounted. Josh had to walk back to the main road and get Dan's mule back on its feet so it could follow.

While Rebecca was helping Dan open up his cabin and retrieve his possessions, Scud and Josh examined the tunnel.

"Good place for bodies," Scud observed.

"I was thinking the same thing. If we can get her to agree to it, our problem would be solved," Josh replied.

They took Rebecca into the tunnel and made the suggestion to her.

She didn't reply for a few minutes then she said, "It would be perfect if we could seal it closed and if it was my claim, but I wouldn't feel right burying my family on someone else's land."

When they came out, Josh approached the old man and asked, "Do you want to sell your claim?"

"Why would you want to buy this?" Dan asked. "It's worthless. I've prospected the whole thing. There's no gold."

"We need it for another reason," Rebecca answered and went on to explain her need for a burial spot for her family.

"So you want to put them in the tunnel and blast it shut?"

"Yes."

"I will trade you the claim for that mule," he said as he pointed at Scud's mule.

"You pile all that stuff on a good mule and try to ride her as well, and she'll end up the same way yours did. We will trade you two of our mules for the claim, your musket and pistol, and that keg of blasting powder in the tunnel,"

Josh offered.

"That is fair," the old man replied.

"We will be out here tomorrow morning to get papers signed and complete the deal."

That evening Rebecca had a local banker make out a property transfer that only required the property name and those of the people involved. The next morning they drove the wagon out to Old Dan's claim. He was ready to go when they got there. They pulled the wagon up to the tunnel entrance, and Scud, Josh, and Rebecca carried the coffins to the back. They left Rebecca alone for a few minutes with the bodies. Dan then set out the powder to explode and collapse the tunnel. He lit the string of powder and got on Lobo behind Josh. They raced to the end of the trail, where the others were waiting. The explosion shook the ground under them and set off a small rockslide that covered the tunnel entrance. They then returned to the cabin to fill out and sign the transfer.

"Who do I put on this as the new owner, you or Scud?" Rebecca asked Josh.

"Put your name in there. Your family is buried here. It's your claim."

Scud unhitched the two mules, and they loaded one with Dan's gear. He passed the guns over to Josh.

"Look after these. They shoot well if you take care of them."

They watched Dan as he headed for the main road.

After he had gone, the three sat on a bench outside the cabin and ate the meal they had missed earlier.

"What do I owe you for the mules?"

Rebecca asked.

"Just one mule," Josh replied. "The other one was a trade for the guns. We'll figure something out later."

Rather than make the trip back to Sierra City, they decided to stay at the cabin on the new claim and prospect the old claim the next day before returning home. They had brought enough food to last a couple of days. That evening Josh and Rebecca sat by the campfire while Scud cleaned up the cabin.

"Are you still planning to go back east?" Josh asked.

"I don't know, maybe like you said, wait until spring to decide. Right now I have to get work so I can live and save up to make the trip if I want to. I also have to figure out how to keep this claim. I don't want someone opening up the tunnel and disturbing their resting place. I just don't know, Josh. You people have been so kind to me, Tenny rescuing me from the bandits, and you and Scud coming up here with me. I want to repay all of you somehow."

"We aren't looking to be repaid," Josh replied. "I would like you to stay with us for the winter so we can get to know each other better."

"I can't do that. I have to find work either in Downieville or Marysville, or maybe Sacramento. It's important to me to be able to look after myself. I know I'll find something."

"Just don't make it too far from us so that we can visit each other."

"I'll try," she replied.

That night Scud and Josh slept in the cabin, while Rebecca bedded down in the wagon.

They rode the animals to the old claim the

next morning in order to prospect the ground above the pit, as old Dan had suggested.

Scud set out the plan.

"We hunt rock with gold. You walk this side," he said to Josh. Then to Rebecca he pointed to the opposite slope. "You walk that side."

"Are we looking for loose pieces of rock with quartz veins?" She countered.

"Yes, that is called float since it sort of floats downhill from its source," Josh explained.

They made slow progress trying to force their way through the thick underbrush and keep an eye out for mineralized rock. By noon the sun had them all soaking wet with sweat. Rebecca was the first to let out a yell just as Scud stumbled across some large boulders with quartz veins. He broke open a couple of the pieces by smashing them together and could see the tiny golden flecks.

"Got gold rock," he bellowed, bringing the other two down to the valley bottom.

"That's the same kind of rock I found up there, but I didn't see any gold," Rebecca observed.

"We'll go and have a look," Josh decided. "That must be the source of this rock."

They climbed up the east slope to the spot where Rebecca had found the pieces of quartz. They searched all over the area, scraping away the soil cover where possible. This exposed some areas of bedrock that was laced with veins, but none of the quartz showed any visible gold.

"I think we need to go back down to the bottom to find out where that gold rock came from."

"You're probably right," Josh replied. "It doesn't look like it came from here."

Back at the valley bottom, the three walked slowly up the old creek bed. The gold-bearing float continued for about fifty feet above Scud's original find. Past that point, it was gone.

"The source has to be near here."

They spread out and wandered up the east slope, but there was no continuation of the trail of gold-flecked rock. On the west side there was a substantial cover of soil with a thick spread of alder. However, there was an occasional piece of quartz-bearing rock poking through.

"We need some tools to clear this stuff away so we can get to the bedrock," Josh observed.

They explored the west slope area until dusk, picking up a few pieces of rock that had worked their way up through the cover. Most contained some gold.

That evening they settled in for the night with great expectations of locating the vein the next day, but such was not to be.

The clouds moved in after dark and by midnight flakes of snow were starting to drift down. Rebecca awoke the next morning covered by an extra blanket of white. The storm had intensified, adding additional depth to the cover by the minute.

"Leave soon or not get out," Scud announced as he emerged from the cabin.

Rebecca appeared from behind the wagon.

"I've got the mules hitched up and the horses saddled. Let's go."

They quickly piled their possessions into

the wagon, closed up the cabin, and broke a path through the snow to the main trail.

"Looks like we're going to postpone finding that vein until next year," Josh remarked as they passed the narrow trail up to the old claim. He smiled as he turned to Rebecca.

"That's another reason for you to stay. You could be a rich woman by this time next year."

She rode up beside him and took his hand.

"If I am, we'll all share in it."

As they proceeded down the road to lower elevations, the snow turned to sleet then to a steady downpour of rain. The roadway quickly became a sea of mud, slowing their progress and causing the animals to lose their footing on some of the side hill spots.

"I'm beginning to wish we'd stayed in the cabin," Rebecca mumbled through the scarf wrapped around her head.

"I don't know," Josh replied. "The way that snow was coming down, we could have been stuck there until spring."

By midafternoon, they had passed through Shady Flats.

"We keep going," Scud announced.

Josh and Rebecca just nodded their heads.

The rain finally quit just after midnight when they reached the Lost Miner Creek cabin. The door was locked, and they had to wake Rachel to let them in. She stoked up the fire, and they stood around the old stove until they were at least warm, if not dry. Rachel dug out some dry clothes for Rebecca, and Elizabeth offered to share her bed. They all retired for the night except Josh and Rachel.

"Do you want to sleep with me tonight?

Your cabin will be cold."

"Not tonight," he replied.

"Why? Are you afraid she might find out we are lying together?"

Josh came up quickly with the answer he had prepared for this moment.

"Yes. She will be moving out in a few days to go to town to find work. She is friendly with your husband. He saved her life, and if she knew about us she would probably feel it was her duty to tell him."

"You're right. I would be very afraid of what Tenny would do if he knew."

Josh and Rachel kept their distance from each other for three days until Rebecca decided to move out. Josh's feelings were mixed. He had become very attracted to her, but his physical need for Rachel was still overpowering.

He held the big horse while Rebecca climbed on, and Scud handed her a small bag of gold dust as he loaded her meager possessions behind her. Before she moved away, she leaned over and whispered in Josh's ear.

"Elizabeth told me all about you and Rachel. It made me sad, but don't worry, I won't tell Tenny anything."

Josh just stood there and watched her as she spurred her horse down the road.

She rode casually into Downieville, already missing her friends back at the creek. She headed for Tenny's home, anticipating that he would put her up for a few days until she lined up work. Melissa greeted her knock on Tenny's door.

"What do you want here?" she snapped.

"I want to see your father. Is he here?"

"No! Go away," Melissa snarled as she slammed the door.

Rebecca was shocked but not surprised. Elizabeth had warned her that Tenny's daughter probably would not welcome her. Fortunately her meager supply of gold would provide her with lodging for two or three days while she searched for employment. She booked into the Bridge House for the night.

Many thoughts raced through her head as she tried to go to sleep. She hadn't really considered until now what type of work to seek. She was thankful her father had let her stay in school long enough to learn how to read, write and do numbers. Eventually she had to quit and help him on their small farm. She knew how to cook, sew, and had always been complimented on her drawing and painting. She would surely be able to find work that she could enjoy and that would provide for her food and lodging. With these positive thoughts, she smiled and drifted off to sleep.

When she awoke, the October morning had brought a chill to the air, heralding the coming season and her new life. So much had happened, and her whole existence had been turned upside down in such a short time. She decided to go see Mr. McDonald, the only person she could think of that might be able to advise her where to look for a job. She learned to her dismay that Mr. McDonald was away in Sacramento. She was delighted, however, when a young assistant, who was obviously attracted to her, offered to help. He pointed out that, since Mr. McDonald had recently taken over the

Mountain Echo, he might be looking for some extra help. He promised to inform Mr. McDonald of her visit and suggested that she return to see him the next day.

Rebecca spent the rest of the day visiting other businesses in the town. She tried the dry goods store, two grocery stores, and the Sierra drug store. Only the manager of the National Theater, a Mr. McClosky, gave her any encouragement. He described some of the shows and plays with famous performers that were coming. He needed someone to sell tickets at these performances. He told her that he couldn't pay much, but she would be able to watch the shows. Rebecca was excited with this opportunity but realized it would not provide enough for her survival.

Her visit to McDonald's office the next day was even more rewarding. Of course, he remembered her from the very sad fate of her family. After relating her trip to the claim and the burial of her folks, she asked him about possible employment with the paper, or suggestions as to where she should look for work.

"Can you read and write?" he asked.

Rebecca assured him she could and proceeded to read the front page of their paper flawlessly. The example of her writing was equally impressive.

McDonald leaned back in his chair and thought for a moment. Then he said, "We have expanded our operation recently by purchasing one of our competitors. We hope to increase our list of subscribers by becoming more diversified and appeal to a wider range of readers. One group that has been neglected by both our publications is the women in the community. I need someone to write about news and events of interest to women. Do you think you would be able to do that?"

"I think so. I would certainly like to try."

"Very well. We will give you a chance to see what you can do. I am going to hire you for a trial period at a nominal salary. If you do well, by the end of the year, we will make you a full-time reporter with a regular income."

Rebecca was overwhelmed by her good fortune and was anxious to get started, but she felt obligated to tell Mr. McDonald about the offer from the National Theatre. She was concerned that he would discourage her from working for two employers.

"That is excellent," he observed. "You will be able to write reviews of all these performances for the paper."

The next few months were a whirlwind of activity for Rebecca. The theater had shows on a regular basis. She would sell tickets before the show, watch the performance and then stay up late writing about it for the paper, especially if it was due to goes to press the next day.

She was entranced when celebrities such as Marian Goodenow offered an evening of song. The beauty of her appearance and voice packed the theater with miners willing to hand over their hard-earned gold for acknowledgement by this lady. Fights often ensued, and in one case a murder resulted from competition for Miss Goodenow's favor.

One of the combatants, a man named Moffat, had salted his claim by firing his shotgun full of gold dust into the rock. He then invited Miss Goodenow to pan gold from his rich claim, where she accumulated a sack full of the dust. A few days later after the touring company had departed, Moffat learned that, in spite of his efforts, the lady in question had looked favorably on a Mr. Butler. When Moffat confronted Butler, hurling insults at him, Butler calmly shot him in the chest, resulting in his death a few hours later.

Rebecca's coverage of Miss Goodenow's performance, and the ensuing events established her as a competent writer. Where she had previously been discounted as a young woman interfering in a male-dominated area, she was soon accepted as a fair and honest journalist.

11

The day after Rebecca left to look for work, Rachel asked Scud to go to town for some supplies and take Joachim. She also asked Elizabeth to go along and look after the little boy.

It was a beautiful, warm October afternoon. There had been a series of frosty nights to cut down on the insects, and the leaves had turned to display their autumn colors. Josh had gone out in the morning to repair a portion of the fence up by the pond, where the cattle had broken through the day before. Scud had helped him round up the cows before the trip to town, but fixing the fence was left to Josh. The work was hard. It involved cutting the posts and rails, digging the holes, and driving the posts into the ground. He had worked up a good sweat by the time Rachel arrived with lunch and a cold drink.

"I think you need a swim to cool off."

They walked slowly up the path to one of their favorite areas, the grassy bank above the pool. She spread out the blanket and put the small food basket and a bottle of cold water down. She slipped out of her simple cotton dress and walked into the water as Josh watched with mixed emotions. Although she had gotten a little heavier and thicker around the middle, the attraction of her smooth tanned body, glistening in the sun, pulled him to her. And then he thought about Rebecca and the feelings for her that were emerging.

"Aren't you coming in with me?" Rachel asked as she slowly walked out of the water and stood facing him. Without waiting for him to answer, she began removing his clothing until they were standing naked together. He could feel the warmth of her body and the desire building up inside him. He pulled her close, and they tumbled onto the blanket. The interplay of their bodies was all that he longed for, as he had for the past few months, but somehow this time it was different. He was lying with Rachel with her body wrapped around him, and all he could think about was Rebecca.

When they separated, Rachel searched his face as she said, "You're thinking about her, aren't you?"

The question surprised Josh. He hesitated a few minutes before he answered, "I don't know how I feel. I think about her a lot and would like to see her again, but I want to be with you. I feel it's somehow wrong lying with you and having feelings for her too. I expect telling you this will make you angry and not want me any more."

"I'm not angry, Josh, I understand. What we have is not the same as what you want with her. You and I need each other's body to satisfy our own. You need a woman to lie with just as I need a man. We are fond of each other, but this is not like the love for which people marry. I once had that with Tenny, but he destroyed it. Your father satisfied my body's needs. When he died, I finally turned to you."

They lay back on the blanket, letting their bodies warm in the afternoon sun. Josh must have slept, for when he awoke with Rachel still beside him, he discovered he needed her again. This time their lovemaking was slow and sensuous and completely fulfilling to both of them.

"I have something to tell you," Rachel said as she slipped into her dress. "I'm going to have our baby. It should come sometime this winter."

Josh's warm glow from the pleasure he had experienced gave way quickly to the cold feelings of panic.

"What are you going to do?" he asked with alarm.

"Just have the baby. There's nothing you have to worry about."

"But how will you explain who the father is?"

"Who will need to know? I don't think Tenny will care. I don't expect to see him around here again. Scud will understand, and your sister already knows. As far as anyone else is concerned, I am a married woman having a child. That's all they need to know."

"What about Melissa?"

"Yes, she could be a problem. I don't know what she would do. You just need to keep it from Rebecca that we sleep together."

"She already knows," Josh replied.

"How?"

"Elizabeth told her."

It was late afternoon when they walked back down the path. They stopped at the fence line, where Rachel helped Josh put the last two rails in place.

That night as she nestled in his arms, Josh lay awake with all these thoughts racing through his mind. In the early hours of the morning, he finally came to a conclusion. In spite of what she had said, he couldn't leave Rachel. She had given him so much pleasure that he didn't want to face the idea of being without her. He needed to put these thoughts about Rebecca out of his mind and appreciate this loving woman that was going to have his baby.

That evening when they returned from town, Elizabeth reported she had visited with Rebecca and brought back the news that Tenny had left and was traveling to the south. She said that Melissa was living alone and was still as mean as before.

As autumn faded into winter, Rachel's pregnancy became progressively more noticeable. She abandoned making any trips to town for fear that her condition would become a topic of conversation among acquaintances. She especially didn't want her daughter to learn about it and pass the news on to Tenny. She knew it was inevitable that he would find out, and although she had told Josh otherwise, she feared his reaction. The memories of his violence that night on the trail with the Indian warriors still haunted her.

Josh was fascinated to feel the movements of the baby when she held his hand to her belly.

He was mildly resentful that this unseen creature had stolen the pleasures of her body from him, but Rachel continued to assure him that everything would be the same once the baby was born.

As the new year dawned, Rachel was forced to spend much of her time in bed, enduring the pain and discomfort. Elizabeth took over most of her chores as they all awaited the arrival of the newest member of the household.

The first week in January was marked by the worst blizzard of the winter. The snow filled the trails and drifted up against the windows. They worried as to whether they would be able to get out for a doctor if Rachel had problems with the birth, but John Sarsfield arrived without incident as the blizzard blew itself out.

"He is your child," she announced to Josh, "so he will carry the Sarsfield name. He is not a Woods. We will care for and protect him together."

Tenny Woods was an unhappy and troubled man. Since the search for the bandits, his life had fallen into a boring, monotonous routine. He realized he missed the excitement of the hunt and needed a more adventurous existence. And surprisingly, he missed Rachel. It was very difficult to admit, and he consistently fought against the desire to go see her and find out if they could resume their marriage. He had finally admitted to himself that he had hurt her deeply, and she would probably have no wish to have him back. When he mentioned to his daughter that they should take a trip to the cabin, Melissa was adamant in refusing to go.

"I don't want to ever see any of them again," she screamed.

This also bothered him. Although she was turning into a beautiful young woman physically, she was not a likeable person. He was growing tired of her constant complaining and demands for money, but he felt a strong obligation to provide a home for her and look after her needs.

He had taken on a job as assistant pastor at a local church, but that had not worked out. The church members had complained that his talks lacked messages that went with their religious beliefs. Tenny knew this was true and that he was only mouthing the words without any sense of conviction. He thought back to Pastor Joe telling him that it didn't matter if he believed what he was saying, as long as it was what they wanted to hear and brought them comfort. Even so, he still felt like a phony. His one-on-one and small group sessions were more productive, but they were also becoming irritating. He was tired of hearing people complain about their problems. He just wanted to get away from all of it.

One evening on returning home from the church, he met Rebecca on the street. He was happy to see her again and learn about her recent trip to the claim and her new job. He asked her why she hadn't called upon him when she came to town. She replied that she had but was turned away at the door by Melissa. After they parted, and he thought about it, he was further troubled that his daughter could be so callous as to refuse help to his friend. He thought about confronting her with his displeasure but realized that with the way she had been acting, it would be of little use and would further sour what relationship they had left. That evening he decided to get away and take a trip south, visit a few of his old friends, and try and figure out where life was taking him. He had enough money to pay for the rooms for his daughter and look after himself with no more preaching or counseling. Though many still called him 'Preacher', he now resented this label.

The next morning he hitched up the mules to the wagon, packed a few belongings, and set out on the road south. This time Melissa did not seem to be unhappy to see him go. Over the months that followed, he discovered that many of the familiar small camps were now deserted. The people had left when there was no more easy gold to be found. Many of his followers in the other towns and villages had also pulled up stakes and moved farther up the valleys, where the lode mining was becoming more profitable. His journey eventually took him back to Mokelumne Hill, where he had spent the winter of 1851. As he expected, his friend Pastor Joe had long departed the area. With winter approaching, Tenny could see no point in staying and decided reluctantly to make his way back north. The trip had been a disappointment. He had expected that things would be much the same as they had been before, but so much had changed that he felt like a stranger wherever he went.

Since Calico had gone to Sacramento to have his shoulder treated, Tenny had not heard from him. He wondered how he had made out and so, on his return, he decided to take a side trip and try and locate him. Asking around in the City, he learned that his friend was working for the Sacramento County as a deputy sheriff. After inquiring at the sheriff's office, he found Calico living at a local boarding house. They talked well into the night, reliving their adventure chasing the bandits up to Quartzite Peak.

"I miss the adventure and excitement we had then," Tenny admitted. "Maybe you wouldn't want that every day, but my life is getting dull with nothing happening. My old way of life as a traveling preacher no longer has any meaning for me. I would think your job here would be more interesting."

"It is. Most of the time I'm just arresting drunks or breaking up fights, but we do get a few murders and stabbings and some claim jumping out in the camps. If you want to stay in the City for the winter, I think I can get you on as a part-time deputy. That might give you some of the adventure you're looking for. You would have to be available when we are forming a posse or for keeping order at events where there is going to be a lot of people. You would also be asked to fill in for regulars when they can't work. You won't make much money, but it would be enough to get you a room and keep you fed."

Tenny thought for a moment then decided he had nothing to lose.

"I'd like to try it. It could be interesting, and I don't have anything better to look forward to this winter. I'm in no hurry to return home."

"Good. We'll go down in the morning to meet the sheriff and see what he has to say."

Tenny was hired that afternoon for a monthly pay that barely equaled what he would have formerly found in the collection plate when he gave his sermons. As Calico had said, it would be enough to keep him alive with very little left over for extras. He still had his pouch of dust, and his only other expense was providing for Melissa back in Downieville. He made the rounds of the city with Calico during the first week, getting to know the problem spots and some of the troublemakers.

The next week he was on his own. He was apprehensive in taking his first shift, but it was a rainy Thursday evening, and the night passed without incident. It was his Saturday tour that was the test. That was a warm summer evening, and the town's folk were out celebrating the end of a wet week.

.

J STREET, SACRAMENTO, NEW YEAR'S DAY, 1853
serreotype by R. H. Vance

Tenny's scheduled route took him along the waterfront, where most of the evening's revelry normally took place. It was late in the afternoon and the men from the mines, as well as the towners, moved from bar to bar, sampling the entertainment and meeting up with friends. Although Tenny now abhorred drunkenness, it was not a crime in the City if the drinker kept his actions under control. As the evening progressed, the scenes on the street and in the saloons got wilder as the whisky continued to flow. While Tenny was walking by one of the more troublesome establishments that Calico had pointed out, a man came crashing out through the front window, landing in a heap on the dirt road. As he struggled to get up, another man charged out through the door and started kicking him. Tenny yelled for him to stop, but too many of the bystanders were cheering and encouraging them to keep fighting. Tenny had enough. He waded in, grabbed the second man, and pulled him away from his victim. The man wrestled free, turned, pulled a knife, and ran at Tenny. He dodged the attack and tripped the man, who fell on the steps. Tenny could feel that familiar uncontrollable anger rising within him. Before the man could get up, Tenny kicked the knife from his hand, picked the man up and drove his head into the porch railing. He was now out of control, the venom spilling out with every blow to the unconscious victim.

"Get him off, before he kills Charlie," someone yelled from the crowd.

It took four of the bystanders to pull Tenny away. They carried the unconscious man into the bar and laid him out on one of the tables, while someone else went to get a doctor. In the ensuing confusion, Tenny hurriedly left the area and returned to his rooms. He couldn't understand what was happening to him and why he was unable to suppress his anger. He felt helpless and that he was losing control.

That night the voices returned, but this time it wasn't God speaking to him. When he first heard them, he sat up in bed soaked in sweat. He lit the lamp and looked around the room, knowing in his heart he would find no one.

The voice was that of Ed Jensen.

"Why did you abandon the search and not look harder to find me? I was so lost and so cold, and I couldn't get back. I was waiting for you to find me. Why did you not come?"

Tenny started to cry when he heard Gladys

speak.

"You shouldn't have left me alone so much. I was so lonely after Ed was gone. I could have enjoyed life if you had stayed home more. "

Rachel, who appeared to be floating above him, interrupted her.

"You abandoned me too. Why did you treat me bad when I loved you? Why did you stop loving me? Why did you leave?"

When the voices were finally silent, Tenny was left with an empty sadness. Everything they said was true. He had walked away from everyone who had loved him. Further sleep that night was impossible. He got dressed and wandered the streets until the first light of dawn. Later that morning as he was sitting down to coffee and biscuits in his room, a knock came to the door, and Calico walked in.

"I hear you got into a hell of a mess last night. Do you want to tell me about it?"

Tenny related the events as well as his memory would permit.

"I can't remember it all," he said. "I guess I blacked out. This fellow came after me with a knife, and the next thing I knew he was lying on the ground bleeding, and these others were pulling me off him."

"Well, the sheriff came to see me this morning. He heard about it last night from some of the locals. He's going to have to suspend you until it blows over. He doesn't even want to see you for at least a couple of months. It might be a good idea if you went home for a while. That fellow you beat up is in bad shape, and he's got a few friends that will probably be looking for you. It might not be too safe to stick around here."

" You're probably right. I'll think about it," Tenny replied, "but now I need to get some sleep."

Calico left, and Tenny stretched out on the bed, but his mind resisted sleep. There were too many thoughts running through his head. He feared that the voices would return if he let down his guard.

He must have dropped off, for Rachel appeared beside the bed. Her form was so real that Tenny reached out to touch her, but there was nothing. She had moved to the end of the bed and was standing next to the two Cheyenne warriors. None of them said a word. Tenny vaulted out of bed as the apparitions disappeared.

He sat with his head in his hands, desperately tired.

"Someone is doing this to me. I don't know who or how. I need help. I don't know what to do."

All afternoon he paced the small room waiting for night, but sleep was totally out of the question. With darkness around him, he felt a bit safer, at least enough to venture from his room out into the street. As he wandered through town, keeping away from the waterfront, he continually felt the eyes of the passersby and heard them speaking to him. Twice he answered, but they looked at him in shock and crossed the street to avoid him. He slowly realized that, although he distinctly heard the voices, no one had actually spoken to him. As he walked further, there were more voices, even with no one on the streets. He shook his head vigorously trying to dislodge them, but they only became jumbled, all talking louder and louder, trying to outdo each other. Tenny sat on the ground and held his head in his hands as the pain began. He didn't know how long he had been there, but when he opened his eyes the first strands of pink were sweeping over the hills.

A week of torment passed. Tenny managed only two or three tortured hours of sleep each night, and he quit eating. When Calico came to see him one evening at the end of the week, he hardly recognized this ragged scarecrow that answered the door. What really shocked him was the constant look of terror in his friend's eyes.

Tenny was suspicious but reluctantly let him into the room.

"What has happened to you? Should I call for a doctor?"

Tenny slowly mumbled it all out, "I can't sleep. I can't get rid of the voices, and at night they keep coming here to stare at me. They won't leave me alone. Everywhere I go, they are there. I don't know how to get away from them."

"What are you talking about? Who are they? What voices?"

"People I know and people I don't know and even people that are dead. They are all accusing me and telling me about all the bad things I have done."

Calico was silent for a few minutes. He was beginning to understand the fear in his friend's eyes and the torture he was going through. He also knew that he had to convince Tenny to leave and go home.

"Do you know that I am really here and speaking to you?"

"Yes, of course, but many times I believe they are real until I reach out to make contact. I don't know what to do," he cried.

"I think I'd better take you home. You can't live here any longer like this. You need someone, such as your daughter, to be with you and look after you."

"It won't make any difference. The voices follow me wherever I go."

Calico could see the pointlessness of trying to reason with him. Something had gone wrong with his friend's mind, and he was unable to look after himself.

"If you stay here like this, it will kill you. We will pack all your things tonight. I will come and get you in the morning and take you to Downieville."

That night as he settled in, he hoped that Calico's visit had calmed him enough to sleep peacefully. He had finally been convinced that going home was for the best. For the first time in days, he felt relaxed.

When Calico arrived the next morning, Tenny's calmness and apparent rationality was a pleasant surprise. They hitched the mules to the wagon, Calico tied his own horse to trail behind, and they set off.

Being alone had suited Melissa just fine. She had no one to tell her how to live, and it fit in well with her emerging personality. When her father left, she was somewhat saddened and apprehensive to see him go, but as the autumn progressed she became more confident in her own ability to cope and look after herself. She was involved in a small way in supporting a temperance publication called The Old Oaken Bucket until it failed due to lack of support from the mining community. She continued to visit Sally Johnson, when she was sure her husband would be at work, to improve her writing and speaking skills. By late autumn, however, she became convinced that she had gathered about as much knowledge and guidance as she needed from this woman and terminated her visits. Her minor speaking engagements on temperance to women's groups and church meetings were giving her an increasing sense of confidence. These sessions brought her in a small income, but it was far less than she felt she needed to pursue the life style she sought. She had to find another source of money as the gold dust her father had left was just about used up.

One afternoon a knock came to her door. The moment she opened it, she backed up with fright into the room. The man at the door was the same one that had attacked her mother at the store five years previous.

"Please don't be afraid," he said. "I won't hurt you. I came looking for Tenny Woods, the Preacher."

"He's not here," Melissa answered tentatively but with a bit more confidence.

"Do you know when he will be back? I want to talk to him about our hunt for those bandits."

"I don't know. He left a short time after he returned from that hunt. He said he was going to visit some friends down south. I don't know when he's coming back."

"You're not Rachel, are you? You look the same. Are you her sister? I don't remember ever having seen you before."

"Oh, you've seen me before," Melissa snarled. "I was there when you tried to rape my mother a few years ago."

Michael Reilly was at a lost for words. He had felt shame about that incident and had apologized. He did remember an awkward little girl around the store, but it was not a beautiful young woman such as this. He was silent for a few moments.

"I am so very sorry for that. I was drunk at the time and had lost control, but I know that is no excuse."

"Did that convince you to stop drinking?"

"No, but I don't allow it to take over my life any more."

"That is good. Drink can destroy your life. Maybe I can help you stop completely."

They had been standing in the doorway. Finally Melissa felt safe enough to invite him in.

"Will you to tell me about the hunt for those bandits. My father didn't talk about it very much before he left."

Michael entered the room, sat down in an armchair, and waited while Melissa prepared tea.

When she returned and settled herself, he launched into his story.

"After my brother was killed, I left the group. I heard they killed the bandits and rescued this girl. That is what I wanted to ask your father. What happened after I left?"

When Michael got up to leave, he asked Melissa if he could come and see her again. He said he would like to take her for dinner at the hotel some evening.

Melissa had to think quickly. She was sure that if he knew how old she was, he might be reluctant to be with her. He was, however, obviously well off, and a few dinners at nice eating-places would be a pleasant change from what she was cooking for herself. She agreed to accompany him the following evening if he assured her there would be no alcohol.

The next evening became the first of many events they attended together during the following autumn and winter.

When Tenny was returned home in December, Melissa was shocked by her father's appearance. The man that had left only a few months before was robust and healthy. When Calico brought this wizened, gray-haired person into the room, she didn't recognize him immediately. Tenny was exhausted from the trip, so after Calico had put him to bed, he sat down with Melissa and told her what had happened and what she must do.

"You're father is sick, and you need to help him get well. He hasn't been sleeping or eating regular, and his mind is playing tricks on him. He hears voices and sees people that aren't there. I don't know what you can do about that, but at least you can see that he eats and spend time with him. He seems to think you are the only one who cares about him. He is going to need you to understand and comfort him for a while."

"I'll do what I can," Melissa replied.

After Calico had gone, she looked in on her father.

"What am I going to do?" she thought. "How can I go after the things in life I want if I have to look after him? I should cart him out to the cabin and leave him with his wife."

She knew she wasn't going to do that. She hated to admit it, but she needed him and his money as much as he needed her.

Tenny's condition improved slowly through the winter. He appreciated the care that Melissa reluctantly parceled out, and she began to regain the affection for him that she had felt when she was younger. She regretted putting her own interests on hold, but she considered it a fair exchange, his financial support for her care and attention.

Michael Reilly's interest in her continued and seemed to grow as he escorted her to dinners, plays and other events. He even avoided his usual drinks with his meals when he was in her company. He made a point of spending time with Tenny, slowly extracting the story of that part of the hunt that he had missed. He had seen Rebecca about town and was surprised to learn that she was the girl they rescued. In March he asked Melissa to marry him. It was a surprise to Melissa and caused her to briefly examine her feelings for him. To her, there was no doubt. She tolerated his company but thoroughly enjoyed his presents and the social life he was exposing her to. She didn't want to marry anyone. She had no interest in the life of a married woman, submitting to the physical demands of her husband. She had observed her mother and Jonathan on a couple of occasions, and the whole thing disgusted her. Her dilemma was that she wanted to delay her reply to his offer in such a way that he would not decide to discontinue his visits and gifts. The next day she informed him that she was honored that he would want her, but her first responsibility was to see to her father's complete recovery before she could look to her own desires. This seemed to satisfy Michael, and the relationship continued at a more subdued pace.

Tenny continued to hear voices and see apparitions, but they were not as often or as frightening. The constant look of fear had gone from his eyes, and his suspicions of those around him had lessened. One night after a particularly trying day, when Melissa had been away, his old mentors, Bishop Cavanaugh and Vanderslyke, visited him. They stood on either side of the bed and denounced him for leaving their ministry. He awoke with a yell that brought Melissa immediately to his side to comfort him. He had to reach out and touch her to make sure she was real.

Before Calico returned to Sacramento, he went to visit Rebecca. He found her at the newspaper office writing her report on the previous night's play. He explained Tenny's condition to her and wondered if she could check on him every once in a while and report to him if their friend was getting worse.

"I don't trust his daughter to give him the care he needs."

"I'll try," she replied, "but Melissa doesn't want me around. I don't know why, but she turned me away when I first arrived in town. I'll try to go and see him when she's not home."

Fortunately she was able to make a number of visits throughout the winter. Tenny was delighted to see her and looked forward to her coming. When Melissa heard of it, she was furious but realized the beneficial effects on her father were more important than her anger over the girl coming to the house. She faced Rebecca on the street one day after the first couple of visits to voice her displeasure.

"I know he wants to see you, so you can continue to come, but just make sure it's when I'm not there."

Before she could answer, Melissa turned abruptly and walked away.

Life at the cabin revolved around Johnny. Josh never ceased to marvel at this little person he had helped to create. He was now totally committed to Rachel and his son with his thoughts of Rebecca confined to the odd occasion when he would see her in town, or she would come out to visit. At these times the old pangs of desire would surface until he forced them out of his mind.

Elizabeth especially took an interest in caring for the little boy, allowing Rachel the opportunities to go to town or visit with her friends in the valley. She had decided earlier to be open about her son and the identity of his father, but putting it into practice was another matter. Deep in her heart she still feared Tenny and what he might do when he found out.

12

Independence Day was a popular holiday in the Valley. All the towns and camps celebrated the Fourth of July, usually with parades, speeches, fireworks, and certainly some serious drinking. Toasting to anything, even remotely patriotic, went on all day and usually well into the night. The holiday was notable in Downieville, as it had been the site of the only hanging of a woman in the State. Many of the locals that had witnessed the event in 1851 still had vivid memories of the brave Mexican woman that had leapt from the scaffold to her death.

Everyone at Lost Miner Creek was excited about this year's celebration, and they all picked out their best clothes to wear to town. Rebecca had been out to the cabin the previous week and had told them that Melissa was to give one of the speeches to a ladies club at a local church. She had been instructed to cover the meeting for the paper and invited Elizabeth to join her.

Rachel had wavered back and forth as to whether to expose Johnny to the eyes of her friends. Finally with Josh's urging, she decided it was time the world knew about her son. Although her resolve was strong, she was nervous about what might result when Tenny or Melissa found out.

Elizabeth offered to look after Johnny while she and Rebecca went to hear the speeches. Melissa was last on the program with her short talk on the evils of drink and the rewards of abstinence. All the seats in the hall were occupied, forcing the two girls to stand at the back. Halfway through her speech Melissa became aware of their presence. She stopped in the middle of a sentence for a beat before she was able to continue. As she approached the end of her talk, Johnny began to cry, turning the heads of most of the audience away from the stage. When the meeting broke up, Melissa charged to the back and without acknowledging Rebecca's presence, faced Elizabeth.

"Whose baby is that?"

Elizabeth was surprised by the question but answered with a smile.

"It's mine, of course. Whose did you think it was?"

"I don't believe you. Who would want to have a baby with you?"

Elizabeth smiled again as she walked away.

"That should give her something to think about. What did you think about her little talk?" Rebecca asked.

Elizabeth thought for a moment then answered, "She seemed to know what she was talking about and had a lot of ideas, but I think she doesn't really believe what she's saying."

"Yes, I felt that too."

"Well then, why don't you write your review that way?"

"Let's go down to the office and you can help me do it."

Melissa was troubled. She felt sure Elizabeth had lied to her, but she couldn't be positive. She was angry because she didn't know what was going on. Even though Elizabeth was a year older than her, she still looked like a little girl: short, thin, and very plain. Melissa could not imagine a man being attracted to her unless one of the miners had taken advantage of her innocence. With these thoughts working through her mind, she decided to go home and look in on her father. Tenny's demons had gradually returned in force over the course of the spring and summer. The relationship between father and daughter was being strained by the almost constant care she had to give. He couldn't sleep. His prowling about their small living space and his occasional screams of terror were continually disturbing her nights. She would have liked to move out and let him look after himself, but she had little money of her own. Her only other option was to accept Michael's proposal, but she had no desire to marry him and become a kept woman.

Tenny was asleep when she looked in. So as to not wake him, she left immediately to go listen to some of the patriotic speeches. She stood at the edge of a crowd as the Mayor gave his annual talk. Her eyes roamed the assemblage until she caught sight of a familiar figure. Her mother stood a few feet in front of her surrounded by a large group of people. She was surprised to notice how much Rachel had aged since she had last seen her. She had grown more matronly with a few strands of gray laced through her raven hair. As Melissa moved closer, her surprise changed to shock. Rachel was holding that baby, and Josh was standing close beside her with his arm around her waist. All of a sudden the whole thing became clear in her mind. The baby was her mother's, and Josh was the father. She had to leave. The realization was too much for her to understand. How could this be?

Over the next couple of days, this new bit of knowledge took control of her mind. She lost interest in the evils of drink, at least for a while. She pondered how she could use this revelation to her benefit. Should she tell her father? She decided against taking that action in fear of what effect it would have on him in his present state. The next day the Citizen was published. She picked up a copy and quickly scanned it to see if her talk with the ladies' group had been mentioned. She found it at the bottom of the back page under Rebecca's byline. The last paragraph read;

A talk about Temperance was given by Miss Melissa Woods to close the program. Miss Woods presented considerable information on the subject but appeared to lack any emotional connection with the topic. Perhaps, she is too young and inexperienced to feel its importance.

Melissa was livid. "They came to the meeting to laugh at me. They were planning to do this all the time," she thought. Every time she reread the report, she got angrier. Finally she ran down the street and burst into the newspaper office. Rebecca was sitting at her desk and looked up with others in the room as Melissa came rushing in.

"Why did you write this in a way to make me look foolish?' she yelled.

"I just report what I see and hear," Rebecca said calmly.

"You are a liar. You did this on purpose."

Rebecca said nothing. She just looked at her accuser with a slight smile on her face.

It was more than Melissa could stand. She picked up an inkwell sitting on the desk and threw it at Rebecca, spilling ink all over her clothes, the desk, and the paper she was composing. With that, Melissa stormed out, slamming the door behind her.

As she walked slowly home, she started to calm down. Her anger was rapidly being replaced by a desire for vengeance.

"I won't let them get away with this," she thought. "But what can I do? I must have a plan to make them pay for doing this to me."

She considered drastic measures such as setting fire to the cabin or somehow causing injury to the two girls but discarded these ideas because of the danger of being caught. Finally she decided that her father could be the instrument of her will. If he knew about how she had been insulted, he might take action. She hurried her steps to reach home and tell him.

Tenny was in one of his more lucid periods when she arrived. The previous night had been one of his good ones with no visitations or voices. Although his mental state had been slowly deteriorating throughout the spring and summer, he still had stretches of normalcy that would last as long as a couple of days. Melissa walked in with the newspaper, showed him Rebecca's article, and waited for a reaction. Tenny read the brief article with interest but made no comment. When none was forthcoming, she demanded to know why he couldn't see the insult to her.

Tenny thought for a moment then replied, "You have to realize it takes time and practice to speak strongly in front of an audience. You have to be very experienced or totally believe in what you're saying to convince people. You can look at Rebecca's words as an insult or as a helpful truth to encourage you to get better. It took me months of traveling with other speakers to become effective. I spent time listening to them and observing their tricks and methods of carrying an audience before I felt confident. You probably need to do the same. I know Rebecca well enough to believe she would not write this to insult or hurt you."

Melissa was disappointed with her father's reaction. What he said was probably true, but her anger made her unable to accept it. That was not the important thing to her at the moment. Throughout the day she pondered her course of action. She knew she would never be content to let it go. Finally that evening she made her decision. She would tell her father about the baby.

At first Tenny didn't believe her when she told of the incident at the church.

"How can you be sure that it wasn't Elizabeth's child?"

Melissa paused for a moment and then

related seeing Rachel holding the baby and Josh with his arm around her.

She waited in vain for an immediate reaction. Tenny stood up, looked closely at her for an instant, and then walked into his room. This was not what she had expected.

Tenny lay on his bed staring at the ceiling. The rational part of his mind had expected something like this. He knew Rachel was a very sensuous woman that required a man's attention, which he had been unable to give. However, it was only seldom that Tenny's rational side ruled his actions. How could she couple with a mere boy just to satisfy her physical needs? It wasn't right. He had known she'd lain with Jonathan and hadn't cared, but this was different. It was an insult to him as a man to have his wife in the arms of a boy. His mind couldn't come to grips with the enormity of the situation. To escape making a decision on the information, he fell asleep even though it was early in the evening. He awoke clearheaded the next morning but was no nearer determining how he should feel or what he should do about it.

That night the demons returned. First it was Rachel hovering over the bed then Josh and the Cheyenne warriors, and each of them was holding a baby. The babies all had strange adult faces, and they were laughing at him. He could hear their laughter getting louder and louder. They wouldn't be quiet. He put his hands over his ears, but he could still hear them.

"Be quiet. Go away. Leave me alone," he yelled.

Startled, Melissa rushed into the room. Her

father was lying on the floor, soaked in sweat. His heart was racing, and he could hardly breathe. She soaked a rag in cold water and held it to his head until he calmed down.

"I'm going out to the cabin tomorrow," he announced.

"I'll go with you," she smiled.

The next morning, while Tenny harnessed and hitched the mules to the wagon, Melissa saddled the horse that Michael had given her. She had on a new riding habit for the occasion. She looked forward to the day with some satisfaction, although she had no idea what was going to happen. Tenny was quiet as they rode along. Halfway to the cabin he stopped.

"I'm not sure I should be going out here," he confided. "I don't belong here. Maybe it's none of my business any more. I should just leave them alone."

"No, she's still your wife, and she has been unfaithful to you. She should be punished. They all should suffer for causing you this shame."

With these words, Melissa spurred her horse down the road. Reluctantly Tenny followed, letting the mules plod along at their own pace.

It was a quiet day at the cabin. Elizabeth had finally panned enough gold from the thin streak in the bank to buy herself a horse and saddle. She had talked Scud into going with her to pick it out and had awakened him at dawn to get going. They took Joachim along to share in the excitement. Josh had stayed to clean up gold dust that had collected in the crevices of the sluice. He heard a wagon pull up to the cabin and was surprised that Scud and his sister had gotten back so soon.

Tenny tied the mules to the rail in front. He sat there for a few minutes unsure of what to do. He finally got up and walked to the door.

"Go in! It's your house," Melissa urged even though she knew it wasn't his any longer.

Tenny slowly opened the door and stopped. Melissa was right behind him and almost knocked him over in her rush to get into the room. Rachel was sitting at the table nursing Johnny. She turned, looked up, and asked, "What do you want?"

Tenny could feel the anger beginning to rise inside him, and the pain was starting to grow in his head. He felt like he was floating in another dream. Rachel and the child appeared almost transparent. He wanted to touch her to make sure she was real. As he moved closer, she backed away, grabbing a cast iron pan from the stove. When he was close enough, she swung the pan catching him in the shoulder. Tenny screamed with the pain, stumbled back, and almost fell. His anger was all consuming as he picked up the poker from beside the stove.

"Give me that little bastard child. It's a spawn of the Devil. It needs to be destroyed," he yelled as he backed Rachel into the corner.

"I'll kill it," he cried as he swung the poker at the little body, smashing its skull.

Rachel stood in shock as the wave of nausea poured over her, and the tears started to flow. She dropped the lifeless body and flew at Tenny screaming as she swung the skillet at his head. Tenny stepped back quickly and caught her in the neck with the poker. She dropped the skillet as she tried to catch her breath. He was now totally out of control. His anger had consumed him, and he kept swinging the poker, finally knocking her off her feet. He continued to beat her as she lay on the floor moaning with pain. Mercifully she passed out as the blows continued.

Josh was unaware of what was happening until he heard the screaming and rushed up the hill. Standing at the door, Melissa was transfixed by the scene inside but made no effort to interfere. She caught a flash of movement out of the corner of her eye and spotted Josh as he came into view.

"Father," she yelled. "Josh is coming."

Automatically Tenny reached for his pistol and fired as Josh appeared coming toward the door. The ball caught him in the chest, driving him back into a tree, where he fell. He banged his head on a rock as he went down. He caught only a momentary glimpse of Tenny and Melissa before he passed out.

The sound of the shot and the gun in his hand brought Tenny back to reality. He stopped and looked around, not really sure of where he was. When he saw the two broken bodies on the cabin floor, his head slowly began to clear, and he realized what he had done. He sat down, held his head in his hands, and started to cry.

"I've killed them," he wailed. "I've killed my sweet Rachel. Why? Why did I do this?"

He crawled slowly over to Rachel's body and cradled her head in his lap, swaying back and forth as he sobbed. He was aware of slight tremors coming from her. Looking closely, he could see the weak movement of her chest up and down and felt what he thought was a pulse in her neck. He placed her head gently on the floor and walked back to Melissa, who was still standing at the door.

"We must go for a doctor. I think she is still alive. We must try and save her," he said as he walked toward the wagon. He paid no attention to Josh, who still lay unconscious in the yard.

As he started to climb into the wagon, Melissa grabbed his arm.

"You can't go back to town. Mother won't live long enough to get a doctor, and if she dies, they'll charge you with murder and hang you."

"I deserve to pay for this. It's not right, what I've done. I don't know what came over me. I don't even remember doing this."

"That doesn't matter," Melissa replied. "You need to go away. Mother won't live, and Josh and I are the only ones that know you were here. It is my word against his, and I know that they will believe me when I tell them that Josh tried to kill my mother. I can take care of all of this. Just give me your gun, take my horse, and go as far away as you can. Don't try to get in touch with me or show up until this is all over. Go quickly."

Tenny stood for what seemed to be an eternity to Melissa, trying to decide between what he should do and what he wanted to do. He couldn't make the decision until finally, with her constant urging, he climbed on her horse and rode away from the cabin.

Without checking to see if her mother was alive, Melissa jumped into the wagon and drove the mules as fast as they would go back to town. When she arrived, she burst into the sheriff's office screaming, "My mother has been murdered in our home, and the murderer is still there. I shot him. You must come."

"Just calm down young lady."

The sheriff got up from his desk and led Melissa to a chair.

"Just sit here, and tell me calmly what happened."

Melissa forced herself to relax. This was no time to wreck her plan by seeming to be too emotional.

"I went out to see my mother this morning. Before I arrived, I heard screaming, and when I got there I saw the cabin door open and Joshua Sarsfield striking my mother. When he saw me, he rushed toward me. I was afraid for my life. I had my father's pistol with me, so I shot at him. I guess I hit him as he dropped to the ground and didn't get up."

"Did you look in to see if your mother was alive?"

"No, I was too afraid that Josh could still come after me. I just wanted to get out of there and get help."

The sheriff thought for a moment then called to his deputy. "Sam, go get Doc and tell him to saddle up. Then hitch up the mules. We need to make a fast trip out to the valley."

He turned to Melissa and said, "Young lady, you better come with us and show us where to go."

Melissa wanted to go home but decided she better go with them and show more concern than she felt.

When Josh regained consciousness, the pain in his head and chest was intense, and it hurt to breathe. As his vision cleared, he became aware of two men standing over him. They said nothing as they lifted him to his feet. He tried to walk but was too unsteady and had to be helped over to a log where he could sit.

"I'm going to have a look at your chest," the doctor said. "This may hurt."

Josh could see the other two men carrying Rachel to the wagon.

"I have to see to Rachel. Is she all right?" Josh asked.

"She is hurt very bad, but she is alive. The baby is dead."

"Johnny is dead? What happened? Who did this?" Josh could feel the tears streaming down his face.

As the doctor examined the wound, he said, "You are a very lucky man. That nugget you have around your neck stopped the ball. It saved your life. I'll have to peel the rest of the gold out of your chest and fix you up back in town."

They loaded Josh into the wagon beside Rachel and Johnny's body. He held her hand. It was warm, but there was no response.

They met Scud, Elizabeth, and Joachim on the road. They were returning to the cabin but turned around when the sheriff explained what had happened.

"I don't care what Melissa told you. She lies. My brother wouldn't hurt Rachel or his son."

The sheriff looked closely at Melissa, who avoided his gaze.

When they reached town, Rachel and Josh were rushed to the doctor's house. Elizabeth shopped around for rooms, where they could stay. While the doctor took care of Josh's injuries, Sheriff Irwin asked him for his version of the events at the cabin.

"I didn't see much," Josh answered. "I was cleaning a sluice down by the creek when I heard the screams. I ran up the hill and saw Tenny and Melissa at the cabin door and …"

"Wait a minute," the sheriff interrupted, "you say you saw Tenny Woods there?"

"Yes. It was Tenny that shot me. That was all I saw before I passed out. When I woke up, you people were there."

"That story doesn't fit with what Mrs. Woods' daughter told us. She said it was you that killed the baby and beat Mrs. Woods."

"That's not true. Why would she say that?"

"I don't know. I will have to leave it to the Grand Jury to determine what the truth is. I would also like to have a talk with Tenny Woods. In the meantime, I will have to arrest you. As soon as the doctor agrees, I will come and escort you to jail."

After the sheriff had gone, and the doctor finished his treatment, he said, "As I told you before, that nugget you wore around your neck probably saved your life. It stopped the ball, but the impact broke some of your ribs, and the trouble you are having breathing suggests your lung may be injured. I will keep you here for a couple of days before I call the sheriff."

In the meantime, his assistant was assessing Rachel's injuries. He approached the doctor as he was finishing with Josh.

"Mrs. Woods is in bad shape. I don't know if she's going to make it. She's lost a lot of blood, and there are bones broken all over her body. I just don't know."

"All we can do is patch her up and hope for the best."

Josh interrupted, "Please let me know if she wakes up. She'll want to know about our baby."

"Are you telling me that was your child?"

"Yes, Johnny was our son."

Two days later Rachel was taken to the temporary home Elizabeth had found, and Josh was escorted by the sheriff to the County jail at Durgan's Flat.

The Grand Jury was scheduled to sit the following week to consider the evidence against Josh and determine if he was to be indicted for trial.

Rachel drifted in and out of consciousness for the next few days, but even when awake she was unaware of where she was or what had happened. She was unable to speak and still in considerable pain, forcing the doctor to administer small doses of morphine during his daily visits. Elizabeth was busy from morning to night tending to her needs and looking after Joachim, Scud had returned to the cabin but came to town every day to look in on his sister. Two days after the beating, he buried Johnny in the upper pasture beside the pool.

On Monday morning Mr. Musser, the District Attorney, informed Melissa that even though she was a minor, she would be called before the Grand Jury to give testimony.

She was apprehensive until she was assured that Josh would not be present. She felt more confidence when she learned the session would be closed to the public. The search for Tenny Woods had proven unsuccessful, and although it was felt that his testimony would be critical, the session went ahead. Melissa repeated the story she had told the sheriff, not wavering in any detail. Her answers to questions posed by the jury members were clear and to the point. With each word that came out of her mouth, her confidence grew. Since there were no other witnesses, the foreman announced that a decision would be rendered the following day.

A knock at the door of his home interrupted Mr. Musser's dinner that evening. He opened it to find a young blond lady standing on the porch.

"Sir, my name is Rebecca Santine. I'm a reporter for the Citizen, but I'm also a friend of Rachel Woods. I just came from visiting her. She is conscious, and the doctor is with her. She has been told that her baby is dead and that Josh Sarsfield has been charged with his murder and her beating. When she understood this, she told us what really happened. The doctor suggested I come and get you, as you would be interested in her version of the events. She is very weak, but she is conscious, so you must come quickly."

Musser followed Rebecca to the boarding house. He found Rachel sitting up in bed and Elizabeth feeding her some soup. When the doctor identified this visitor to her, she motioned him closer so she could speak to him. In a trembling voice that was barely above a whisper, she gave him her story.

"It was my husband, Tenny Woods, that did this to me and killed my son. He came at me like he was crazy and kept beating me with the stove iron."

"Did he shoot Josh Sarsfield?"

"I don't know," she mumbled as she began

to lose consciousness.

"Did you see Josh?"

Rachel didn't answer. She was no longer awake.

"This changes everything," Musser announced. "I need to talk to the Grand Jury foreman, but I think we can get Josh released when the Jury hears this."

The next morning, when Musser repeated Rachel's words, the Grand Jury was quick in deciding not to issue an indictment against Josh. They also called for a warrant to be issued for the arrest of Tenny Woods. After consideration of Melissa's story, it was suggested she be called to account for her perjured testimony and arrested as a possible accomplice to her father. Melissa did not wait around to hear any of this. She hurriedly left the courtroom and disappeared.

Josh was released from the jail that afternoon. He tried to walk to the boardinghouse, but he could only go a few steps without sitting down to catch his breath. The pain in his chest was all he could stand. Scud finally had to come and get him. In spite of his discomfort, he stayed by Rachel constantly, taking over her care from Elizabeth. They settled in with the prospect of spending the winter in town and concentrating on Josh and Rachel getting well. Rachel's periods of consciousness became more frequent and lasted longer. More memories of that terrible day continued to emerge.

Melissa's hurried flight from the courthouse was undetected. The last thing she had expected was for her mother to live, much less testify. She was in a panic and knew she couldn't go home. That would be the first place they would look for her. She had to find a place to hide until things cooled down. She could think of no one that would help her. The only person in Downieville she felt she could trust was Sally Johnson, but she knew that Sally's husband would turn her in without a second thought. The whole town would know by evening that she was a fugitive. Her father was on the run, and she had been adamant in telling him not to contact her. Now she wished she knew where he had gone. The only one she could think of that might help her was Michael. After all, he had asked her to marry him. Maybe he still had enough feeling for her to offer protection even though she had postponed her answer to his proposal. She believed that it was her only option. She knew where he lived, so she quickly had her team hitched to the wagon and was out of town within an hour. She decided it would be too risky to even go home for her clothes and possessions.

It took her most of the day to find Michael's cabin. She had to bypass her old home on Lost Miner Creek. Fortunately there was no one there to see her.

Michael was outside his cabin repairing a piece of harness when she pulled up.

"Well, this is a surprise," he exclaimed. "To what do I owe the honor of this visit?"

"You haven't called on me for a while, so I thought I would visit you."

"It's getting a bit late for a visit, don't you think? But, what the hell, come on in and have a drink."

"You know I don't drink, Michael, but I'd like some tea if you have any."

"I'll have a look," he said as he opened the door for her to enter.

The single room was a mess. The dirt floor was littered with clothes and whisky bottles. Unwashed dishes and pots were stacked beside a basin half-filled with scummy water. The single bed was unmade. Melissa found the whole scene disgusting and was having trouble finding a clear place to sit down.

Michael stoked up the fire in the stove, rinsed out a pot, and splashed in some water from a barrel in the corner. Eventually a cup of tea was produced. Melissa had considerable trouble drinking the foul brew.

"I figured that when you turned me down it was the end of the line for us. I could see little reason to keep spending more time with you. I was beginning to get the feeling you were just using me to take you to nice places and buy you gifts."

Melissa slowly realized she had made a mistake in coming here. Michael was slurring his words and was obviously drunk, but it was dark and she had no idea where else she could go. "Just get through tonight, get out of here tomorrow, and go far away," she thought.

"I guess I should tell you the truth," she said. "My father has been away for a while, and he neglected to pay the rent on our rooms. I was told today that I had to leave immediately. If you can put me up for a couple of days, I will find other lodging."

"I don't suppose you want to share the bed

with me," he offered.

"No!" She exclaimed. "I'll lay my bedroll over here by the door."

"It's up to you," he replied.

The next morning Melissa awoke early as Michael stepped over her to go outside.

"I have to ride to town for a few supplies. You're on your own. I don't expect to see you when I return."

When he was gone, she got the fire in the stove started, boiled some water, and had a bath. She washed her hair and shook the dust from the trail out of yesterday's clothes. She was just loading her meager possessions into the wagon when Michael returned. He jumped down off the horse, grabbed her by the arm, and led her back into the cabin.

"Let me go, you're hurting my arm."

"Just sit down," he snarled as he pushed her onto the bed. "We need to have a talk. I learned some very interesting things about you in town this morning."

Melissa was silent. Fear of his anger forced her to get up quickly and run toward the door, but Michael caught her arm and threw her back on the bed.

"The sheriff is looking for you. There is a warrant out for your arrest. They want to ask you a few questions. They don't like it when someone lies to the court, and I don't like it when someone lies to me. That story about being kicked out of your rooms was a lie, and you have been lying all along to me about your age. I found out you are only fourteen. You tried to make me believe you were a grown woman. You're only a little girl. I should tie you to a mule and take you in to the sheriff right now."

"No," Melissa cried, "They will throw me in jail. I would die in jail. Just let me leave, and I will go far away, and you will never hear from me again."

"I have a better idea. Take off your clothes."

"Please don't make me do that."

"Take them off, all of them. Let's see if you're a woman or a little girl."

When Melissa made no move to obey, he tore all her clothes from her body.

"That's better. I couldn't have your mother, so you will have to do."

He lowered his pants, threw her on the bed, spread her legs and began thrusting as soon as he fell upon her. Melissa almost passed out with the pain as he entered her. She began to sob and couldn't stop until he was done.

"You had better get used to that. You are staying here and will do as I say, and you will be available to fill my needs whenever I want you. The rest of the time, you can keep this place clean, cook the meals, and take care of all the duties of a wife. If you don't do what I tell you or try to run away, I will find you and take you to the sheriff. Do you understand me?"

Through her tears, Melissa nodded that she understood. She also understood that somehow she had to find a way to escape this monster.

Throughout the fall, winter, and spring Melissa was a prisoner. She was treated, not like a wife, but as a slave. When he was away, he locked her in the cabin. She continually tried to escape, but her efforts were in vain. Almost daily she was subjected to Michael's bizarre sexual demands. She was forced to sew old clothing and sacking if she wanted anything to wear and was supplied with only a bare minimum of food to provide the meals. At no time was any kindness shown or words of appreciation expressed for her efforts. She was continually subjected to his anger and physical abuse. Her only relief was the time Michael spent in town drinking, which was usually every day. As the year wore on, he got progressively meaner and more demanding. Melissa's body became a painful collection of bruises in varying states of healing. Her spirit was broken to the point that she didn't care if she lived or died. As time went on, she seriously considered taking her own life but couldn't find the courage to do it.

She discovered in the early spring that she was pregnant. She kept her condition from Michael as long as she could. She feared his anger when he found out, but he simply said,

"Get rid of it. I don't care how you do it, but get rid of it."

One night in late September, as Josh was lying beside Rachel, she awakened, held him tightly, and whispered, "I love you."

Josh held her closer, and immediately she fell asleep.

By the time Josh awoke the next morning, she was dead. They buried her beside her son.

"She was just too broken up inside, and it wouldn't heal. She suffered too much to continue. I expect she just wanted to escape the constant pain," explained the doctor.

They moved out of the rooms at the end of the week and returned to the cabin. There was no reason to stay in town with Rachel gone. It was an empty house without her. Josh's sadness was overwhelming, and he lost interest in life. Each day he just went through the motions of living. He would walk up to the pond regularly and sit by Rachel's grave and talk to her. At night he would lie awake for hours trying to relive the moments of their love, but the memories were starting to dim with time. Elizabeth and even Joachim tried to cheer him up. Rebecca came out every week to sit and talk with him until the weather got bad. Josh looked forward to her visits. He still cared very much for her and looked forward to seeing her, but he felt guilty that he was betraying Rachel's memory by having these feelings. He was getting stronger. He could walk easily without pain or shortness of breath by Christmas, and by spring he was back to being able to put in a full day of work.

Josh had told Rebecca during the winter that he wanted to go after Tenny in the spring, when his body had healed. She was worried. She knew Josh was no match for the older man if it came to a showdown. She doubted that Josh was capable of killing another human even in his present state of grief and anger. She knew Tenny would have no problem in causing his death. When he had first brought him back home, Calico had warned her that Tenny was crazy, but she hadn't believed him. Now, with the beating and death of Rachel, she had no doubts.

On a previous visit to the cabin, she had

asked Scud to go with Josh and protect him if he set out after Tenny. The big man sensed the depth of her feelings for Josh and had agreed.

On an April morning, Rebecca rode out to the cabin to announce that the sheriff had given up his search for Tenny and Melissa. They had found no trace of either of them.

"A warrant for Tenny is still out there and has been sent to the other counties, but there have been no replies."

The news hit them hard. They had felt sure Tenny would be picked up quickly and made to pay for his crime and that Melissa would be called to account for the lies and the trouble she had caused. Josh felt the anger rising.

"I can't let him get away with this. I'm going after him."

"Josh, you can't go alone. He will kill you," Elizabeth said.

"Your sister's right. You are not a killer, but he is, and he's crazy. You try and take him in, and he will shoot you without a thought, and I couldn't live with that. You can't go alone. I will go with you," Rebecca observed.

"I go."

Scud had been quietly taking it all in and remembered his promise to Rebecca.

"You don't need to put yourself in danger. You have Joachim to raise," Josh said.

"I go. She my sister. He go jail. Elizabeth stay with Joachim."

Josh knew from experience that it was useless to argue with the big man once his mind was made up.

"Alright, but we need to be able to move quickly and cover a lot of ground. I've got some ideas where he might have gone. I know the names of some of those camps and towns where he used to preach."

Rebecca thought for a moment then said, "You won't be able to move fast enough with Scud driving those mules with the wagon. He can take that big horse of mine. I'll get you some copies of the warrant from the sheriff if you two will meet me in town in a couple of days."

That night Josh had his first untroubled sleep in months. He was anxious to get on the trail after Tenny. He finally had a chance to set things right and pay part of the debt for the love and joy that Rachel had brought to his life.

13

Scud was devastated by Rachel's death. He very seldom showed any emotion, and this time was no exception, but Josh and Elizabeth knew him well enough to know that he was really hurting inside even as he went about his daily life as before. As a boy, he had learned early to control his emotions. His exposure to other people had been very limited, and since he didn't know how they would react to him, he had made very sure not to give them reason to treat him badly. He had never known his mother, who had left Caleb soon after he was born. When he was ten, Caleb hooked up with a Mohawk lady for a brief period that produced Rachel. Even as a baby, Rachel became his whole world. When Rachel's mother left Caleb to return to her own people, Scud was desolate and constantly looked forward to the times he would see them again. As she grew older, Rachel would come to the mountains and spend the summer with Scud and her father. They were inseparable, and these were the happiest times of his life. He taught her all he had learned about the forest, the animals, and plants that lived there. As Rachel grew older she passed on the knowledge she had gained from her mother's people. When Tenny came into her life, Scud basked in the warmth of her joy with the new love. Both their spirits were lifted higher by the birth of Melissa, and Scud learned to care for this little girl, but somehow he knew the child was not like her mother. When Caleb died, and he moved to the village to be with Rachel, he soon found that he could barely tolerate Tenny. For her sake, he hid his dislike and agreed to look after the store to earn his keep. As the love between Rachel and Tenny began to sour, his dislike for Tenny grew. When Tenny decided to sell out and go west, Rachel pleaded with him not to go, but in the end she reluctantly went along. She was unhappy, and her unhappiness was Scud's unhappiness. He had considerable forebodings about making the trip, but Tenny would listen to no objections.

Scud had decided long ago there was nothing else for him in life except looking after his sister and trying to make her life more pleasant. When Jonathan arrived, her spirits picked up for that brief interval until his death. With Josh, he could see that she was finally truly happy.

Now she was dead. He would have gladly died in her place. The fury and hatred he felt for Tenny continued to be bottled up inside. He was basically a gentle man, and these strong feelings disturbed him. He didn't know what to do. He couldn't hunt him down and kill him, yet he wanted to see him punished. The only time he had killed a man was when the Cheyenne warriors had invaded their camp and attacked Rachel. He felt remorse for that sudden act of violence for years after.

When Tenny and Melissa had parted, Tenny rode aimlessly to the south. He had no purpose or plan and was still dazed by the turn of events. He had meekly obeyed his daughter's directions and heeded her warnings to stay away from settlements where people might remember him. His nightly visions were always with him, but he no longer feared them and almost looked forward to their company at the end of his day. During the day there were voices, and he often saw fleeting glimpses of familiar figures on the trail. He stayed away from people, and consequently he spent most nights sleeping under the stars.

His wanderings brought him by coincidence, or unconscious plan, back to Mokelumne Hill. By now he was thinking a bit more rationally and began to be concerned that he might be a man wanted by the law. He took the chance and looked into the local post office for any 'wanted' circulars with his name. It was with some relief he found none posted on the wall. The town was much smaller and quieter than he remembered it from that winter five years previous. The gold was now tougher to find, and most of the folks had moved on to easier diggings. Tenny had no trouble locating the cabin on the edge of town that he had stayed in. It was now boarded up and rundown. Locating his friends, the previous owners, proved unsuccessful. They had moved on. Tenny opened up the cabin and decided to stay for a few days, but the few days stretched into weeks, and soon the cold weather returned heralding another winter. He decided to stay put and move on when the warmer weather returned. He wanted to get in touch with Melissa to find out what had happened and if he was safe. However, he was reluctant to send a message and reveal where he was.

His demons were still with him, although not as often since he had stopped traveling. He thought it was because he had come to accept them as part of his life. Most of all he regretted his attack on Rachel. He longed to see her again and tell her how sorry he was for what he had done. He was sure she would forgive him and want to be with him again if she knew how he truly felt. He was, however, afraid to return to Downieville.

The day after Josh had announced his decision to find Tenny, he and Scud went to town to meet Rebecca. She saddled the big horse for Scud and handed them the 'wanted posters' and arrest warrants she had obtained from the sheriff.

"Sheriff Irwin wants to see you before you go."

When they arrived at the sheriff's office, he was waiting for them.

"You two realize we been looking for Tenny Woods for over six months now without any idea where he is. His daughter is gone too. We think they probably hooked up and boarded a ship. We're guessing they are long gone out of the country by now. What makes you think you can find him?"

"Well, we know him and where he used to travel when he was preaching. We feel he is still around here somewhere, probably farther south, where he used to make most of his trips. We need to find him. He killed Scud's sister and my son. I'm not going to quit until he gets what he deserves."

The sheriff was quiet for a moment then said, " I'm going to deputize both of you. That will give you some authority to get help in other counties, but it will also put the responsibility on you to bring him back for trial, if you find him."

His last words brought some relief to Scud. As much as he hated Tenny, he knew he couldn't shoot him on sight, but he was afraid that Josh might be angry enough to do it. Both he and Josh were now obligated not to kill Tenny but to bring him back.

On the way back from the sheriff's office, Rebecca announced, "I want you to come with me to Sacramento and talk to Calico. He's a deputy there. If I'm with you, he'll listen to what you have to say and may have some ideas where Tenny might be holing up. It's worth a try, and maybe he'll go with you. Although Tenny was his friend, he won't accept what he has done."

They packed up their gear and supplies and by noon were on their way to Sacramento. Rebecca borrowed a friend's horse to make the trip. They reached the city by dark and headed to the local sheriff's office to find Calico. As he was out on patrol, they had to wait until the next morning to meet up with him at his boarding house. Rebecca introduced Josh and Scud and told him the whole story of the events of the previous year.

"This doesn't surprise me," Calico observed when she had finished. "The last time I saw him, I felt he was a bomb ready to explode, but I didn't think he would do anything like that."

"Can you go with them?" Rebecca asked. "I'm afraid for their safety."

Calico thought for a moment and then replied, "No, there are too many problems here right now, and I need this job. I'd like to help. He needs to be brought to justice, and I have an idea where he might be. He once told me he spent a winter at some little camp down in Calaveras County, and he was thinking of moving there. That would probably be a good place to start looking. If I can get away from here soon, I'll come and help you if you need me then."

Josh and Scud left that afternoon, heading south, and Rebecca returned to Downieville.

Scud had a rough idea in his head of the route Tenny had taken in the past. Whenever they rode through a camp or town that he had heard Tenny mention, they stopped and asked the local lawman or some of the old-timers that had known him if they had seen him recently, but no one had.

To Josh and Scud, it seemed like Tenny had vanished off the face of the earth. In two months they had passed through every village and camp along the way with the same answers to their questions. No one had seen or heard anything recent about 'the Preacher'. By the time they reached the Calaveras County line, Scud was about ready to give up, but Josh kept pushing. At Mokelumne Hill they got their first break.

It was a soft early June morning when they rode into the sleepy little town.

"According to those folks we talked to yesterday, this is the main town in the County," Josh said. "We should go find the sheriff and tell him what we're doing. Maybe he can help us."

When they entered the sheriff's office, they found a slim older man sitting with his feet on the desk, reading a newspaper.

"You the sheriff?" Scud asked.

"No," the man replied. "The sheriff has gone to Stockton. He should be back tomorrow. I'm a Deputy. James Sorren is my name. I'm looking after things while he's gone. What can I do for you fellows?"

"We're deputies from Sierra County up north. We've been looking for a man who committed murders. We got reason to think he might be around these parts," Josh replied.

"Have you got a warrant and a picture of this fellow?"

"No picture. Here warrant," Scud said as he pulled the paper from his pocket.

Sorren looked over the warrant and said, "Tenny Woods. I've heard that name before, but I can't remember where. What else can you tell me about him?"

"He used to come down here a few years back and preach."

"That's it," Sorren interrupted. "The Preacher. I remember him. I went to a couple of

284

his talks. He was pretty good. In fact he stayed here one whole winter. I haven't seen him since, but I've been away from here for a while. You say he killed two people?"

"My sister. His baby," Scud replied.

Sorren was quiet for a moment then asked, "You want some help in this? I can lead you to people that would remember him and would certainly know if they saw him again."

"That would be good We can use the help. We haven't had any luck so far," Josh replied.

"We'll check it out with the boys over at the Chronicle, then go see the Reverend."

Nobody at the newspaper had ever heard of the 'Preacher', but they were anxious for the story about what was going on.

Reverend Fish had been at Mokelumne Hill since '51 and was a mainstay of the community. His wife had opened the first school, and the couple was well respected throughout the area.

They found the Reverend at home in the parsonage.

"Yes," he replied to their questions. "I remember Tenny Woods. He was a good man until he lost his faith. It is very sad to hear he has sunk so low as to commit this terrible crime. I haven't seen him, but I have heard that he is somewhere around here. You might ask at the General Store. I don't know how else I can help you."

They thanked the Reverend and headed for the General Store.

Tenny had felt secure all winter and was beginning to think he could live safely in this small town as long as he wanted. That was until he saw Scud, Josh, and another man walk out of Reverend Fish's home.

He thought, "Why would they be here unless they're looking for me?"

He followed the three men at a safe distance until they entered the General Store.

In the store, the Mexican girl that met them at the counter was about Josh's age. The name Tenny Woods was unfamiliar to her, but when they described him, she thought she had seen someone that looked like that.

"There are a lot of old men here that have that wild look with hair all over their heads and face."

The owner of the store overheard them, came out from the back, and asked if he could help. He looked a lot like Tenny, medium height, gray beard, and tangled hair raging across his head and down his neck, but he lacked the fierce look in his eyes. When Sorren mentioned having sat through the 'Preacher's' talks, the owner's face brightened.

"I remember him. He was a young, neatly dressed, clean-shaven fellow with a pleasant way about him. What you are describing is a scruffy old man, but there is this fellow that comes in here every couple of weeks for a few supplies. I thought I recognized him from somewhere but couldn't place who he was. It's clear now, it must be your man."

"Have you seen him recently?" Josh asked.

"He was in this morning, bought a few things, and left without saying a word. In fact, he seldom has anything to say."

"Can you tell us where he lives?"

"Can't say that I can for sure. I never asked,

and he never offered the information. When he comes to the store, he is on his horse, so I'm guessing he's staying outside the town somewhere."

"Any suggestions where we should look?" Sorren asked.

'Well, there's some abandoned cabins up in the hills east of here. It was a busy camp a few years ago, but most everyone pulled up and left when the gold ran out. I think that would be the first place I'd look. It seems to me that was where he stayed a few years back."

Tenny sat in the shadows until they came out of the store, mounted their horses, and headed out of town. By the time he had his horse ready to ride, he could still see their dust in the distance, moving in the general direction of his cabin.

The cabins were easy to find. Almost a dozen of them were perched on the hillside above the old placer creek. They were in various states of disrepair, and most were boarded up, but the three closest to the creek shows signs of recent use. An old man and an old woman sat in front of the first one, watching a bunch of chickens scratch about the small yard. They welcomed their three visitors and informed them that only the far cabin had anyone living in it. The man kept to himself, and they didn't really know much about him.

Tenny had rode hard and reached the valley first by a shorter route. He watched as the old couple down the trail talked to his pursuers. When he saw them riding in his direction, he moved away from his cabin and further back into the woods.

"This looks like it," Josh observed as he rode up, jumped off Lobo, slowly slid the cabin door open, and eased into the small single room. "It's empty, but he's been here. His Bible is on the table."

"We can come back early tomorrow and catch him," Sorren suggested.

"No. We stay. Wait for him," Scud replied.

"Alright, I'll ride out in the morning and see how you're doing," Sorren announced as he prepared to head back to town. Josh and Scud moved their horses to a nearby grove of trees to make camp and wait to see if Tenny returned.

Tenny remained hidden at the edge of the woods as he watched Scud and Josh settle in for the night. He knew now that it wasn't safe for him to stay any longer. He had finally recognized the third man as the deputy sheriff. To Tenny, that made it official that the law was hunting him. Before he could leave, he had to get back to the cabin. He needed his gold pouch and pistol, which were buried in a corner. His only chance was to wait until they were asleep, sneak back to the cabin, and then get out of there as quickly as possible.

The shot woke Josh immediately. He looked for Scud, but he was alone. The big man's empty bedroll lay nearby. In the bright moonlight, he could see the cabin from the edge of the trees. He started to move in that direction just as Scud stumbled out through the cabin door, took two steps, and collapsed heavily to the ground. In the background, he saw a form running from the rear of the cabin up the slight incline into the forest. When he reached his friend, he immediately noticed the blood collecting on his shirtfront.

"Tenny shot me," was the coarse whisper. "Not want hurt him. Just take him back. Told Rachel dead. He start yelling. Shot me."

Josh tore up his shirt and pressed it into the wound as well as he could. The bleeding slowly lessened as the big man slipped into unconsciousness. Josh could see he had lost a lot of blood. He thought of riding to town for a doctor, but decided to stay with his friend and wait for sunrise and Sorren's return. He also wanted to follow Tenny, but he didn't want to leave Scud in this condition.

As the ground warmed with the morning sun, a dense fog moved slowly up the hillside. Josh wasn't aware of Sorren's arrival until he was right beside him.

One look at Scud and Sorren exclaimed, "We have to get a doctor right away. He's in bad shape. You stay here with him, and I'll ride back into town and fetch the doc."

Sorren returned about an hour later, followed by the local doctor driving a wagon.

"We need to get this man to the hospital right away," the doctor announced after a brief examination. "His wound is serious. We may not be able to save him."

It took the entire effort of the three of them to load Scud gently into the wagon.

"Will you take him back and see that he's looked after?" Josh asked Sorren. "I'm going after Tenny. I can't let him get away with this."

"You're no match for him. You'll get killed. Wait til I see if I can get the Sheriff to put together a bunch of experienced men to track him down."

"No! He killed my woman and my son and now has almost killed my friend here, and he tried to kill me. I've had enough. I'm going after him. It's going to be either him or me that rides away from all this."

Sorren could see and hear the determination in this young man and that there was no point in arguing with him.

"At least, take a decent gun," Sorren said. "Here's my new Springfield. That old gun of yours don't look like it would be much help if he starts shooting."

Josh agreed and replied, "I need to get a message to my sister in Downieville. Just send it to Rebecca Santine at the Citizen. Elizabeth needs to know what has happened and to come care for Scud."

"I'll look after it," Sorren replied.

Josh watched with concern as the wagon disappeared down the road. He wondered if he would ever see his companion alive again.

Riding Lobo and using Rebecca's big horse for packing, Josh headed up the faint trail behind the cabin. He traveled at a good speed through the open woodland, ever vigilant for any movement. His anger was slowly subsiding, and the fear he had felt toward Tenny since his younger years began to return. He fully realized the danger in his mission, but he knew that to be able to live with himself, he had no choice.

The path ended at the base of a small scarp where evidence of past campfires was spread over a flat, grassy area. It had been a long tough day, and Josh was physically and emotionally tired, but he resisted the urge to settle for the night. He forded a cold mountain stream and picked up a trail of recently blazed trees on the other side.

"Looks like new claim staking," he thought. "Maybe somebody's working their ground near here. I should check it out and see if anyone has seen him riding through."

He followed the blazed line to the discovery post of the claim, but there was no sign of anyone or any recent work.

Josh sat on a log, took a drink from his canteen, and considered his plight. He no longer had any lead to follow and was moving strictly on instinct. He tried to put himself in Tenny's place and determine what logical move the man would make, although he was sure Tenny had abandoned logical thinking a long time ago. Did he know he was being hunted? He would surely expect someone to come after him. The thoughts of Tenny circling around in back of him and attacking from behind crept into his consciousness. He didn't know what to do, but he did know he would have to be more aware.

He continued to move up into the foothills, keeping to the valley bottom, where stretches of alder and willow hid his passage but gave him a clear view of the ridges on either side. A couple of times he imagined he saw movement higher up to the south, but it was too far away for him to be sure. He traveled at a steady pace throughout the day without any sure signs to follow. Nightfall found him beside a small pond, which served as the source of the creek he had been following. Rather than bed down in the open area beside the water, he moved up into the trees where he had an unobstructed view of that part of the valley. He hobbled the

big horse but let Lobo run free. He had learned
to trust his horse to stay close and set up a
ruckus if it sensed danger.

The next day was much like the first. Josh
saw little sign of human presence, with the
exception of a myriad of faint trails leading in
all directions. Most of these were game trails,
and few showed any evidence of use by
humans. He was becoming frustrated, and the
temptation to yield to the futility of the chase
preyed on his mind. The thoughts that he kept
hanging on to were the memory of Rachel in his
arms and the love she had shared with him. He
knew deep in his heart he would never quit.

By the third day, he was deep in the
foothills. The slope was less steep, and the trees
had thinned out into a mature fir forest. He had
awakened to a heavy frost that lasted well into
the morning hours. Late in the afternoon his
ears picked up a noise, which he immediately
identified as rushing water. As he moved toward
it, the noise grew louder. Soon he could identify
human voices. At the edge of the forest, in a
gentle valley, was a camp with a hydraulic
pump washing down gravels from the slope.
Five men were working the operation, but they
stopped when Josh appeared. They gathered
around as he rode into camp. Two of the men
had guns leveled at him.

"You come back to pay for the food you
stole?"

"What are you talking about?"

"Someone broke into our food tent last
night and took a bunch of food."

"Well, it wasn't me, but I've got a good
idea who it was. I been chasing after this man

for the past three days."

Josh proceeded to tell his story of the murders, the trial, and his pursuit of Tenny. When he had finished, the men were silent for a moment until an older man, who appeared to be their leader, spoke up.

"You say this man killed your baby son. Why didn't the sheriff up there go after him right away?"

Josh went on to explain how he had been accused of the crime until Rachel regained consciousness.

"By then, Tenny was long gone."

The miners put him up for the night, fed him, and loaded him up with supplies before he set out the next morning.

"I would guess your man is going to head east into the high country, especially if he knows somebody is after him. There are a lot of places to hide up there, and if he goes far enough and gets through the Pass, you'll never catch him. Do you want one of my boys to go with you in case you run into trouble?"

"No, but thank you. This is my fight, and I don't want to risk anyone else getting caught up in it. At least you've got me on the right track now."

"Well, I'll tell you what we'll do. If your man comes back this way, I'll send one of the boys to try and find you and let you know."

Josh rode all day following an old trail that snaked its way up the slope. It was rocky and partly overgrown, but the occasional horse print in the soft earth encouraged him to think that he might be on the right trail. He could feel he was getting closer and was convinced when a shot rang out, and the ball embedded itself in a tree behind him. He slipped out of the saddle into the low brush beside the path, pulled Sorren's musket from the scabbard, and crouched down beneath the foliage. He scanned the forest ahead for any signs of movement. After a few minutes, he crawled slowly out onto the path for a clearer look, but as he started to rise to a kneeling position, another shot whined over his head. This time he could see the movement of a horse along the ridge. He took aim and fired above the animal. The horse took off, and he could see a man running after it. Both figures were out of sight by the time Josh had reloaded. He waited a few minutes then remounted and rode slowly through the thick forest toward where he had last seen them. He followed their trail along the ridge until it opened out into a wide meadow. He spotted the faint speck of horse and rider descending into the next valley and knew that if he could see Tenny, he could be seen as well. He decided to stay back and wait for darkness to get closer.

He moved into a small group of trees, lay down, and fell asleep immediately. The land was bathed in moonlight when he awoke. He moved slowly north toward his last sighting of the horse and rider. His old fears of the man made him cautious and alert to any movement. As he rode up the gentle slope to the ridge separating the two valleys, he picked up the faint smell of wood smoke on the breeze blowing up from the next valley. Unfortunately, travel in that direction was impossible due to the sheer drop on the other side. A trail that showed signs of recent use ran along the top of the ridge.

Josh had to decide whether to follow the trail into the high country to the east or to try and descend into the main valley. The fog began to roll in as he sat pondering his decision. Within minutes it was too thick for him to safely make a move in any direction. As he tried to get his bearings, he could hear the faint mumble of men's voices, and a group of four riders materialized out of the mist almost immediately. They were surprised to meet a lone rider on the trail. Half a dozen pack mules followed the men, who were on horseback. They stopped, and a tall black man greeted Josh.

"Are you lost out here, young man?"

"No, I'm chasing a murderer," Josh replied, showing the men his Deputy's badge.

"Could be the man we passed an hour ago. We thought it was kind of suspicious when he rode into the trees as soon as he spotted us. Tell us what he did."

The rest of the group dismounted and gathered around to hear the story. When Josh had finished, one of the other men in the group spoke up, "You say this man you are hunting has the name Woods. There was a man by that name used to come to Angel's Camp. They called him 'the Preacher'. Is that the same man?"

"It is," Josh replied, "but he's turned from preacher to killer."

As the men mounted up and moved off down the trail, Josh now knew that Tenny was headed for the high country and was only a couple of hours ahead of him. What Josh didn't know was whether Tenny would continue to move or wait in ambush for him somewhere along the trail. He realized there was no way in this rugged country that he could go around and get ahead of him. He would just have to follow and take his chances.

Josh rode slowly picking his way through the mist until first light. During the day he stayed off the trail but moved along the forested slope below the ridge. There was no further sign of Tenny.

Darkness found him tired, hungry, and getting discouraged with the chase. The bright moonlight of the previous night had been replaced by a gray leaden sky and a cold damp wind blowing down from the mountains. Josh knew he could go no farther without sleep. Just off the cliff trail, he found a level area in the trees with a small stream and enough grass for the horses. He hobbled the big horse again and let Lobo run free. His meal consisted of a few hard biscuits the miners had given him.

It was a cold night, but he knew lighting a fire to keep warm would make it too easy for Tenny to find him. He wrapped himself in the bedroll, making sure the Springfield was within reach, and he was asleep within minutes.

14

The ride back to Mokelumne Hill was rough. Scud drifted in and out of consciousness most of the way, and the continual bouncing of the wagon along the rutted road started the bleeding again. The doctor stopped it and rebandaged the wound, but he kept Scud in the hospital until he could be sure the big man was on the way to recovery. Sorren hired a messenger to take Josh's note to Elizabeth.

Rebecca got the news two days later and rode out to Lost Miner Creek to deliver the letter. The girls hitched four mules to the wagon, loaded in Joachim and some supplies, and Elizabeth headed for Mokelumne Hill.

Rebecca continued to worry about Josh and the dangerous mission he had chosen. She decided to try once more to get Calico's help. When she arrived in Sacramento, he was just getting ready to go on shift.

"I desperately need your help," she pleaded. "I'm so afraid for Josh out there and on his own hunting for Tenny."

"You're right. I need to go down there. I know what Tenny Woods is capable of. Your man hasn't got much of a chance against him. Let me make some arrangements here. We can be on our way in a couple of hours."

They rode fast, traveling all night, and arrived in Mokelumne Hill early the next day. Later that afternoon, Elizabeth met them when she pulled into town.

Elizabeth was surprised at her level of concern over Scud's condition. Since Rachel's death, he had transferred his affection and protection to Elizabeth. They had made many trips to town together for supplies, and until now she hadn't realized how much she depended on and needed him. She was anxious to see him and help him recover from his wounds.

They had no trouble locating Scud at the hospital. They talked with the doctor and were relieved to learn that, although seriously injured, the big man was recovering. With the doctor's directions, Rebecca and Calico were able to find Sorren at the Sheriff's office. The doctor advised Elizabeth not to try and take Scud back to Lost Miner Creek for at least a couple of weeks until he had healed further. She rented some rooms in a boarding house and with everyone's help, they were able to move him and get him settled. The doctor promised to visit a couple of times a week.

"We're leaving to find Josh," Rebecca announced.

After he had discussed the situation with Calico, Sorren responded, "I think it's a good idea if I go with you. I was concerned right from the start about Josh traveling alone up there. There are too many bad things that can happen to a young green fellow, especially with this murderer roaming around."

Then he said to Rebecca, "I think you should stay here. You could be in danger as well."

"I can look after myself," she replied defiantly. "Tenny knows me. I don't think he would cause me harm."

"She's probably right," Calico put in. "She is a very capable lady who has been through a lot, and besides, this is the love of her life we're trying to protect."

"I guess there's no changing your mind, but wait until tomorrow. I'll talk to the sheriff again and see if he will put together a group to go up there. He wouldn't before, but it's worth another try."

Since it was getting late in the day, they agreed to wait until they heard from Sorren again.

He was back the next morning in time to have breakfast with the group.

"How's your patient?"

"He slept through the night," Elizabeth replied, "but with a whole bunch of moaning and tossing around. Doctor says that he's gonna get better, but it will take a while."

"I talked to the sheriff. Just like before, he's not going to get involved," Sorren continued. "I guess we're on our own."

"What do you mean?" Rebecca asked.

"He agreed that I should go along with you. I know the country up there and have a few ideas where Tenny Woods might have gone.

You are going to need some heavy clothing, a warm bedroll, and enough food for a week."

They set out at noon, starting at Tenny's cabin and moving up the trail behind it in the same direction Josh had taken. They rode all day without incident.

Sorren announced after they had spent the better part of the next day in the saddle, "Old man Martin and his sons got a gold operation over in the next valley. We need to ride over there. They might have seen Josh, and maybe we can get a hot meal and a place to stay tonight."

The sun blazed its way over the eastern mountains, blasting Josh out of his deep sleep. For a few moments, he forgot where he was until his mind cleared, and he saw Tenny sitting on a log across the clearing. He was holding Sorren's Springfield pointed at Josh.

Beyond Tenny, Josh could see Rebecca's big horse tied to the pommel of Tenny's mare.

Both were grazing just off the cliff trail.

Josh lay still for a few minutes until his mind cleared. He tried to wriggle his way out of the sleeping robe but stopped when Tenny yelled, "Stay where you are!"

Josh forced himself to relax. He could see that Tenny's level of agitation could be set off by the slightest action on his part, but he had to figure a way out. He lay and stared at the older man, looking for a chance to get free.

Tenny was shaking. His mouth started to open and close, and drool seeped out at the corners. Then he began to scream, "She came to me and told me you were coming for my soul, just like you stole hers. Last night she came to me again and told me you were here. She says you are the Devil. She wants you dead. I want you dead. You are going to die."

With those last words, he quickly raised the musket, pulled the hammer back, and fired. Josh tensed and rolled to the side, but he could feel the ball penetrate the robe and enter his leg. He cried out from the pain. He was trapped in his bedroll and couldn't get out.

"Now you will die," Tenny screamed as he tried to reload the musket, but his hands were shaking too much, and he dropped the bag of powder spilling it all over the ground. In frustration, he threw the gun into the bushes, got up, and stumbled over to the horses.

Josh tried to pull himself into a sitting position, but the pain was too intense. Finally by grabbing on to the robe, he was able to partially raise himself up. As Tenny started to climb into his saddle, Josh reached behind his bed, located his knife, and pulled it from the sheath. Tenny hoisted himself onto his horse just as Josh threw the knife with all the force he could muster. It missed Tenny by a wide margin but embedded itself in the flank of Rebecca's big horse. The animal bolted from the shock, lost its footing in the loose rock, and stumbled over the cliff face, dragging Tenny and his mount with it. Josh could hear Tenny's scream as he plunged into the abyss. He finally managed to pull himself out of the bedroll and crawl painfully over to the edge of the cliff. He looked down, but there was no sign of horses or rider in the dense foliage below.

He tore strips out of the bloody robe to tie

around his leg and stop the flow. It wasn't broken, but he could feel the ball still deep in the flesh. He tried to get it out, but the pain was too much to bear. He knew he had to ride out of there and get help. He whistled, and Lobo trotted out of the woods a few minutes later. Josh had been too tired to take the saddle off his horse the previous night. Now he was glad he'd forgotten. He didn't think he could have put it back on in his present shape. He called his horse over to stand beside him. When he was younger and smaller, he had taught Lobo to lower his body so he could climb on. The horse had not forgotten the simple command, making Josh's task of getting into the saddle much easier.

He didn't know if he could make it to town with the ball still in his leg. It continued to bleed, and he didn't seem able to stop the flow completely. His only hope was to ride to the miners' camp and get some help there. If he rode steady, he figured he could be there by evening. He blindly retraced his path, almost passing out a number of times from the pain. Lobo seemed to sense where he wanted to go.

Sorren, Calico, and Rebecca were sitting around the miners' campfire when Josh rode in. They rushed up and grabbed him as he started to slide out of the saddle. With the four Martin boys holding him firmly, Sorren dug the ball from his leg. Copious amounts of whisky cleansed the wound, and Rebecca bandaged it as Josh lay unconscious on the ground.

The next day he described what had happened.

"I've got to go into that valley, have a look, and bring the body out," Sorren announced. "I know the area. There's a lower path that goes in along the base of the cliff. The brush is thick, but there shouldn't be any problem finding him. Besides, I want my gun back."

"I'm going with you," Josh said. "I have to know for sure that he's dead."

"You can't even walk without pain. Why do you want to put yourself through this?" Rebecca asked.

"I can ride, and I want my knife."

"Then I'm going too."

"Alright," Sorren replied, "we get out of here early tomorrow morning, ride hard into the valley, find the body, and get back to town."

They rode out at dawn. Josh could feel a stab of pain with every step that Lobo took, but he said nothing. Only Rebecca could tell by the look on his face the torment he was enduring.

The valley was narrow with a small creek winding slowly down from a wide marshy area. There were no trees, but the ground was covered with an almost impenetrable mass of alder, willow, salal, and patches of devil's club.

Moving through the brush was slow and tedious. By early afternoon they had found the horses. They were impaled on the rocks but still tied together. Josh retrieved his knife, and Rebecca shed a few tears over her dead horse. Sorren looked for his gun until Josh remembered he had seen Tenny throw it away on top of the cliff. What they didn't find was Josh's pack, which had been tied to the big horse, and there was no sign of Tenny Woods.

They spent most of the afternoon looking for Tenny. They searched systematically, working in circles out from the horses, but there was no body. The only sign that anyone had even been there was a strip of shirt that Calico spotted fluttering on a bush halfway up the cliff.

"He has to be here somewhere. Nobody can survive a fall like that," Sorren observed.

"Maybe that bush up there broke his fall, and his body is stuck there," Calico suggested.

"If it is, someone has to climb up and find out," Sorren said.

"He's right. If Sorren is agreeable, I suggest he and I stay in here and extend our search for the body. It could take a day or two, but if it's here, we'll find it. Rebecca, you need to take Josh back to town and see that his leg gets fixed up."

They were silent on the ride out of the valley until Rebecca finally asked the question that was in both their minds,

"What do you think happened to him?"

Josh thought for a few minutes then replied, "His body could have gotten hung up on that ledge or thrown into an area we didn't search. I still can't see any way he could have lived through that, but what scares me is that he is still alive and out there somewhere."

"The important thing to me is that you survived. I was so worried that I wouldn't see you again."

"Rebecca, you know it was something I had to do for Rachel and Johnny. I think, no matter what happens now, I am free to go on with my life."

Her tears started to form as they rode on.

The next few weeks were spent at Mokelumne Hill until Scud was well enough to travel. Rebecca stayed with Josh until she was convinced his leg would heal. When Sorren and Calico returned a few days later, they reported that no sign of Tenny had been found after three days of intensive searching. The fragment of shirt caught up by the bush on the cliff face led nowhere. Sorren did, however, retrieve his Springfield.

Rebecca returned to Downieville and her job. The editor was excited about her story of the hunt for Tenny Woods. He requested a full report to go on the front page of the next issue of the Citizen.

Josh stayed with his sister and Scud. Scud had lost much weight during his recovery and was still unable to walk very far without tiring. It was the middle of August by the time they returned to Lost Miner Creek.

One evening as Rebecca was coming back from a performance at the National Theater to her office in order to write a review for the next day's paper, she almost ran into a man who came lurching out of the hotel entrance. He was obviously drunk. She took no notice of him at first, but a second look made her realized that she knew him from somewhere. Then it came to her. This was the man she had seen with Melissa the previous year.

"I know you. You are Melissa's friend."

Michael looked at her suspiciously then replied, "Yeh, I know her, and I know who you are. You're the girl that Tenny Woods rescued from those bandits. I was on that hunt, but pulled out when my brother was killed. I hear that old Tenny is in a lot of trouble for killing his wife."

"Do you know where Melissa went?" she

asked.

"I might," he replied. "Why don't we go back in here, have a drink, and talk about it."

Rebecca was reluctant to spend any time with him, but she wanted to find out if he had any idea where Melissa had gone.

The bar was practically empty. They found a table and Michael ordered a whisky.

"What do I get in return if I tell you?"

Rebecca ignored the question and stated, "She's wanted by the sheriff. If you're hiding her, they can arrest you as well."

"I don't think so. The sheriff cancelled the warrant for her arrest a while back."

"How do you know this?"

"I asked him, told him that I used to be her boyfriend and was concerned about her."

"So where is she?"

"Out at my cabin. I haven't told her that the warrant was cancelled. Why don't you ride out with me tonight and see for yourself?"

"Not tonight. I'll come out there in a day or two."

Rebecca's went to see the sheriff the first thing the next morning. He confirmed that the warrant for Melissa's arrest was no longer outstanding.

She had gotten directions to his cabin from Michael and decided to ride out there that afternoon. She was shocked to see how far Melissa had fallen. Her clothes were barely more than rags, her hair was matted and dirty, and her skin discolored with open sores and bruises.

She was also due to have a child soon.

"Why are you here?" She asked as Rebecca

rode up to the cabin.

"Michael told me you were here. I came out to see for myself."

"Well, you've seen me, now please go away."

"Why do you hate me?" Rebecca asked. "I've done nothing to hurt you."

Melissa's voice was softer as she replied, "I don't hate you. I just hate my life and who I've been in the past. Nothing matters any more. All my hopes and dreams are gone, and there is no one that cares about me anymore."

As Rebecca rode back to town, she wondered if she should have told Melissa about the warrant, but this girl had done so much to hurt Josh that she couldn't bring herself to do it.

Rebecca rode out to Lost Miner Creek a few days later with her news.

"The paper is giving me time off to go out and explore my claims. They want me to write a story about it, and they will hold my job for me until autumn. Will you all come out there with me like you said last year?"

Scud thought for a moment then said, "Elizabeth and I not go. I not strong yet."

"You know that I'll go with you," Josh said. "There's nothing keeping me here now. We will need to fix up that cabin if we're going to stay in it for a while. I've got some lumber and tools here that we can take."

"I'm glad you are coming. It would be too lonely without you, and I have another surprise for you, but we need to go for a ride first."

Rebecca led the way as they rode farther up Lost Miner Creek.

"Where are we going?" Josh asked.

"You'll see very soon."

They rode up the creek trail a ways then took a side path toward an old log cabin.

"That's Reilly's cabin," Josh announced, and as he did, a young, very pregnant Melissa opened the door to throw out a basin of water. She wore the same dirty, tattered rags she had on when Rebecca first saw her, and her long, black hair hung in clumps. Josh figured her to be either native or Mexican, but when they got closer, he was shocked as he recognized Melissa.

"Why did you come back?" She directed the question at Rebecca. "Didn't you see enough when you were here before?"

"This time I brought Josh. He needs to tell you what happened to your father."

Melissa looked at Josh expectantly as he dismounted. He walked over to her, took her hand, and made her sit on a log by the door. Tentatively he put his arm around her. She didn't draw away.

"I'm almost sure your father is dead."

"What do you mean 'almost sure'?"

Josh went into detail describing all that had happened.

"We didn't find his body. That's why we're not sure."

"Do you think he could have survived that fall?"

"I don't know. It was a terrible drop, but I suppose it's possible. We did find a piece of cloth on the cliffside in some bushes that could have broken his fall."

When he was finished, he added, "What I don't understand is, who was the woman that he was talking about coming to visit him?"

Melissa showed no emotion. She thought for a moment before she finally replied, "That would probably be my mother. He began to believe long ago that she visited him at night. He has had voices talking to him, and at night he sees people. That has been going on for quite a while. I thought last year that he was starting to get better until I told him about your son."

"Where is Michael?" Rebecca asked, "Is he in town drinking again?"

"I don't know, and I don't care. I hope I never see him again. I either have to get out of here and give up to the sheriff or kill myself. I can't live like this any longer. He wants me to kill this baby inside me. I can't do that, even if I knew how."

Before they left, Melissa again pleaded tearfully with Rebecca not to tell the sheriff where she was living.

"If I decide to give up, I will do it myself."

Rebecca was hesitant but agreed.

As they rode off, Rebecca described to Josh how she had located her.

"The next day after talking to Michael I went to see the sheriff to find out if there was still a warrant out for her for lying to the Grand Jury. He said they had issued one but decided that because she was so young and just trying to protect her father, they cancelled it. So that afternoon when I knew Michael was in town again, I rode out here to see her. She appeared very embarrassed that I saw her condition and the mess she was living in. She was very sad about her life and asked me to leave."

Josh reined in Lobo and faced Rebecca.

"Wait a minute. Are you telling me that there is no warrant out for her, and the sheriff is letting her go free? Why haven't you told her?"

"After what she did to you, lying, and getting you put in jail, I think she deserves this."

"No," he replied. "No one deserves what she has suffered, no matter what she has done. We can't do this to her."

He turned Lobo around and headed back to the cabin. Melissa met him at the door and looked up questionably at him.

"Melissa, we've got something more to tell you. The sheriff does not want you. There is no warrant. They've decided not to arrest you for lying."

Melissa started to speak but slumped to the ground as the tears began to form. Josh picked her up and wrapped her in his arms as the sobs wracked her body. She cried silently for a few minutes before asking, "Why did you not tell me before?"

Rebecca answered, "Josh didn't know, and I was angry for what you did to him. If Josh can forgive you for that then so can I."

"I understand your anger. For a long time I have been sorry for how I treated all of you," she said as she wiped away the tears. "I've wanted to leave Michael and this place for so long, but I've always been afraid I would be locked up. Josh, I am so sorry for what I did to you. It was so unfair. I felt I was helping my father, but he was wrong for what he did. He killed my mother and your son. It was so wrong, but he is my father, and I believed it was my duty to protect him. I knew his mind was going, but I couldn't abandon him."

They sat for a few minutes, no one saying anything.

Finally Josh asked, "Do you want to go back with us? We can take you to town and help you get started on a new life. Scud and I will deal with Michael if he becomes a problem."

"Yes."

Scud and Elizabeth were surprised and suspicious to see Melissa again.

That evening at the cabin, Melissa made her peace with them.

"I am so sorry for the way I've treated you all these years. I believe I have suffered enough meanness this year to appreciate the hurt I have caused you."

Elizabeth dug out Rachel's clothes and gave them to her daughter.

"I think now she would want you to have these."

The next morning, before they left for town, Scud produced a small leather sac and gave it to Melissa.

"Your mother's gold."

They loaded her meager possessions into the wagon, drove into town, and let her off at the hotel.

As she was getting out of the wagon, Josh took the talisman from around his neck and handed it to her.

"I want you to have this. My father treasured it and believed it brought him good fortune, and it did save me when Tenny shot at me, but to me it has only been a piece of gold. If there is any power in it, I feel you need it more than I do. I have everything I want now."

Melissa held his hand as a tear slowly

rolled down her cheek.

"Thank you."

Afterward, Josh helped Rebecca pack her clothes and supplies into the wagon. When they were finished, he put his arms around her and kissed her. She clung to him and said, "I love you, Josh. I'm so happy we are finally going to be together."

APPENDIX

Glossary of Mining Terms

Adit - A nearly horizontal passage from the surface by which a mine is entered and dewatered. A blind horizontal opening into a mountain, with only one entrance.

Assay To analyze the proportions of metals in an ore; to test an ore or mineral for composition, purity, weight, or other properties of commercial interest.

Barren - Said of rock or vein material containing no minerals of value.

Bedrock - Solid rock underlying soil, gravel or loose boulders.

Claim - A mining right that grants a holder the exclusive right to search and develop any mineral substance within a given area.

Colors - The specks of gold seen after the successful operation of a gold pan, when sand and gravel has been panned to remove the bulk of light minerals.

Crib - A roof support of prop timbers or ties, laid in alternate cross-layers, log-cabin style. It may or may not be filled with debris.

Deposit - Mineral deposit or ore deposit is used to designate a natural occurrence of a useful mineral, or an ore, in sufficient extent and degree of concentration to invite exploitation.

Disseminated - Ore deposits consisting of fine grains of ore mineral dispersed through the host rock.

Drift - A horizontal passage underground. A drift follows the vein.

Formation - Any assemblage of rocks which have some character in common, whether of origin, age, or composition.

Float - A general term for loose fragments of ore or rock, esp. on a hillside below an outcropping ledge or vein.

Gold - a yellow malleable ductile high-density metallic element resistant to chemical reaction, occurring naturally in quartz veins and gravel mining.

Gold Dust - Fine particles, flakes, or pellets of gold, e.g., as obtained in placer.

Hydraulicing - Excavation by means of a high-pressure jet of water, the resulting waterborne excavated material being conducted through flumes to the desired dumping point.

Long Tom - A trough for washing gold-bearing earth. It is longer than a rocker.

Outcrop - An exposure of rock or mineral deposit that can be seen on surface, that is, not covered by soil or water.

Miner - One who is engaged in the business or occupation of extracting ore, coal, precious substances, or other natural materials from the earth's crust.

Nugget - A large lump of placer gold or other metal.

Overburden - Layers of soil and rock covering a mineral deposit.

Placer - A deposit of sand or gravel that contains particles of gold, gemstones, or other heavy minerals of value.

Placer Gold - Gold that is obtainable by washing the sand, gravel, etc., in which it is found.

Panning - A technique of prospecting for heavy metals, such as gold, by washing placer or crushed vein material in a pan. The lighter fractions are washed away, leaving the heavy metals behind in the pan.

Portal - The structure surrounding the immediate entrance to a mine; the mouth of an adit or tunnel.

Prospecting - To search an area for valuable minerals and ores, such as gold or silver.

Prospector - A person engaged in exploring for valuable minerals or testing discoveries of the same.

Pyrite - A hard, heavy, shiny, yellow mineral, FeS_2 or iron disulfide, generally in cubic crystals. Also called iron pyrites, or fool's gold.

Rocker - A small digging bucket mounted on two rocker arms in which gold-bearing alluvial sands are agitated by oscillation, in water, to collect gold.

Seam - A stratum or bed of placer gold.

Shaft - A primary vertical or non-vertical opening through mine strata used for ventilation or drainage and/or for hoisting of personnel or materials; connects the surface with underground workings.

Sluice - A long troughlike box set on a slope of about 1:20, through which placer gravel is carried by a stream of water. The sand and gravel are carried away, while most of the gold and other heavy minerals are caught in riffles or a blanket on the floor.

Sluicebox - Long, inclined trough or launder containing riffles in the bottom that provide a lodging place for heavy minerals in ore concentration. The material to be concentrated is carried down through the sluices on a current of water. Sluiceboxes are widely used in placer operations for concentrating elements such as gold and platinum, and minerals such as cassiterite, from stream gravels.

Tunnel - A horizontal, or near-horizontal, underground passage, entry, or haulageway, that is open to the surface at both ends. A tunnel (as opposed to an adit) must pass completely through a hill or mountain.

Vein - A zone or belt of mineralized rock lying within boundaries clearly separating it from neighboring rock. It includes all deposits of mineral matter found through a mineralized zone or belt coming from the same source, impressed with the same forms and appearing to have been created by the same processes.

Windlass - A device used for hoisting; limited to small-scale development work and prospecting because of its small capacity. A drum or a section of tree trunk set horizontally on rough bearings above a shallow pit or shaft; used to raise or lower buckets in exploratory work. Handles at each end of the drum allow for manual rotation.

Also by Guy Allen

Novels Available as EBooks

Amyot

A Mystery Novel with a Northern Saskatchewan Wildcat Oil-Drilling Setting

Bush Camp

An adventure novel with a Northern British Columbia mining exploration camp Setting

www.guyallen.ca

Guy Allen is a retired geological engineer with many years experience in mineral, and oil and gas exploration in North America. He and his wife Geri divide their time equally between British Columbia and Washington State.

91940014R00180

Made in the USA
San Bernardino, CA
29 October 2018